# 'Triple Intrigue'

# By

# Neal Hardin

ISBN  9781655442889

For my good friends,

Linda and Graham Scholey,

Anne and Alan Myers

## Acknowledgement

With thanks to my friend, Alison Henesey for her advice, guidance and suggestions, and also with thanks to my friend Mark Bones for his suggestions.

## Authors opening gambit

Someone once told me that all stories are like jokes. Some stay in the memory for a long time and can be recounted over and over again, whilst others are instantly forgotten and assigned to the trash bin. The three stories I'm about to tell you, fall under the banner of 'intrigue'. Hence the title of the book.

The 'Black Cab' considers the exploits of Steve Relton, the driver of an iconic London cab. He meets a man who pays him to deliver a briefcase to a house in Primrose Hill. Relton soon wishes he never accepted the job.

In, 'Firestarter', an arsonist is loose on the streets of north London. DI Stephen Taylor must find him before any more lives are lost, but that just turns out to be the beginning of the nightmare.

In, 'Six Amigo's', Rob Bennett invites his closest friends to join him in New York City for his 'stag' party. Little does he know what his friends have in store for him.

# 'Black Cab'

# Chapter 1

The stream of vehicles going around Trafalgar Square raced to the next set of traffic lights. They were desperate to get there before they turned from green to red. On a dark, dingy and rainy late afternoon in the middle of March, London had a bleak and an unappealing backdrop to it. Like a wet weekend in some cold and miserable seaside town, in which nothing much happened. There were a few tourists standing close to the base of Nelson's column.

For those hardy souls inquisitive enough to be out on such a damp early evening, the lights shining out from the front of the National Gallery did suggest that there was something interesting to see and enjoy. Steve Relton checked in his mirror, then slipped his cab into the inside lane in preparation for turning into Charing Cross Road.

He had had many interesting and varied days on the roads of the capital in his fifteen years as the driver of an iconic black London cab. Today was never going to be an ordinary day. Not that such a thing as an ordinary day driving a cab in London existed.

Relton was made of the right stuff. He had the two Ds in abundance - a determination and a desire to succeed. For those in the *know*, know that to succeed in becoming a *bona fide* fully licensed and equitable London black cab driver requires the applicant to complete a gruelling test of his or her knowledge of the city streets. Every authentic black cab driver must learn the streets of London like the back of their hands, then pass a test before they can be let loose on the streets of the capital. Passing the test shows that the driver has the knowledge to ensure that customers are ferried to their desired destination in the shortest time by the quickest and least costly route possible. Those chosen few who drive a London black cab for a living are not allowed to use 21st century inventions such as a satellite navigation system to help them find their way. The navigation system has to be in their heads. Every driver has to obtain 'The Knowledge' before he or she can gain a licence.

Steve Relton had 'The Knowledge'. Born and bred on the streets of Brentford in west London, he had grown up in a family of black cab drivers. His dad had been a driver for thirty years. His uncle Harry had driven a cab for forty years, before his untimely death a couple of years ago. His cousin Pete was a black cab driver. All had needed the right stuff to succeed and to be able to earn a decent living.

Relton had gained his licence fifteen years before. He had inherited his first cab from his dad. Four black cabs later he was still driving the streets for twelve hours a day, for six days a week. On the streets of one of the most vibrant, cosmopolitan cities on the face of the planet. He knew that if he worked long hours, he could make as much as eighty thousand pounds a year. In his fifteen years, he must have done enough miles to circumnavigate the globe several hundred times. He had fed thousands of gallons of diesel into the tank, enough to fill a decent size swimming pool, and gone through enough tyres to fill a landfill of his own.

In his time, he had seen it all: examples of horrendous driving, stupid morons on bicycles, idiots on motorbikes and empty-headed pedestrians. The number of accidents must have run well into three figures. People knocked over. Roadworks that seemed to last for ever. Diversions that took him down dead-end streets. Everything that London could throw at him. Yet he came back for more, six days a week, twelve hours a day. It couldn't knock him down and when it did, he got up, brushed himself down and carried on. At forty-two years of age, he anticipated that he only had maybe another twelve years at the wheel. Not many drivers made it past their mid-fifties in this game. The wear and tear on his limbs, the pollution and having to stay alert, would eventually eat into him, and leave him fatigued and burnt-out. It was a young man's game, and whilst he wasn't exactly at the stage of ordering a Zimmer frame, the warning signs were there. Such as an increasing impatience with the traffic which he didn't have five years ago, and a wholly unhealthy opinion of the world.

He had had a few famous people in the back of his cab. A couple of sports stars, television people and the like. He had experienced every kind of human emotion and every kind of passenger. The talkative ones who wouldn't stop talking, to those who didn't say a word. The argumentative ones who wanted to know why he was going that way, to those who told him the route and those who had no idea where they were going. Then some of them got to their destination then denied they wanted to go there in the first place. He had met them all. On a few occasions was he able to say: Do you know who I had in my cab the other day? Then there were those who gave him a good tip to those who had attempted to run without paying. He had had his fair share of jumpers in his time. He never regretted becoming a cab driver. It was far better than an office job or working on a building site humping bricks, or standing on a factory production line, wishing your life away. He didn't have a boss telling him what to do. Driving a cab was the only thing he had known for over half of his working life, so he was either his own boss or his own worst enemy. He couldn't blame anyone else he if didn't go to work.

Steve Relton was happily married to Sonia – the love of his life. They became sweethearts at school, courted for a few years, fell out, courted again, and were married at the age of twenty-two. Their one and only child, Hailey, was eighteen years of age, going on twenty-eight, as her mother would often comment. Hailey attended a local college not too far from their north London home. They lived on a pleasant road in a residential area off Shaftsbury Road in Harrow. Their house was a three-bedroomed property, consisting of a downstairs reception, a sitting room, a decent size kitchen and a lounge at the rear which looked out onto a spacious garden. Relton had neglected the garden, but promised to do it once he had done the next phase of work on the houseboat he was renovating. 'So never,' Sonia had sarcastically muttered under her breath. He protested. He had only been out the previous evening cutting the grass and clearing the flower bed of leaves that had fallen from their neighbour's tree.

The best thing about living in Harrow was its proximity to the centre of the city. It was ideal for his work and popping into the West End if it took their fancy, though they very rarely attended any type of arts or cultural events. They weren't the type. A good movie and a couple of cans of beer with a curry was his idea of a good night.

Beside his family, the love of his life was the houseboat he had bought on the Thames. It was moored at a pier on the Chelsea embankment, close to one of London's most iconic and beautiful bridges – the regal Albert Bridge. Like a lot of loves, if the truth be told, it had turned into a bit of a millstone round his neck. In reality, it was little more than a barge that had once sailed along the Leeds and Liverpool canal in the 1960s, before being transferred to the Thames to become someone's idea of a bespoke home on the river. It had cost Relton twenty-five thousand pounds, eighteen months ago at an auction. He had already spent somewhere in the region of another twenty thousand pounds gutting out the interior, putting in a new floor, a new roof, and fitting out a new interior. It still required a complete new electrical rewire and a new generator. It also required new plumbing and a kitchen, or galley to use the correct term. The bilge pump had seen better days. It had fast become one of those endless pits of expenditure. The more he put in, the more he discovered that something else needed doing. He estimated that he needed to spend another twenty thousand pounds to get everything done to the standard he wanted.

Little wonder that Sonia had done her nut and nearly laid into him when he purchased it without her agreement. "How much?" she had cried when he told her. It was surprising that she hadn't killed him there and then. The Marie-Claire was his hobby, his project in life. After all, after driving through the streets of London, day in day out, fighting with the traffic and having to deal with the road rage and the occasional nasty passenger, he needed some salvation, something to give him the will to continue. He would get the Marie-Claire repaired and ready to be sold for double what he paid for it, come what may. Everyman needed a labour of love. The houseboat on the River Thames was Steve Relton's.

# Chapter 2

The month of March was going to be remembered as little more than a damp squib, much like the previous two months so far this year. This day had been cold enough for Relton to put on the car's heater on the fourth click on the dial. It was six-thirty in the evening. The evening rush hour had another hour to run. London was on the move. As the night crept in, the lights of the city were beginning to pierce out from the darkening streets, to reflect in the sheen of wet that a sudden cloud burst had dumped on the streets. Relton had only just turned the windscreen wipers off. The passenger in the back of his car was chatting away giving him chapter and verse on the state of the nation. All he could do was agree and say 'right' and 'yeah'. It was an occupational hazard. On this occasion he tended to agree with the majority of the guy's opinions.

He kept his eyes on the road, though the traffic along Charing Cross Road was hardly moving. Today, so far, had been okay. He had been on the road from eight in the morning to catch the final hours of the morning rush hour, then carried on through the day with some off-road time for half an hour at lunch time when he joined a rank outside St Pancras International and Kings Cross railway stations. He had ferried a couple of young executive types from St Pancras to Liverpool Street station to catch a connecting train to Norwich, or somewhere in that neck of the woods. As luck would have it, he stayed in an area roughly two or three miles around the City of London financial district.

For his recent forty-second birthday, his daughter had bought him a CD of the very best of Ennio Morricone. He had played it over and over again in his cab. 'Chi Mai' was now playing and it seemed somehow apt for the ambient feel of the night and the neon glow of the city. If he could stay in this area for the next hour or so he might think about turning the 'For Hire' sign off and calling it a night at seven. After all, he didn't have a boss on his case. He was a free spirit, with a licence to roam or go home if he chose to do so.

He had just gone through the lights at the Oxford Street and Tottenham Court Road junction when a pedestrian stepped off the pavement and raised his hand. He was a dark-complexioned guy in a dark raincoat, with a shoulder bag over his shoulder and a wheeled suitcase at his feet.

Such was his eagerness to attract Relton's attention, the orange glow of the 'For Hire' sign on the top of the cab must have been like a beacon of rescue in the otherwise onslaught of traffic coming along the road. Relton reduced speed, looked into his mirrors, indicated to pull in, and slipped into the side of the pavement. The passenger opened the back door and placed his case onto the floor. He plumped on to the back seat, then he said two words Relton seldom liked to hear at six-thirty of an evening: 'Heathrow Airport.' He didn't even say please.

Relton was obliged to take him, it was in the code of conduct. Fighting to get across to the western edge of the city to the beginning of the M4 at this time of the night would mean he wouldn't be home for seven o'clock. No way.

He had chatted to Sonia on his mobile phone an hour before, to tell her that with luck he would be home for seven. He had asked her what she was doing for the evening meal. When she had uttered the immortal words 'lamb casserole' he had salivated. One thing was for sure, Sonia prepared a wonderful lamb casserole. Alas, it would have to go in the microwave to be reheated. It never tasted as good as the oven-cooked version. He thought about contacting her, but what the hell. It was another occupational hazard. He'd live with it.

He turned the 'For Hire' sign off, adjusted the meter and set off up Tottenham Court Road to the junction with Euston Road.

"Which terminal?" he asked.

"Four," replied the passenger.

Relton turned on the CD player for 'Once Upon a Time in the West' to drift out of the speakers. He put it on a low volume.

"Going anywhere nice?" he asked.

"Home," came the one-word answer.

"Where's that?"

"Milan," he replied.

Relton could gauge by the guy's tone of voice and body language that he had no wish to indulge in banal conversation or any other type of conversation come to that. After years of reading the signs and the signals, he knew he was onto a loser from the word go so he shut up, turned the volume up a couple of notches, and settled down to drive the eight miles to the airport. He fought his way through the volume of traffic heading west to the start of the M4.

One hour and thirty minutes later he was dropping the passenger outside the Alitalia sign hanging from the underside of the canopy at Terminal four. The time was seven fifty-five. He contemplated calling it a day. He was tired and he was hungry. The lamb casserole might be okay to eat from the microwave.

He had just put the fare into his cash bag and was just about to set off home, when he heard a sound. Someone standing on the kerbside was tapping on the window at the passenger side. Relton looked across to see the face of a man pressed close to the window. He pressed the window button and let it slide halfway down. Relton could see that he was a distinguished looking fellow with a pleasant face, nice eyes and smile. Alas, he couldn't pick him up from here.

"You'll have to go to the queue," he said. "Over there," he pointed at the long line of people, two hundred yards further up the road. "I can't pick up from here."

The guy opened his mouth and clenched his teeth. "No time," he said. "There's a hundred bucks in it for you if you get me to the city." Relton had ferried many Americans in his time. This guy spoke with an east coast accent that wasn't as far north as Massachusetts or one of the other New England states, but not as far south as the New Jersey shoreline. Which suggested to him he hailed from the Connecticut or the New York area. Relton was going to insist that the guy joined the queue at the rank further along. But the

16

guy had clearly offered him a hundred-dollar tip. What the heck, he thought.

He waited for a moment, "Okay. Get in," he said; knowing full-well that he had just broken an unwritten code of conduct. No picking up from outside of drop off. He felt bad about it. Still he wasn't a charity. If he didn't do it, someone else would. As soon as he had dropped him at his destination, he would definitely go home.

The American thanked him. He opened the door and climbed into the back. He was carrying a silver metal case that looked like a solid piece of kit. He also had a compact suitcase, as if he wasn't expecting to be in the city for a long period of time. He plumped into the seat, sat back and crossed his legs. The overhead light in the roof allowed Relton to see him in a clear light. He was a smart-looking man with a nice tan, and a cool expensive dress sense. He was close to the same age as Relton, average height, average build, though well- groomed, suited and booted.

"Where to?" Relton asked.

"The London Minerva in…" he paused for a moment… "the City of London," he said with a question mark in the tone as if he wasn't sure where he was going. He shifted slightly in the seat to sit in the middle, then dipped his hand into the inside of pocket of his heavy overcoat.

"The London Minerva," asked Relton for clarification.

"That's it," said the guy. "It's on Can…non Street," he said stressing the two syllables. It was definitely a New York or New Jersey accent with a kind of an easy-going drawl similar to the way

Frank Sinatra spoke. Relton knew the hotel. It was one of London's newest, poshest and finest hotels that had been closed down and then renovated for the 2012 Olympic Games.

Relton changed track. He ejected the Morricone disc and fed Pink Floyd's 'Division Bell' into the player. He slipped into the line of traffic and headed out of the airport. The time was a shade after eight. He drove past the line of passengers waiting at a taxi rank, knowing full well that he should have demanded that the passenger go there. Too late. He was on the road.

The passenger didn't say a word. Relton turned down the volume and listened to the Floyd and 'Poles Apart.' By the time the cab was on the periphery of the airport, the rain that had stopped at five o'clock came back with a vengeance. As soon as the cab was on the M4, it was soon hammering down onto the top of the roof like bullets from hell.

Relton put the windscreen wipers on quick. The Floyd sang 'the rain fell slow'. It didn't. It was bucketing down and pinging onto the bonnet and the roof.


It must have been a mile or so down the motorway that Relton noticed that the passenger had turned around and was looking out of the back window. He didn't think a lot of it at first but, when thirty seconds later he looked into the mirror again, he could see that the American was still looking out of the back window at the headlights of the vehicles behind him. He thought he would try to engage him in conversation.

"Here for long?" he asked.

"Pardon me?" asked the American and turned his head forward.

"Are you here for long?" he asked again.

"A few days," he replied quickly.

"Tell me, where are you from?" he asked.

"What?"

"Where are you from?"

"Philly," he replied quickly.

"I've never been there. Is it nice?"

The guy didn't reply.


Within the next ten minutes they had reached the edge of west London and the elevated section of the M4 in the Brentford area. The floodlights surrounding Griffin Park football ground were on and the lights in the tower blocks out towards the edge of the river beamed out like bright white lights suspended in mid-air against the dark backdrop of the cloud-filled sky.

In the next two hundred yards, the traffic came to a grinding stop at the scene of a shunt. Up ahead the tell-tale blue and white flashing lights of a police patrol vehicle, mingled with the flashing orange lights of a recovery vehicle, rippled across the rain-soaked windscreen. Relton cursed.

"Something wrong?" the Yank asked.

"A prang," he replied.

"Pardon me?"

"An R.T.A...Road traffic accident. This is going to take longer than I anticipated," he said apologetically.

Just sit back and enjoy the music, he said to himself. The introduction to 'High Hopes' flowed out of the speakers. Relton had no chance of getting home any time soon for the meal. There were still ten miles to go before they hit the heart of the city, despite this being the dying embers of the rush hour. As they approached the scene of the accident, the traffic slowed to little more than two miles an hour. The rain had eased to little more than a pitter-patter, as the sky cleared to the west.

In the next five minutes, the speed of the traffic in front picked up as the vehicles sneaked passed the accident. They were gradually edging towards the fringe of Chiswick. Relton glanced back to see that the passenger had returned to looking out of the back window.

"You okay?" he asked. "Have you lost something?"

The Yank said, 'Urrggh'.

"Lost something? You okay?" he asked again.

Then the urbane American said something very rarely heard in the back of a London cab. Relton certainly hadn't heard it before in the fifteen years he had been doing the job.

"We're being followed," he said. He still had his head turned to the back window.

Relton thought he said they were being followed. Or maybe he had said something that sounded like that. He looked in his wing mirror. All he could see were the bright, white dazzling headlights of the cars behind.

He glanced back to look through the opening in the mesh metal grill separating the cab from the passenger space. "What?" he asked.

"The car behind is trailing us. He's been on your tail since we left the airport."

"You serious?" Relton asked.

"You bet," came a terse two-word answer.

Again, Relton looked into the wing mirror for a long few seconds. The white beam of the headlights of the car behind sent ripples of light dancing across his eyeballs. He blinked several times to clear his vision of white specks.

"Why?" he asked.

"Why what?"

"Why are we being followed?"

"Take my word for it," he said stiffly.

Relton said 'whatever' under his breath, but just shallow enough so the passenger didn't hear him. The congestion in front cleared in the next two hundred yards, allowing the traffic to pick up speed to fifty miles an hour. He wondered if this was some kind of April Fool's day stunt, a couple of weeks early.

"Lose him," said the Yank suddenly. "There's another hundred bucks in it for you." Relton had forgotten about the initial hundred for picking him up in a restricted area. That was two hundred pounds. He didn't know who he was supposed to lose. But the guy sounded serious. He wasn't going to question his judgement, not when he was throwing money around like candy.

"Whatever you say," he said. "I'll shake him off."

The guy might be a raving nutcase for all he knew or he could be onto something. Relton didn't know which was nearer the truth. He couldn't recall anything so bizarre as this in a long time. The last time anything crazy happened in his cab was a year before, when a rather attractive looking woman in her twenties stripped to her bra to try on a new blouse. It had been like a scene in some silly Rom-com movie. This was more like a suspense movie. He had heard stories from other cabbies who had been encouraged to lose following cars. Then it was usually a husband trying to shake off a jealous wife, or vice-versa. This was something different.

As he headed along Chiswick High Road, he suddenly veered into the right-hand lane for a late right-hand turn and slipped into the lane. Lo and behold, the car behind did the exact same thing. Maybe the American was onto something here. Relton felt his heart beat quicken. He sat up straight and gripped the steering wheel. He swung the cab across the road and headed down Chiswick Lane at a speed over the thirty mile an hour limit. The pool of water in the road threw up a sheet of moisture that splattered against the windscreen. The headlights of an oncoming car blinded him for a brief moment. The driver of the next approaching car beeped his horn because the taxi was taking a fair amount of his side of the road. Pink Floyd stopped singing and it was silent in the taxi.

The car behind stayed close enough for it to loom in the windscreen mirror. It was just a few feet from him at best. It was a bigger car, bigger engine, and far more powerful than the cab. If he was going to shake it off, it would require a monumental amount of effort and skill. At the next junction he took a left onto the Great West Way, put the pedal to the metal and headed towards Hammersmith Flyover. He accelerated then took a slip road at the last possible moment before an elevated section of the road. The car behind did the exact same manoeuvre. It was a high-powered Mercedes, black body, wide windscreen and chrome bumper. Relton thought it was a S350 model. His heart was beating like a drum. The taxi screeched around a corner and wobbled from side to side. It was like a roller derby. The car behind was easily keeping up with him. Up ahead, about one hundred yards away, the road split into a four-way junction at a set of traffic lights. The lights were on red. It was make-up- your-mind-time in thirty yards. Relton reduced speed and got into the middle lane to go ahead, then at the last possible second, he gambled. He swung the wheel anticlockwise, steered the car into the left-hand lane and cut in front of a double decker London bus waiting at an amber light. He managed to squeeze through a tiny gap missing the front of the bus by millimetres, as a car came from his right-hand side. The driver of the bus was soon on the horn. The driver of the car swerved to miss him and nearly took out another car in the second lane. The following Merc was too cumbersome to get around the bus, and got boxed in by the car behind the bus. The driver of the Merc was forced to go directly ahead onto Shepherds Bush Road, while Relton spun the taxi left onto Glenthorne Road.

At the next T-junction, he took another left, then left again, and came out onto the King Street section of Hammersmith Road. He had succeeded in losing the Merc, though he had been incredibly lucky. He had nearly been wiped out by the bus and the other car coming from his right. His heart wasn't so much beating as pounding on his chest wall. The bus driver – whoever he was – had reacted well not to collect his back end.

At the junction near to Hammersmith tube station, Relton got onto the flyover and headed east into central London along with the other traffic zooming along the A4 towards the junction with Warwick Road.

Relton cursed under his breath, but he hadn't felt so alive in a long time. A crazy night was going to turn even crazier.

Chapter 3

The American didn't say a word for five minutes. He clammed up and just sat back as if nothing had happened. Maybe it was his occupational hazard. Relton didn't want to say anything or ask a question because he feared the answer. He had just earned a two-hundred-pound bonus by not only risking his livelihood, but his life.

They were soon in Kensington and heading into the West-End. In this part of town, the traffic had thinned out considerably. The spray on the roads wasn't so much of a problem; indeed, the roads in this part of the city were nearly dry. At Gloucester Road he took a left and headed up to Hyde Park. On reaching Kensington Road he turned right and sprinted up to Hyde Park Corner then onto Piccadilly and into the heart of the West End. He quickly became lost in a whole procession of black taxis.

The Yank suddenly stirred from the back seat. "How far?" he asked.

"To the city?" asked Relton.

"To the hotel."

"Another couple of miles," replied Relton. He gripped the steering wheel and kept his eyes on the road ahead. Even a seasoned cabbie like him could become disoriented and lost in these parts. It needed every ounce of concentration he could muster to negotiate the narrow spaces, and to anticipate the changing lights. The high-rise towers in the city were not that far away, just a mile or so. He was going to drop off the passenger, get his dough, then go home. After he had had something to eat, he was going to soak in the bath for an hour. He felt physically and mentally drained. It was as if a tap had opened and his energy had drained out. His plan was to go home and relax, but he didn't anticipate that the Yank would open his mouth and ask him a question.

"Can you do something for me?" he asked.

"Like what?" Relton replied.

The Yank took hold of the metal case he had at his feet and lifted it up so Relton could see it. Relton could hardly miss it. It was three feet long from top to bottom, by two feet wide, by six inches deep. It looked like a heavy-duty security type of briefcase often seen in the hands of security guards leaving or entering a bank. The light in the roof reflected in the silver metal surface. He reduced speed as the taxi came to a halt in the traffic.

"Like you take this to an address for me."

"What!" Relton exclaimed.

"There's another two hundred bucks in it for you."

"That's another two hundred pounds on top of the two hundred I've already earned," he replied.

The American didn't say anything immediately. Maybe he had forgotten he had already said he would give him two hundred pounds. He did the math. "That's right. Four hundred," he said as if it meant nothing to him.

Relton turned his head to look into his eyes. "I don't doubt you've got it, but let me see the money," he requested.

The passenger dug his hand into his overcoat pocket and pulled out a huge roll of banknotes. He peeled off eight fifty-pound notes and wafted them a couple of inches from Relton's nose. He could hear them and smell their fragrance.

"Take it to an address for me and it's all yours."

"Why what's the matter with you? Why can't you?"

"I thought that would be obvious."

Now it was Relton's turn to say 'urrggh'

"They'll be watching me."

"Who?"

"The guys who were following."

"I shook them off."

"Maybe. Maybe not."

"Who are they?"

He didn't answer the question, maybe because he didn't know the answer.

"You take this and I'll give you another hundred." He proceeded to peel off another two, fifty-pound notes.

Relton saw a flash of the red notes. "Where to?" he asked.

To an address in Prim...Rose Hill." He took the case again and lifted it up.

"Primrose Hill."

"That's correct."

"What's the address?"

The Yank read out an address without any hesitation. Relton knew the road. It was in a smart part of the district. "Someone will be waiting for you," he said.

"Who do I need to say it's from?"

"Just take the briefcase and give it to a man at that address."

"What's he called?"

"Hank."

"Hank."

"Yeah. Hank Peterson."

This was so off-the-wall it was almost horizontal. "Okay. I'll do it. How will Hank know I'm coming?"

"Because I'll tell him."

Relton reset his eyes on the road as the traffic moved off. A police car with his horn blaring and lights flashing came by on the other side of the road. It zoomed by up the street in a hurry to get to wherever it was going. He watched the back end in the wing mirror until it was out of sight.

The Yank fiddled in a jacket pocket and pulled out a cell-phone. He turned it on and pressed a call button. Relton made sure the CD player was well and truly off as he wanted to listen to the conversation. A few seconds elapsed before the receiver answered the call.

"It's me," said the American. "Yeah.... Listen.... Listen...I was followed from the airport. They could be waiting for me at the hotel." His tone was calm, then he ratcheted it up a decibel ....... "No listen...I can't stay with the case. I've done a deal with the driver of this cab. He'll deliver it......Yeah......What's your name?" he asked. Silence for a couple of seconds. "What's your name?" he asked again.

"Who me?" Relton asked.

"Yeah."

"Steve."

"Steve will deliver the case.... Look after it.... Yeah...Okay..." He ended the conversation and closed his cell-phone with a snap that made Relton jump.

"You know where you're going? Right?"

"Of course." Relton prided himself on having a memory for addresses. After all it's how he made his living. He read out the address then said. "Tell me this."

"What?"

"What's in the case?" He didn't reply. "How do I know it's not a bomb?"

Relton looked behind him to see his response.

"A bomb?" he exclaimed. "Are you kidding me? I've just flown three thousand miles across the pond with a bomb in my possession. I've just walked out of an airport with a bomb. I don't think that would be possible." He had a point. "It doesn't remotely contain anything like that," said the Yank and almost laughed it off as an absurd suggestion.

"Just checking," said Relton.

He inched the cab into the City of London, along Cheapside and by St Paul's. The Yank didn't bother to take in the sights. He couldn't have cared less where he was.

The Minerva Hotel was situated on a one-way street off Cannon Street, near the Monument. It was a high-end, palatial, five-star hotel, catering for a wealthy clientele. It had frock-coated doormen standing outside the entrance and valet parking in an adjoining private car park. The flags of several nations were flying over the entrance canopy. The long, high, plate-glass windows gave a view into the reception area with its chic colour scheme and ambient lighting. Members of staff in uniform were attending to guests at the front desk. This was a thousand-pounds-a-night hotel, for those with few money concerns.

Relton slipped the taxi into the short stay parking bay on the pavement outside of the entrance. As he came to a halt the American edged forward. "Now deliver this for me," he said, then he put his hand through the gap in the mesh. It contained ten fifty-pound notes. Relton took the notes and slipped them into his cash bag. He was going to ask him for a tip but decided against it. He may not have seen the funny side.

"Tell me one more thing," he asked.

"What?"

"Who did I have the pleasure of talking to this evening?"

"Doctor Peter Kinden," said the American.

With the introductions over Kinden took his other suitcase, opened the door and climbed out of the taxi. Relton watched him walk the ten paces to the entrance. The doorman on duty was someone Relton knew – an ex-cab driver called Ray Slater. He watched as Slater pulled the glass door open. Kinden stepped into the foyer and headed to the front check-in desk, where he was greeted by a chap in uniform behind the counter.

Relton glanced down to the floor of the cab and clapped his eyes on the silver metal case. It looked like a solid bit of luggage. He took in a deep breath. What a night it had been! The trouble was, it wasn't over by a long way.

# Chapter 4

Relton watched the American check in. Suddenly the nervous tension in his body came flooding out. He began to sweat buckets. He turned the heating off, turned the radio on, and listened to some new music. He couldn't stick it for more than a few seconds, before turning it off. Seconds later a taxi pulled in behind him and dropped off a passenger. Ray Slater came to greet him.

Relton waited for a moment, then set off to deliver the briefcase to the address in Prim...Rose Hill. He touched the five hundred pounds in his cash bag and smiled to himself. The money would go a long way towards the fund to get the houseboat into A1 condition. A few more customers like that and he would soon have the dough he required to finish the job.

It was twenty minutes before he reached Primrose Hill. The time was nine-thirty. It was chilly out. The weather people were hinting at a warm front over the weekend, but today was Thursday and it seemed as likely to him as winning the National Lottery.

The house was on a nice, tree-lined road that was bordered by three-storey brick homes in blocks or two or five. There was a church on one corner. Relton ventured on for another fifty yards before coming to the address.

It was the end house in a block of five. The front was behind a high privet barrier, that partially hid the house from the road. Relton pulled into the kerb directly opposite but didn't get out immediately. First, he glanced up and down the road. It was quiet. No one was around. The events of the last hour were still reverberating through him. What the hell was the Yank fresh in from the states up to? All kind of shenanigans no doubt, but he didn't come across as a criminal, in fact the contrary. He seemed like a level-headed kind of guy and as straight as the M4, or maybe he was a good criminal and good at what he did.

Relton concentrated on the final task. All he had to do was deliver the case, say goodbye, and get away. There was a meal waiting for him at home and a beer with his name on it. When Sonia asked him how his day had been, he would say quiet. He wouldn't mention the American with the thick roll of fifty-pound notes.

He got out of the cab, quietly opened the passenger door, reached in and took the case. A car came by on the road, the dull thud-thud-thud of music playing at a high volume bounced out.

Through the privet he could see that a light was blazing in the front window of the house behind a pull-down roller blind. There were no lights on in the two upper floors. Overhead the sky was starry and bathed in moonlight. He suddenly fancied a cigarette to ease the tension, then realised he hadn't smoked for two years. He put the case on the ground and closed the cab door. Then picking it up, he approached the front door. There was the reflection of a light in the room to the left. The blind over the bow-shaped bay window was all the way down to the sill. Before he reached the door, he looked at the case and wondered what it contained. He couldn't tell anything by the feel and there was no way he could open it to look inside as there were two solid latches tightly closed. Each latch had a three-digit combination lock and a keyhole to boot. He wondered if there was some kind of device inside which would explode and release a deadly toxic gas if the lid was forced open. Though he had a desire to prise the lid open, it was something he wouldn't attempt.

This was definitely the correct address. He had heard the American speaking to Hank not thirty minutes before, so he must be at home. He reached out and hit the bell. Only then did he notice that the front door was open a few centimetres. He pressed the doorbell again. He waited for a good twenty seconds, but no one came. He knocked, this time on the frame. Still no one came. The light in the room on the left was still on. With the weight of the case pulling on his hand he let it down to the floor then he turned around to see if anyone was watching him. No one was there. Anyway, he was hidden behind the thick privet which hid the front door from the road. A car on the road went by. A breeze got up and shook the top of the privet. It didn't look as if anyone was coming to the door, so he gently pushed on it and it opened with a creak of the hinge. The hallway was in darkness. It was bare, but for a small table to one side. No carpet on the floor just a polished wood floor. There was a stairway going up to the first floor on the right-side wall.

He took a breath, picked up the case and stepped inside. "Hello," he called out. "It's Steve. The cab driver." He expected someone to come bouncing down the stairs or out of the door to the left or through the door at the end of the hallway. No one did. "Hello," he called again this time louder.

The breeze got up and was strong enough to open the door on the left - the one that led into the front room. Shit, he thought. "Hank," he called. Still no reply. For fuck's sake he thought. What's going on here? It was becoming too hairy for words.

He called out for the umpteenth time. As the door leading into the room inched open further, he could hear the sound coming from a television inside the room. Obviously, the person in the room couldn't hear him because of the sound of the television. He just hoped no one was waiting for him behind the door. He was aware of a smell, but couldn't place the scent. The sound of canned laughing was coming from the television. He stretched out a hand and pushed the door wide open. Directly ahead, the television was on and the sound of actors talking and a studio audience laughing out loud filled the room. Then his eyes went to a high chair in between him and the television. Someone was sitting in the chair facing the television, his left hand resting on the armrest. The back of his head was an inch or two above the top edge of the back of the chair.

Relton felt jittery. "Hello," he said gently. He had no wish to scare the shit out of the person in the seat. No reply. Was the person deaf or even asleep? He stepped into the room which contained several items of furniture. Then he noticed the books and the pile of papers and an assortment of documents that were scattered over the floor. The drawers of a chest were all hanging open. Items were hanging out. It was as if a mini tornado had suddenly swept through the room, picked up the contents and literally tossed them all over the floor. The sound of the television went mute as the programme

35

went to a commercial break. Relton felt his heart pounding like a piston hammer. His skin was itching. He was aware of sweat on his brow. The person in front of him hadn't moved a muscle. Gingerly, he approached the chair. It was then that he saw the thin metal coil at the back of the person's neck. The ends were twisted over each other. It didn't register with him immediately what it was. It was only when he had summoned up the courage to look into his face did, he see that it was a garrotte. The man in the seat was dead. His mouth was open an inch. A pair of black rimmed spectacles were over his upper face, hanging half off. His eyes were open. There was a look of surprise on his face as if the attack that killed him had come as a complete unforeseen act. It was a horrible look. There was no evidence of any blood.

Relton wanted to get out of there as quickly as possible. He didn't linger for more than a second, then he was out like a shot. As he passed out of the front door, he realised that he still had the case in his hand. He thought of throwing it into the garden but he couldn't let go of it. He didn't care if anyone saw him. He had no fear of being seen. He just wanted to be away from here. He was fumbling in his pocket to find his keys, opened the cab and jumped into the driver's seat. He dropped the case on the passenger side of the cage. The smell of death seemed to have impregnated his clothes and hair. Everywhere. The stunned, helpless look of the man in the chair was one he wouldn't be able to erase from his memory any time soon. Almost hyperventilating by now, he tried to steady himself and told himself to calm down. He hadn't murdered the man. Someone else had done that. Finally, he was able to collect his thoughts and deal with it the best he could. He got the keys into the ignition, started the taxi and pulled away from the house of death in Primrose Hill.

# Chapter 5

Relton raced home to Harrow. He was in a quandary about what to do. He was literally a quivering wreck. He parked the cab in the drive by the side of his house, turned off the engine, but waited before he got out. After a few moments thinking time, he climbed out.

Once inside his home, he locked the front door. Then he stepped along the hallway to the lounge at the back of the house, opened the door and poked his head in. Sonia and Hailey were both sitting on the settee, one at each end with their legs curled under them. Just sitting in the dark, watching the television, and laughing out loud like a pair of drains. They were watching the same comedy show as the murdered man. Both had changed into their pyjamas, and both had a glass of red wine in their hands. Sonia said something which was lost beneath the sound coming from the television. He didn't ask her to repeat it. He went out to the bottom of the stairs and went up to the bathroom. Once inside he stripped off to the waist, ran hot water into the bowl and had a quick wash. He wanted to rid himself of the stench of death. He washed his hands and face with a creamy lather several times. After drying himself he came down stairs into the kitchen, to make himself a cup of instant coffee and a sandwich of meat and pickle from the fridge.

Moments later Sonia came in, saying that the new comedy show on telly was very funny. He said right. She asked him how his day had been. He said he wasn't feeling so good, and might have a bit of man flu coming on. She told him to go upstairs and have a lie down. He said okay. Sonia went back into the lounge.

As soon as he had eaten half of the sandwich, he went up to the bedroom and fell onto the mattress. No matter how he tried, he couldn't rid himself of the face of that man. His startled expression, the bulging eyes, the open mouth and the grimace on his face. The metal ligature round his neck. His black-rimmed spectacles had been sitting skew-whiff on his nose in an almost comical fashion. His right arm on his chest, the other by his side resting on the armrest. Legs crossed at the ankles. It looked as if he had fallen to sleep. Then someone had come in and put him to sleep for eternity.

Fifteen minutes passed, but Relton couldn't sleep. He was too tense. His mind was racing. The bedside clock said ten-fifteen. He could hear Sonia and Hailey still laughing in the lounge. Oh my God, he thought. What a disaster of a day. If only he hadn't picked up the Italian guy on the corner of Tottenham Court Road. If only he had stuck to his guns and refused to take the American from outside of Terminal Four. If only this – if only that. Fate had determined that he wouldn't do any of those. He tossed and turned for a further five minutes, then decided that it was no use. He had to return to the hotel to give the case back to Doctor Peter Kinden.

He slipped on some clean clothing then went down the stairs. As he reached the front door, he shouted. "Just going out."

"Don't be long," Sonia replied, as he closed the front door.

He got into his cab and looked at the case resting against the side of the cage. What did it contain? He wondered aloud to himself. Why had a man been murdered? And why was he involved? These were just two questions he didn't have an answer to.

He pulled the cab down the drive, over the ramp, swung it onto the road and headed towards the city. He was going to give the case back to the Yank. Tell him the man called Hank wasn't at home. He didn't want anything to do with it. If he had to, he would give him the five hundred pounds, back in a heartbeat.

As he drove towards the City, he decided that he would tell Kinden that no one was at home to receive the case. Nothing about Hank being dead. Nothing about someone giving Hank a metal necklace as a parting gift. Someone with herculean strength, and a professional aptitude, had snuffed him out. Relton was no expert on such matters, but it didn't take a genius to see that Hank hadn't put up much of a fight. There wasn't any evidence of blood. No obvious lacerations on his face or hands. The guy had been sitting in the seat watching television, then someone had crept into the room, got behind him, wrapped a thin metal cord around his neck and just rubbed him out of existence. Then he had ransacked the room looking for something. Maybe it wasn't a 'him'. Maybe it was a 'them'. Maybe they found what they were looking for. Maybe they hadn't.

The traffic was relatively sparse for a Thursday night in central London. It would take him just under twenty minutes to drive the four miles into the city.

It was actually ten-thirty when he steered the cab down the one-way street adjacent to the hotel. There was still a healthy number of people sauntering along the pavement, coming and going, to and from the hotel, even at this hour. Maybe there was a function of some description in one of the conference suites in the hotel. As well as being knowledgeable about the streets of the capital, a cabbie had to have a decent knowledge of the hotels as well as the transport hubs and so on. He knew many of the people who worked at the doors of the major hotels. Those guys in their fancy long coats and top hats were the guys with the knowledge of who was and who wasn't staying in the hotel.

As he pulled into the front of the hotel Relton could see that Ray Slater was still on duty. He would probably knock off at midnight. Slater came forward and opened the back door of the cab, expecting a passenger to emerge. The cab was empty. He stepped forward to the window for an explanation.

"Dropping off some luggage for a guest," said Relton.

"Right you are," said Slater before gently closing the door.

Relton looked across to the front of the hotel and observed the scene inside at the reception desk. A chap was on duty at the front desk that was illuminated in a splash of light from above. On the wall behind him was a line of clocks. Spot lights bathed a carpeted area which contained tables and chairs adjacent to the

41

window. A number of people, were engaged in conversation, were standing to the left of the front desk. This hotel mainly catered for business people and wealthy tourists. It had a five-star reputation and a five-star price tag to match. It had a much-praised Michelin star restaurant. A top French chef, a business centre, and a fitness area which included a twenty-metre swimming pool. All the features you would expect in a high-end hotel.

"Okay," he said to himself, "collect your thoughts." He grasped the metal case and got out of the car, closed the door and set off across the front to the doors where Ray Slater was stationed. As Relton went by him, Slater nonchalantly touched the brim of his hat and grinned. He had done it a thousand times today and would do it again tomorrow and the day after that.

Relton stepped into the reception area and advanced to the front desk with the case in his hand. Violin music was playing at a low level. There was a warm waft of air from a ceiling air vent. The group of people had moved into a carpeted area by the elevators and were chatting in low voices. Someone must have told a funny story or a joke because they all laughed out loud. The guys were in black suits and bow ties and the ladies in their finest gowns. There was definitely a function of some kind going on in one of the banquet rooms on the ground floor. Behind the front desk a feature wall contained a display of clocks that gave the time in various places around the globe. It was already seven-thirty tomorrow morning in Tokyo.

A single display case held a noticeboard on which there was a notice which said: 'Welcome to the International Forum of Medical Scientists.'

Relton stepped to the counter and placed the case at his feet. There was no one behind the desk so he hit the bell on the counter. A tall young man about twenty years of age, with a business-like look on his face soon appeared from out of a door to the left and came to greet him. He was decked in the uniform complete with name badge and all the trimmings. "Yes Sir," he asked. "How may I help you?"

Relton smiled. "I'm here to drop off a case for one of your guests," he said. "He left it in my cab."

"Oh," said the young man. "Do you have a name?"

"Doctor Peter Kinden."

"Kinden?" asked the chap

"Yes, Kinden. Doctor Kinden."

The chap tapped a console under the level of the counter, then focused his eyes on the screen. "Let me see," he said. A long moment passed. "Oh yes. Dr Peter Kinden. Room 529. I will call his room."

Relton smiled, nodded and mouthed thanks. The chap took the telephone, punched a number and waited for a reply. He eyed Relton and gave him a half smile. Relton replied in kind, then his attention was taken by two Asian-looking men in dark suits, who were sitting at a table in the seating area. They were Chinese, Japanese or Korean. Somewhere from that part of the world. Both of them appeared to be glancing towards the front desk as if they were

43

expecting someone. The people who had been standing chatting in the group had moved away from the elevators. The violin music ended, to be replaced by a jazz number. Then Relton was aware of the sound of applause coming from one of the function suites down the foyer. This hotel wasn't only a place to stay, but a venue for conferences and events in large suites that could easily accommodate several hundred people at one time.

Relton refocused his eyes on the guy behind the desk just in time to see his reaction. "Hello Sir. Sorry to disturb you. It's the front desk. I've a gentleman here who tells me he has a case that you left in his taxi this evening." Relton reached down to touch the case as if to reassure himself it was still there. The two oriental looking gentlemen were chatting in whispered conversation. The guy standing at the desk said. "Yes Sir…I will inform him…Thank you." He replaced the handset into the cradle.

"Mister…Doctor Kinden will be along in one minute," he said. Relton thanked him. "Perhaps you may wish to take a seat and wait for him over there," he said, and pointed to the arrangement of chairs and tables.

"If it's okay with you, I'd rather stand here," replied Relton.

The chap looked marginally put out. "As you wish," he declared, then he stepped away from the counter, went back into his room and out of view.

Relton looked in the area where a group of people emerged from further along the foyer. They looked like professional people. They had that aura about them.

Perhaps he should have taken the chap's advice and found a seat because one minute turned into two and two turned into five. He could hear someone in the function room talking into a microphone and asking the delegates to welcome the next speaker onto the stage. A round of applause followed. He looked at the line of clocks attached to the wall. It was ten-forty in London...five-forty in the evening in New York City and noon-forty in Sydney.

The two east Asian-looking men at the table were joined by several other people dressed in evening wear, though they sat at an adjoining table. A further minute passed. Relton recalled the events of the evening and wondered what he was going to tell Doctor Kinden about Hank Peterson. Assuming it was Hank. How would he break the news to him, that the man he had asked him to give the case to was sitting in a chair as stone dead as can be? Perhaps he didn't need to tell him anything. He decided not to say a thing. He would tell him there was no response when he knocked at the door, therefore he was returning the case to him.

A further minute passed. It was now getting on for twelve minutes since he had entered the hotel. He was going to ring the bell and summon the guy behind the counter when a figure dressed in a shiny evening suit complete with a bow tie approached the desk. It wasn't Doctor Kinden. This guy was taller, even more distinguished than the Yank and a few years younger. He had a full head of carefully styled hair, a lighter shade, a darker complexion and softer features. Just then the guy from behind the counter appeared and clapped his eyes on the guy.

"Doctor Kinden. Thank you," he said. "This man has your case."

Relton was dumbstruck. This wasn't the man who had been in the back of his taxi two hours ago. He instantly assumed there had been a mistake. That or else he had had a head transplant in the past two hours. Then he thought maybe there were two Doctor Kindens staying at the hotel. A perfect error to make.

"No. I mean Doctor Peter Kinden of Philadelphia," he said.

"I am Doctor Peter Kinden of Philadelphia," said the stranger.

# Chapter 6

This Doctor Kinden locked his eyes on Relton, then let his eyes drift to the metal case at his feet.

Relton looked at him. "You're not the guy I dropped off here an hour ago," he said. The man looked incredulous and mildly shocked by this revelation. He clapped his eyes on the guy behind the counter, who in turn looked at Relton who glanced at the men sitting at the table, then back to the stranger in front of him. This Dr Kinden was just as polished as the man he had picked up at Heathrow, though maybe a good five years younger and at least three inches taller. He had a long face and a firm, solid chin. In the gold splash of light reflecting from the lighting behind the counter his hair looked almost like gold thread. He was wearing a tailored dark suit and a bow tie at this neck and a blinding white shirt, which all suggested he was attending a function in the hotel.

"Excuse me?" he said.

"You're not the chap I dropped off at the hotel one hour ago."

He rolled his eyes. "I never said you did," he retorted.

His accent was American, location unknown to Relton. He had heard plenty of American accents in his time, but he couldn't hazard a guess at the location of this one.

He gave Relton a kind of grin and they looked at each other for a long moment, thereby creating an embarrassing silence.

"I can't give the case to you," said Relton.

"I didn't ask you to. Look what's this all about? You asked for me," he said tersely. He was right. Relton had asked to speak to Doctor Kinden. That was the name the man in the taxi had given him. He had seen him enter the hotel and check-in, but now he actually wondered if he had imagined it. Maybe he was going mad. No, he wasn't going mad. It had happened. He glanced down at the silver case, then at the guy standing behind the counter who had a kind of dumb expression on his face. Maybe he was dumbfounded by the exchange that was going on.

Relton looked at him. "Have you seen this man before?" he asked.

"Excuse me?" he said, projected his head forward then widened his eyes.

"Have you seen this man before?" Relton repeated.

The guy just stood there with his month ajar.

The new Peter Kinden remained impassive and a kind of silent stand-off took place for a few seconds, until the guy behind the counter grabbed the telephone and said he would call security.

Kinden looked at Relton and they locked eyes again. Relton was the first to blink. He grabbed the handle of the case in his right hand, turned around and beat a hasty retreat out of the foyer, through the glass door and out into the open. The change in temperature from warm to cool took his breath away. Ray Slater nodded in his direction. Relton didn't reply. He quickly walked to his taxi, opened the driver's door and climbed in. As he looked into the foyer area, he could see that the man who called himself Kinden and the guy at the

48

counter hadn't moved a muscle. Ten seconds later he was pulling away. They watched him drive away from the front of the hotel. The two Asian men who had been seated in the seats were no longer there.

Relton felt as if his tail had been rammed firmly between his legs. He had attempted to return the case to the man who said he was Dr Peter Kinden. The man who had stepped to the counter was someone completely different to the Peter Kinden in his taxi. Something very strange was going on. For a moment Relton doubted his own sanity, but he didn't want to start doubting himself. The only thing the men had in common was that they spoke with an American accent. The first Doctor Kinden sounded like a New Yorker; the second Doctor Kinden could be from the west coast or anywhere in between.

Relton drove through the centre of London. It was ten past eleven when he got home. He parked his cab in the drive by the side of his house, took the case and went inside his home. The house was in dark. Sonia and Hailey would have gone to bed. Once in the house he put the case into the cupboard under the stairs with the ironing board, a fold-up decorating table, and hid it under several rolls of unused wallpaper. Then he went into the kitchen and turned the light on. There was a note on the kitchen table which said:

*There is a sandwich in the fridge. Don't forget to turn the alarm on.*

Over the past couple of weeks, the local police had informed homeowners that there had been several attempted burglaries in the area. On a couple of occasions when he had forgotten to turn the alarm system on, Sonia had chastised him. She now resorted to leaving a written note on the kitchen table to tell him that he needed to turn it on.

That night Relton didn't sleep much if at all. He tossed and turned, much to the annoyance of Sonia who he had woken coming to bed. She had to tell him to stay still. She asked him what was wrong. He said nothing. But there was plenty wrong, and he didn't know what the hell was going on or how he was going to get through it.

Relton was awoken in the early hours first by a neighbour's dog barking then by what he thought was the sound of breaking glass. He assumed a cat had knocked over a bottle or a vandal was on the prowl. He eyed the clock on the bedside table. It was four-twenty. The streetlight directly outside of the house was as bright as a searchlight. He got up out of bed, and stepped to the front window to look outside. Overhead it was still pitch-black. Dawn was still one hour and forty minutes away. Nothing moved. As the bedroom was at the front of the house, he could see down onto the top of his cab on the drive and see the back end was sticking out from the corner of the house. Then he heard it again, a crack of glass breaking as if someone was trying to prise out the glass in the front door. He strained his ears to listen. It may have been coming from the lounge because there were a pair of French windows that led onto a patio. Anyone trying to break in would in all likelihood come over the fence at the bottom of the garden, walk across the lawn and try to get in through the windows. It was the obvious weak spot. Hailey slept in the room at the back of the house.

Sonia turned over in the bed and let out a snore. Relton, who was dressed in a pair of pyjama bottoms stepped to the bedroom door, opened it, stepped out onto the landing and looked down the stairs to the bottom and the front door. Now he could hear a scratching noise as if an animal of some description was scraping its claws along a smooth surface. His heart was racing at ten to the dozen. He was almost petrified with fear. Then he recalled that he had set the alarm system. If anyone was trying to get into the house he wondered if they had managed to bypass the system. He continued down the stairs in a slow careful descent, trying to not make a sound, though the stairs did creak.

"What you doing?" someone asked. The shock nearly gave him a heart attack. He looked up the stairs to see Sonia hanging over the bannister looking down the stairs. Her long hair was loose over her face and shoulders. "Shhhh. Be quiet," he said in a forceful whisper. "I think someone is trying to get into the house."

She put her hands to her face. "Who is?" she asked.

"How the hell do I know?" he snapped.

He made it onto the final step. He knew there was a hammer in a cupboard in the kitchen if he needed it. The noise of the scraping stopped and he thought whatever was at the back of the house had given up and gone away. He blew out a massive sigh then sucked in a deep breath. The noise didn't go away. In the next second there was an audible sound as if someone was using a jemmy to prise the back door open. Then it happened, the silence ended when the alarm went off and an ear shattering 'dur-dur-dur' filled the house. Under the cover he turned and hastily opened the door into the kitchen, turning the light on as he entered. He anticipated seeing someone at the door. The coast was clear. Whoever was trying to get in must be at the patio doors in the lounge. His first thought was to get the hammer. If someone was in the house, he wanted to defend himself and his family. If it meant hitting him with the tool then so be it. There was a determination in the pit of his stomach he had never felt before.

Once he had the hammer in his hand he quickly stepped out of the kitchen and opened the door to the lounge and raced inside. The moonlight was cascading through the French windows which were open a couple of inches. The burglar had managed to get that far. The glass in the left-hand pane was smashed. Relton ran forward in his bare feet across the lounge, looked into the garden and just caught the tail end of a figure climbing over the fence and fleeing. It was one of those events that you never think will happen to you, then when it does it seems so incongruous. Then the reality dawned on him. Someone had tried to break into his home. As he stepped to the door, he didn't see the shard of broken glass on the carpet. He stepped on it, and sustained a cut to the sole of his left foot.

Sonia came flying into the lounge. She was wearing a silk kimono over her pyjamas. She had never looked sexier. "What the hell happened?" she asked.

"I don't know," replied Relton shouting above the noise of the alarm. "What I do know is that I've cut my foot." He hobbled to the sofa, plumped into it and looked at the bottom of his foot. There was a puncture hole in his heel. It was a couple of centimetres wide, and deep. Blood was winding its way over the hillocks of his foot. Luckily the splinter hadn't penetrated deep into the flesh. The cut was the least of his worries. Someone had tried to gain entry into his house.

In the next instant the alarm stopped ringing. Hailey stepped into the room rubbing sleep out of her eyes. "Didn't you hear anything?" he asked her. She bobbed her head on her shoulders to let her mane of blonde hair dance.

She yawned "Pardon?" she asked.

"Nothing," he said. Then he was aware that Sonia had hold of the telephone and she was making a call.

Before he could persuade her not to, Sonia was making a '999' call to the police, to report the attempted break in.

# Chapter 7

It took the local police a shade under eight hours to send an officer to the house. Relton wished his wife hadn't bothered to call them, but she was far savvier than him. She knew they had to have a police number for insurance purposes. Therefore, it had to be reported in order that the necessary repairs to the door wouldn't put them out of pocket. After all, why pay house insurance and not claim? It would be like having a dog and barking yourself.

Sonia made the call at four-thirty in the morning. It was just after noon when Relton answered the front door to two uniformed police officers. They didn't look much older than his daughter. Mere kids. Sonia had gone to work at ten and Hailey had left for college an hour later, so he was home alone. He didn't like the idea of having a day off. It meant he wasn't earning money, but someone had to be at home to meet the police. He had found the house contents insurance policy and looked over it in the early hours of the morning. He knew he would be paid out if he ever had to take a prolonged period off work, but he wouldn't get anything for a few days. His cab was on the brick drive by the side of the house leading to the garage.

During the morning he had taken a piece of hardboard, once destined for the floor of the houseboat, and placed it over the pane of glass that was cracked. All he could do with the French windows was to tape them together. A local repair unit couldn't come to the house until tomorrow afternoon. That was the least of his worries.

He had been asking himself for the last several hours who would want to break into his home, and more to the point, why?

The police officers may have been young, but to give them credit, they went about their duty in a professional manner. They looked at the damage, and even went out into the garden to inspect the door from the outside, then they came back inside. They asked him if he had any idea who may have wanted to break in. He said 'no idea'. They asked him what he had seen. "Just the arse of some bloke leaping over the fence at the bottom of the garden," he replied. One of the constables asked him if he was in dispute with anyone? Did he have anything valuable in the house? Had he won any money recently? He said 'fat chance'. As he answered the questions something came over him. He decided that this – for right or for wrong – was an opportune time to tell the police what he had seen in the house in Primrose Hill.

The younger of the two cops had his notebook in one hand and a pencil in the other. The other one was letting his eyes drift across the room. He looked very interested in the photographs of his daughter Hailey in her running gear. Relton explained she was a middle-distance runner at her local sports club.

He was sitting in a leather chair in his jeans and a polo shirt. There was a bandage around his left foot. "There's something you must know," he said.

The two cops looked at each other as if they knew the gravity of the situation. "Such as?" the older, more experienced one asked.

Relton clenched his teeth and sucked on them. "I think the burglar may have been looking for something."

The two cops looked at each other. The younger one asked, "Like what?"

"A briefcase," he replied.

"A briefcase?"

"There's something I need to tell you."

"What?"

He told them about how last night at eight-thirty he had picked up an American from outside Heathrow terminal four. They had already sussed he was a taxi driver by the sight of the cab on the drive. It was a bit of a giveaway.

They let him talk without interruption about everything that had occurred. When he told them, he had visited a house in Primrose Hill and discovered a dead body, then what seemed like a rather non-urgent case of attempted burglary mushroomed into something that was way off their radar. Talking and getting it off his chest, and out into the open came as a huge relief. The second cop gave his colleague a look, then said he would make a call. He went into the kitchen to make a call to his superiors in the local police station.

The younger cop asked Relton where the case was. "In the cupboard under the stairs," he replied. The cop wanted him to show him where, then asked him what was in it. He said he didn't know.

The other constable joined them at the cupboard and asked him to extract the case, which he did. Then they took him and the case back into the lounge and kept him talking. They asked him to repeat his account of events, not once but twice. They asked him the obvious question about why he hadn't reported this last night? This was the sixty-four-thousand-dollar question.

He said he had been too shocked and too fearful.

"What had changed?" one of the cops asked.

"The attempted burglary," he replied. The constable with the notebook made a note of his reply. He was scribbling like there was no tomorrow. After a period of ten minutes or so there was a period of silence. Relton offered to make them a hot drink. They declined the offer. Relton asked them who they were waiting for. *'Detectives'*, the older one replied. They told him to relax and that he had done the right thing telling them. He knew he had done the right thing. There was no need to tell him that. He could feel the weight lifting off his shoulders.

A further ten minutes passed before there was a knock at the front door. The older cop went to open it. Two guys in civvies stepped into the house and sauntered into the lounge.

The guy in the lead introduced himself has Detective Chief Inspector Peter Winn. The other one was Detective Inspector Michael Devlin. The one in charge, DCI Winn was slick and well turned out. He looked like a bit of a throwback to a bygone age when detectives were pillars of the community. Honest guys, who were adored by the public. Too many bad stories over the past twenty years had changed that image.

DCI Winn had a sharp haircut and an even sharper suit and a kind face. DC Devlin was the handsome one with skin the shade of milky coffee. He had nice eyes and perfect teeth. He wore his hair in a modern style. Short down the sides, thick on top. Both were unsmiling and business like. They produced their ID badges at the same time and flashed them in front of Relton. He had little doubt that they were the real article. The one called Winn asked the uniformed cop who had taken the notes to update them on the story so far. He obliged, using the notes in his book. As he spoke, they observed Relton closely to see his body language and see how he reacted. He kept his body language in check, though he did nod his head on several occasions to confirm what he had told them was true. He had picked up an American guy from outside of terminal four and taken him to the hotel in the Square Mile. The Yank had asked him to take the briefcase to an address in Primrose Hill.

"Which address?" asked Devlin.

Relton told him.

"What's in the case?" Winn asked.

"No idea," replied Relton.

On hearing the first full account of the details, Devlin stepped out of the room. Winn asked Relton about the attempted break in and what he had seen.

"Nothing," he replied. "Other than the arse end of a guy climbing over the fence."

Devlin returned to the room after a couple of minutes and looked towards Winn. He told Relton they wanted to take him to the address in Primrose Hill. To which Relton replied. 'No problem'.

Winn suggested to one of the uniformed cops that he stay here to guard the house and that the other one accompanied them in his patrol car to the address. They would take Relton in their own car.

Relton stepped out of the house, accompanied by the two cops in plain clothes and the one in uniform. Missus Curtain-Twitcher at number thirty-six adjusted her nets. Relton felt like flashing the Vs at her, but thought better of it. Word that the police had called at his house would soon be broadcast around the manor on the bush telegraph.

Relton was shown into the back seat of the unmarked police car - a four door Audi. As soon as Devlin was in the driver's seat and Winn was beside him, they set off for the short drive to Primrose Hill. On the way there, DI Winn asked Relton if anything out of the ordinary had happened to him in the past few days. "Only this," he replied. The cops didn't ask him anything else.

On arriving outside of the house Relton expected to see a hive of activity with police officers in 'noddy' suits coming in and out of the house and a line of tape to prevent anyone from getting near to the scene. The reality was something different. There was no one close by, and no activity, but for a single police car parked outside the house. A policeman was sitting in the driver's seat. Now in the light of the day, the street looked even quieter than it had last night. Across the way, behind a low wall was a three-story old people's home. Devlin parked the Audi behind the stationery police car. "Is this the address?" he asked.

Relton looked at the privet hedge. "Absolutely," he said. "And there's the body of a dead man inside the front room. He's been garrotted," he added.

"Is that so?" said Devlin. "Let's see. Follow us."

The two cops and Relton got out of the car, walked through the gap in the privet and up the flight of three steps onto the path and onto the front door which was wide open. A cop in uniform was just stepping out. He said nothing. Relton gripped himself for the scene that would greet him, but then he asked himself where were the 'Scene of Crime' officers? Where was the guy with the camera? Where were the finger-print guys? He had seen enough crime dramas on TV to last a lifetime. He knew they should be here. When he was at the top of the steps Winn turned his head back and said: "This is the house, is it?"

"Yes."

Winn stepped inside. Devlin was bringing up the rear with the young uniformed cop behind him. Relton stepped through the front door. Winn took the round knob on the door to the left, opened it and stepped inside. Relton was behind him and hey presto, nothing. There was no dead guy sitting in a chair. The scattered books and the papers on the floor were no longer there. The room had been rearranged. The chair the guy had been sitting in was now over to the right adjacent to a sideboard which was now at the other side. The plain orange rug on the floor was now tight to the fireplace along its length. Yesterday it was turned the other way. The television now had a wicker bowl full of fruit on it. The clock on the cabinet was now on the mantel piece above the fire place.

Winn looked to Relton. "This is the room is it?"

"Yeah."

DI Devlin looked at Winn then at Relton. "You certain? Because I don't see a dead body, do you?"

Relton was perplexed. "I'm telling you. He was sitting in a chair right here." He indicated where the chair had been. "That cabinet over there was here." He pointed to the wall on the door side. "The rug in front of the fire place was the other way."

DCI Winn looked around the room, then at the wood floor to see if there were any scuff marks on the surface to indicate that a chair had been there. He sniffed. "As you can see. There are no dead bodies in here. Believe me, the officers have searched from top to bottom."

"And believe me, I'm telling you the truth," Relton said in an adamant tone.

Devlin gave a light cough. "He must have come back to life, because I can't see a dead body. Are any of your mates playing tricks on you for a laugh?"

"I don't have any *mates*," said Relton stressing the word mates.

Neither of the two cops made a sarcastic remark though they may have been tempted. Winn sniffed again. "Are you sure you're not under any stress?"

"I get stress every day of the week driving the streets of this fucking place."

"No need to swear," Devlin said.

"Sorry," said Relton. He was dumbfounded. Totally at a loss to explain what was going on. Now he wasn't sure what he had seen. "Whoever had garrotted the guy in that chair," he pointed to it. "Must have come back to move the body and tidy up."

Devlin stepped to the chest of drawers. He opened them and found papers and books all neatly arranged inside. All the books had a medical theme. There were papers and thesis and studies all with titles that required someone with a medical brain to explain the subject matter. He closed the drawer and looked to Relton, pursed his lips and shook his head.

"Are you sure you're not stressed out over something?" he asked.

"It happens," chipped Winn. Relton wanted to storm out of the house and to bang his head against the nearest brick wall. "I know what I saw," he said.

"You must dream up some fantasies in that cab." Devlin said.

"I tell you. There was a dead body right here in this room last night."

Winn brought him down to ground with a bump. "There's no indication of that," he said. Relton had to admit that was the case.

"Unless you killed him and disposed of the body," Devlin said in a tone of voice that suggested he had just considered the theory. "Like the murderer returning to the scene in an effort to distance himself. It happens. Believe me."

"Leave it out," Relton said. He wanted to say something far more provocative but held back. Devlin looked to Winn. "If there's anything, I dislike its pranksters taking the piss," he said under his breath. Devlin appeared to be the provocateur of the two. He was the hard-arsed one. The one who was looking for and wanting a reaction.

Relton wouldn't satisfy his desire for a reaction. "This is no prank," he said in a calm and measured tone.

"There isn't a body here and there is no obvious evidence of a fight or a struggle," said Winn.

It was all too convenient, thought Relton. His failure to report the crime immediately had given the killer the opportunity to return to the scene to clean up, remove the body and any evidence of a struggle. And in doing so made him look like a time-waster and a loser.

He thought it was better to admit defeat rather than antagonise them. He had no need to yank their chains anymore. He would take it on the chin and live to fight another day. A new tactic. "Okay," he said and shrugged his shoulders. "Maybe I got it wrong," he said ruefully.

Winn looked at Devlin. "Maybe the attempted burglary on your house took you over the edge," he said.

"Yeah maybe," he grudgingly admitted. "Sorry for the inconvenience. I'm sorry about this. Maybe I need to see my doctor."

Neither of the cops said anything, but their faces told a different story. Winn dipped his hand into a jacket pocket. He extracted a business card. "Here is my card. Give me a call if you think of anything else," he requested.

Relton thanked him. He took the card and slipped it into his back trouser pocket. "What about the case?" he asked.

Devlin looked at him. "Hand it into the taxi lost luggage place. No doubt someone will claim it in time." They were not interested in the case and must have assumed that like the rest of the story, it was a load of bollocks.

Winn and Devlin escorted him out of the house and down onto the pavement. They asked the officer who had accompanied them from Harrow to take Relton back home, and to collect his colleague watching over the house.

# Chapter 8

As Relton was driven away from the house in Primrose Hill, he felt as low as a snake's belly. He didn't know what was going on. For a few short seconds he even contemplated that DI Devlin was right. He had imagined the entire episode. 'Am I going mad?' he asked himself. No, he wasn't. He had seen what he had seen. The question was where the hell was the dead body? The cops who had been at the house before they had arrived must have searched in every room for a dead body.

Once they were back at his home, the cop who was guarding the house left and joined his colleagues. Relton was left alone to plan his next move. First, he put the case back into the hiding place under the stairs, under the rolls of unused wallpaper, so it was hidden from Sonia's eyes

When she arrived back home at four o'clock, she asked him what the police had said. Not a lot, he replied. It was just another attempted burglary. Another case to go on the list of unsolved crimes. Lucky for them that the alarm system had worked and had prevented the burglar from getting inside. Not that there was much to steal. It was hardly crammed with precious jewels and piles of cash. Relton felt down and on the edge. He told his wife that the police had put it down to the same burglar who had carried out a spate of burglaries in the area.

After a bite to eat at six, he decided to get out and catch the final hour of the evening rush hour. After all, a taxi parked in a drive doing nothing wasn't earning any money. He got onto the road and did what he did best. He slipped Santana's greatest hits into the CD player and lost himself in the heady mix of electronic funk and modern jazz.

His first passenger took him to Hyde Park corner, then from there he went to Kings Cross station. It was lightly raining. Someone flagged him down and asked to be taken to an address in Islington. He was soon back in the swing. He picked up a couple near to Angel tube station who wanted to go into Kensington. They spent most of the ride arguing over where and what they were going to eat. As a black cab driver, you tend to come across every facet and emotion of human life in the back of a cab. If he had the time, he could write a book about the mysteries of human behaviour.

He called it a night at ten and went home. Nothing had occurred. It was a quiet night for a Friday in the centre of the city.

The following day – Saturday – was always a good day for business. Scores of people came into the city from out of town to shop in the West End, or take in the sights and a show in the evening. Sonia was staying at home for the workmen who were coming to fix the French windows. The house insurance would eventually cough up to cover the bill.

Relton was out at nine and roamed the streets looking for trade. He got his first pull of the day on Maida Vale, to go to a business address in Camden. On his way back, he went around Regent's Park on the north side. On reaching Prince Albert Road he hung a right and headed into Primrose Hill. He wasn't going to let it drop. He had to find out what had happened to the body in the house. Who was he? Where was he? Maybe one of the neighbours might know him or something. No matter what the police said, he was going to make some enquiries of his own. Possibly dangerous? Stupid? Yes, but he had to know. The unknown was driving him mad.

Once in Primrose Hill he found the street where the house was located. The one on the corner of a block of five and the one with the high privet at the front and the cream-orange blinds over the windows.

A couple were walking a big, ugly dog on a lead, perhaps heading to the nearby common ground at the bottom of Primrose Hill Road. Otherwise there were few people about. The day, though immersed in dark cloud, was mild and with little breeze. There was no evidence of anyone loitering on the pavement outside the house. He pulled into the kerb and killed the engine, got out of the cab and stepped onto the path leading to the three steps going up to the front door. Nothing stirred. The blinds over the windows on all three floors were down. As he looked to his left, a guy emerged onto the path carrying a racing bicycle. He eyed Relton. He was a tall white guy, approximately thirty years of age with a pale complexion and hair the colour of carrot juice. He was wearing long racing shorts and a real riders' jersey. He even had a safety helmet on his head. He looked at the cab parked in the kerb. Relton made eye contact with him. "Sorry to bother you," he said. "What number is this house?" he asked.

The chap looked towards the house he had emerged from. "This one?" he asked, gesturing to it with a thrust of his head.

"Yeah."

"Forty-two," he replied.

"Do you live in the house next door?"

The guy looked at him with suspicion etched on his face. "Who wants to know?" he asked.

Relton smiled. "Sorry. I'm picking up a passenger from this house, but no one is here. Do you know who lives here?"

The guy questioned him with his eyes. "Not sure," he said. "Think he's an American guy, but I don't know for sure," he said.

"Okay. Do you know where he might be?"

The guy gave him a puzzled face. "Might be at work. As far as I know he's a lecturer at some university, or a college lecturer."

For someone who didn't know him he seemed to know a lot more than he was letting on. "How long has he lived here?" Relton asked.

"About six months I reckon." He edged his bike to the edge of the path as if he was done with answering questions and wanted to jump on his bike and ride away.

"Thanks," Relton said. "One more question, if you don't mind."

"What now?"

"Do you know his name?"

"No, I can't say I do."

"Is it his house?" The guy narrowed his eyes. "Or does he rent?" Relton asked.

"Rent I think," said the guy in exasperation as if he was becoming pissed off by the tone of the questions. In the next second, he put the bike on to the road, swung his legs over the frame, jumped onto the seat and rode off up the street at speed.

Relton got into his cab, started the engine, edged forward then did a U turn and went back the way he came.

For the next couple of hours, he sought to make a living on the busy bustling streets of the capital. There were a number of football games in the capital today. A couple of heavyweight encounters. At the Emirates in north London, Arsenal were entertaining Liverpool. Over in west London the gladiators from the Kings Road, Chelsea, were at home to Manchester City. He would listen to a commentary on BBC Radio London, whilst he combed the streets looking for customers. As he cruised, he reflected. He recalled everything that had occurred. Was it only thirty-six hours since he had picked up the American from outside of Terminal Four at Heathrow? It seemed like a lot more than that.

From three o'clock onwards he listened to the first half of the Arsenal versus Liverpool game then turned the radio off at half time to put in a call to Sonia. The workmen, who were fixing the patio doors, had only just left the house. It took them less than an hour to take the glass out of the door, then replace it with a fresh pane. The door frame was slightly warped, but it still closed and locked tight. The men told her it would require replacing in the next few months or so. More expense, thought Relton. He still had loads of work to do on the houseboat. He needed more expense like he needed a hole in the head. Perhaps they could claim the money from a criminal compensation scheme.

He told Sonia he would be home at six for a quick bite to eat, then he would go out again. Saturday night in the West-End was always busy. The shows, the clubs and the concerts, really pulled in the punters. It would be busy from eight o'clock right into the early hours of the morning. He intended to stay out until one in the morning, then come home. He was already feeling tired.

His next passengers were a middle-aged Spanish couple who he picked up from outside a hotel in Kensington. They were heading to the Roundhouse in Camden Town, to attend a concert by a band whose name didn't register with him. The chap spoke excellent English and was very chatty, though his partner didn't speak a word, or chose not to.

Relton asked him if he was on holiday. He said 'yes' then changed it to 'no' then changed that to 'maybe'. He told Relton he was in London to attend a conference at the Queen Elizabeth Conference centre. It was a meeting of world-renowned medical scientists. The 'Forum of International Medical Scientists'. It was a biannual event. The previous conference was in his home city of Madrid. This year it was London. In two years' time, it would be the South Korean capital of Seoul.

Relton wondered where he had seen the 'International Forum of Medical Scientists' before. Then it came to him. It was on the noticeboard in the Minerva Hotel. Relton saw an opportunity. He asked the chap if he was a medical scientist. He said he was. Relton then asked him if he knew an American called Doctor Peter Kinden. The chap knew his name though he had never met him. He said Kinden was an eminent doctor from the United States, who was renowned for the research he was doing into using gene therapy to find a cure for certain forms of cancer. Then he said something interesting. Doctor Kinden was due to deliver a keynote speech on Friday at the conference on the findings of a research programme he was leading, but he had had to return to the United States at short notice due to a family illness. Relton asked him who had told him this. He replied the organisers of the conference, of course.

The chap asked Relton why he was interested in Doctor Kinden. Relton said nothing really, just that he had heard his name on a television report into the research he was carrying out. Then Relton chanced his arm. He asked him if the name Hank Peterson meant anything to him. Of course, replied the doctor. Hank Peterson was an associate of Doctor Kinden's. They were working on the same research project. Hank Peterson wasn't just a Doctor, he was Professor Hank Peterson of Harvard University.

Relton asked him if he knew or had seen Professor Peterson. He said he knew the name, but had never met him, nor had he seen him at the conference. You won't, thought Relton, because he was stone dead. But he didn't tell him that.

The doctor told him that the forum had begun yesterday and would close on Monday afternoon with the final speech to be given by the head honcho of the forum.

A couple of minutes after the conversation had concluded, Relton dropped him and his partner outside of the Roundhouse on Chalk Farm Road. The time was six o'clock.

After dropping off the Spanish couple, he turned the radio on, to catch up on the football results. Arsenal had drawn one-one with Liverpool. Chelsea had lost two-nil to Manchester City. Brentford, the team he followed from afar, had lost three-nil up north, at Sheffield United. That was the least of his worries.

He turned on his smart phone, brought up the internet, and searched for the 'International Forum of Medical Scientists'. He soon found some information and read it. The meeting for the forum looked like a pretty big deal. Doctors and medical boffins from all over the globe had congregated in London for their bi-annual conference. They were the people who discovered cures to end the diseases and illness which blighted the human race. Apparently, the event was sponsored in joint cooperation by the United Nations and the World Health Organisation, so it was a major conference.

# Chapter 9

On this Saturday night the weather was clear, but chilly. A sleet-tipped breeze had descended over the city and the people on the street were well wrapped up against the elements. There was that smell of late winter snow in the air. It would become, if anything colder as the sun dropped and the night came rolling in. At seven he took a break and joined a long line of cabs at the taxi-rank adjacent to the side of St Pancreas Station. The next passengers in his cab were travellers from the Manchester area, in London for a long weekend. They wanted to be taken to look at the Shard and view Tower Bridge from London Bridge in the failing light.

By eight o'clock the night had fallen and the lights in the city were on. As he went across the centre of the city in a northerly direction, he looked into his mirrors to see that a large, silver-bodied car was close to him. It could have swept by him in a heartbeat, but the driver elected to stay close to him for some unknown reason. He put his foot down to see if the car would keep up with him. It did and remained close to his rear.

He headed off down Bishopgate towards Liverpool Street before taking a left onto London Wall. He looked into his wing mirror. The car was still keeping pace with him yard for yard, little more than a couple of feet away. It didn't look like the same car that had followed him on Thursday evening from the airport. This car was if anything larger, but not the same model. The other car was a

Mercedes. This one was a silver top-of-the-range Ford saloon. Far more powerful than his one thousand cc diesel engine.

He hung a left at Moorgate and carried onto the square outside of the Bank of England. Okay, he thought to himself if this is how you want to play, bring it on. Adjacent to St. Paul's cathedral was a controlled zone, and a narrow road that can only be accessed by taxis, buses and emergency vehicles. A hand-held device in his cab would activate a pair of retractable bollards in the form of two steel poles that sunk into the ground, then re-emerged as soon as the vehicle had passed through. Without the device, normal street vehicles cannot get access. Ahead, where the road narrowed, he could see that the bollards were up, to block access. As he reduced speed and neared the two protruding metal objects, he reached for a clicker device in the door pocket and pressed a button. It automatically lowered the bollards. He drove through the opening then looked into his rear-view mirror to see that the two bollards had instantly come up to block entry. The car behind drove into the opening then had to swiftly apply the brakes to stop from crashing into the raised bollards. He smiled to himself then laughed out loud. He had got one over them. But perhaps, who 'them' were was another matter. It was at this point that he decided to get off the road and go home. The time was eight-fifteen. He felt tired, but at least he knew he hadn't imagined any of it. There really were people in a car trying to follow him.

As he made his way across town, he recalled what the police had told him. 'Put the briefcase into lost luggage – someone would claim it.' Then he had an idea. Rather than head off in the direction of Harrow he took a right turn and headed into South Kensington. He knew of a store on Gloucester Road that bought and sold second hand luggage and briefcases. If he could find one that matched the silver case, he could feasibly give it to the opposition. For he was involved in a game of cat and mouse, a game in which someone wanted the case and whatever was inside it. When he got to the store it was closed. In the darkened window display, there were literally several dozen briefcases, though he couldn't see one that matched the one he had under the stairs. He thought there was a reasonable chance he could find one in there. He would return to the store early tomorrow morning.

Sunday was supposed to be the day of rest, but there was no such thing as a day of rest for Steve Relton. Sunday was the day he usually worked on the Marie-Claire, the houseboat moored on the Thames, that bottomless pit of expense he was handcuffed to. Still, when it was completely renovated, he could look at it and say 'I did that'. And no matter what it could be worth, that was a lot more worthwhile than any financial reward.

Sunday was the day he gave Marie-Claire his undivided attention. He worked for six days of the week, spending as much as twelve hours a day sitting on his backside in the cab usually in slow moving traffic, chatting to some interesting people, but it was usually people who had little to say or the time or inclination to chat to a cabbie. Today was his day – a day to be creative. He had painted the houseboat from back to front, inside and out, put in a completely new floor and various cabinets and cupboards. He had put in a seating area down one side. All he needed to do was work on the electronics, the plumbing and the job would be seventy-five to eighty percent complete. The day he finished would be the day he could rejoice.

He collected his tools from the garage, put them into Sonia's Nissan runabout and left the house. He had an agreement with Sonia that he could use her car on Sunday, in order to give the cab a rest day.

His plan was to first visit the store on Gloucester Road to see if he could find a replica case, then carry on to Chelsea embankment and Cadogan Pier where the houseboat was moored. He loved the feel of the boat gently bobbing in the water. One of the best things about the pier was its close proximity to Albert Bridge, one of the most beautiful, ornate and picturesque bridges over the Thames. On a warm summer's day there was no better place to be than on the barge, sitting at a table under a parasol, with a glass of wine in his hand and a paperback in his lap.

The boat had caused plenty of stress with Sonia, mainly over the expense. At one point it had resulted in their relationship going through a sticky patch. If it wasn't for Hailey being at home and at college, and needing their support, the boat could have been the straw which broke the camel's back. Relton had promised Sonia that as soon as he had finished renovating it, he would put it up for sale and get the money back plus a lot more. On that account she had reduced her resistance. That was a year ago. He thought he still had at least three month's work to complete.

The Sunday morning traffic was easy going. He soon made it onto Gloucester Road and found the second-hand store selling briefcases. He parked outside and ventured inside. There was an assortment of briefcases and every kind of luggage piled high from floor to ceiling. It was like a traveller's bric-a-brac heaven. The proprietor was a small, balding, elderly guy in a loose shirt and knee length shorts. He greeted Relton as he entered.

"Looking for anything special?" he asked.

Relton described the metal case as best as he could. Detailing the measurements, the two, three digits combinations next to the catches with the key holes. The steel like body.

The guy told him it sounded like a Samsonite model called a 'Deluxe'. Virtually unbreakable unless you hit it with a ten-pound lump hammer. The bad news was that he didn't have one. Relton asked him if he knew where he could find one. The old chap ran his hand over his mouth then stroked his chin. He suggested he might try the Stables market in Camden Town market. There was a guy there who might have one. He only stocked second- hand Samsonite merchandise or good fakes.

Relton thanked him. He debated whether he should go to the houseboat or divert to Camden Town. After thinking about it for a minute he elected to head off to Camden. It was still early – only five to ten. The market didn't usually get into full swing until the early afternoon. If he got there now, he would avoid the midday crowds.

He set off in Sonia's car and turned on the radio to listen to the local BBC Radio London news. Things were going to get a lot more interesting.

The third item on the news – after the international and national stuff – was a report about a body found in Primrose Hill Park at eight o'clock last night. A young couple out walking a dog had found the body of a male partially concealed under a bush in a small park. Relton pricked up his ears. He felt his heart thump and his stomach turn. Was this the body of the man he had discovered in the house? The report didn't supply any more details or a description, but concluded by saying that the police were making house to house enquiries in the locality. Then the newsreader turned to the sports news. Relton turned off the radio.

Within a couple of minutes of turning the radio off, his mobile phone rang. In order that he didn't break any law he pulled into the kerb and came to a halt. Sonia asked him where he was. He said he was still on his way to the houseboat – the traffic in the Chelsea area was heavier than normal due to a burst water main along Cheyne Walk – a lie. She sounded exasperated and mildly agitated. Two police officers had come to the house to speak to him. What the hell was going on? They wouldn't tell her what it concerned. Good, he thought. He quickly told her it must have something to do with the burglary. Maybe they had caught the villain. She said they wouldn't send two detectives for that. She had a point. Winn and Devlin, he assumed. They wouldn't send the 'dynamic duo' to deal with a piddling attempted burglary. No, these boys had bigger fish to fry. He said he would be home in an hour, and no, he had no idea why they wanted to speak to him.

After talking to Sonia, he drove the couple of miles or so to the fringe of Camden Town. On any given Sunday from midday onwards, the roads closed and turned into a pedestrian market for locals and tourists to wander up and down. There were numerous stores selling everything from high-end clothing to stalls selling one-wash t-shirts, to stores selling old CDs and DVDs. The diversity of people and languages was really what made London the most diverse city, not only in Britain, but within Europe.

He and Sonia had come here many times to visit a music store selling old-style vinyl LPs. Then they'd buy some fish and chips and walk along the streets just taking in the atmosphere. It had been several years since they were last here. At this time in the morning some of the stalls were still setting up and it wasn't as busy as it would become during the afternoon. He strode over the bridge going over Camden Lock and into the Stables building. The Stables was a veritable Aladdin's cave of small stalls selling everything and anything from new-age jewellery to second-hand paperbacks, to stores selling leather goods and electrical goods to herbals remedies.

Relton went deeper inside, then down a flight of stairs and into an underground cavern that was dominated by a large sculpture of three horse heads. He had to discover if there was a stall selling second-hand briefcases and general luggage. The market was a maze of tiny walkways and thoroughfares. He must have walked for a good five minutes browsing before he came across what he was looking for, a stall selling all kinds of bags, holdalls, suitcases and brief cases. The smell of leather, mingling with the smell of spicy food drifting out from a nearby stall, was almost overpowering. Relton made eye contact with the Asian guy behind the display unit. "Do you have a Samsonite Deluxe?" he asked.

The man looked at him through bright walnut eyes. 'Err,' he looked on the shelves that were out of sight to the customer at the other side. Then he leaned down, pulled at something and lo and behold, he pulled out a case and lifted it up. It was the same model as the Samsonite he had in the cupboard under the stairs. Far more battered, older and not as shiny as the one Doctor Kinden had given him, but it was the same model. Maybe not a genuine Samsonite, probably a fake, but it still resembled the case. It required cleaning in order to get the metal hinges and the metal clasps gleaming but that wouldn't take long.

"How much?" Relton enquired.

"Twenty quid," replied the store holder.

"Done," said Relton. He purchased the replica case then left. Rather than head home, or to Cadogan Pier, he ventured into the City and to the Minerva Hotel.

# Chapter 10

Ray Slater had once, several years ago, been a black cab driver, so he knew the score. He knew that people such as the entertainment press, and the London paparazzi would – from time to time – ask for information about who was staying in the hotel. If the paps got wind that a big star was in town they would put out a message to all the door staff to look out for a certain 'A-lister'. If that 'A-lister' was staying in their hotel then a quick phone call could earn them a couple of hundred quid. They also wanted any tittle-tattle about anything going on in the hotel behind closed doors. Who was bonking who? The higher the celeb, the more the money.

Slater had worked as a doorman at several of the major hotels, such as the Savoy, Claridge's and the Ritz. In truth he was little more than a 'meeter and greeter', who would touch the brim of his top hat to a guest and tell the bell boy wheeling the luggage carrier to get a move on. Relton knew him from way back when. Slater and Relton's fathers had been mates. If he asked him nicely, offered him a small bung in the form of a crispy twenty-pound note, Slater might just get him some information he wanted.

As Relton pulled up outside of the hotel he could see it was his lucky day, Ray Slater was working the Sunday morning shift. On seeing the car, Slater stepped forward to meet the driver. He would have been wondering why an ordinary car had pulled up in front of the hotel. The customer wouldn't require valet parking for this vehicle.

"Ray," Relton said. "How you doing?"

Slater eyed him then glanced back to the front of the hotel as if he suspected he was being observed. "You can't park here sir," he said in a loud voice. "Just go with it," he added in a low voice. Maybe he had heard about the scene at the front desk last Thursday night.

Relton winked. "Can you do something for me?"

"Keep talking," said Slater and edged to the open passenger side window. The brim of his tall hat cast a shadow over his face.

"Last Thursday I dropped off a guy at close to eight-thirty. A Yank, said his name was Kinden, but now I'm not so sure who he is. I want to know if he checked in under a different name".

"Yeah, I was on duty. Keep talking." He glanced back to the foyer for a second time.

"Can you do me a favour? Find out if he used another name and get it for me?"

"Who wants to know?" he asked.

"I do."

"I'll see what I can do for you."

"Also, there is a guy in 529. Can you let me know if he's still here?"

"I'll see what I can do," he repeated.

One of Slater's jobs was to observe the coming and goings and to report any suspicious activity to hotel's security manager. If there was anyone who would know if the guy in 529 was still here, it would be Slater. If he didn't know straight off, there were ways and means of finding out.

Relton dipped a hand into a pocket. "No," said Slater. "Give me some money later. I'll see what I can do. Leave it an hour or two." He straightened his back. "Now as I told you once, you can't park here," he said loudly.

Relton smiled. "Be seeing you." He pulled away from the front of the hotel. His next destination was his houseboat, then he would put in a call to DCI Winn.

He drove to the Chelsea Embankment and parked close to the river on Royal Hospital Road. From there he walked the two hundred yards to the embankment. He had his hand wrapped around the briefcase handle. Once at the pier, he opened a metal mesh gate in a fence with a key. Before stepping down the ramp to the pontoon in the water, he closed the gate and locked it. Then he headed down the gangplank, onto the pontoon, then along the pier to his houseboat. All the people who had boats moored here knew him well, so he never received a second look. They were like an owner's club, and there was a strong bond of camaraderie. Those he talked to often complemented him on the fine job he was doing restoring the barge to its former glory. They appreciated his efforts. It wasn't easy combining the task with doing a full day's work.

He walked along the pier to a point near to the bottom, stepped along a short plank and up onto the stern of the boat. Before going down into the interior, he opened the flap leading into the interior then took a glance back. No one was watching him. He opened the flap and stepped down into the interior of the boat. It was one long open space to the exit at the other end.

He had completed two-thirds of the project. At the forward end – the bow – was an arrangement of seating along the sides, then a line of storage cupboards. The seating could be transformed into a double bed in a few seconds. At this end of the interior there was still plenty of work to do. He was going to put in a galley area, then a shower unit, and that would be it, other than the plumbing and the rewiring for the electrics and new circuit boards. On the floor there were several small bottles of propane gas he used for heating and cooking. These would be replaced in time by radiators and a stove. He had fitted in a new floor, sanded it and applied several coats of hard wearing vanish. The whiff of varnish was still strong. It looked great. The cupboards he had fitted along the length looked okay. It really was a labour of love. The glass he had put into the portholes was gleaming, along with the original brass fittings which he had got to sparkle like new.

He needed the can of polish he had put into one of the drawers, and a couple of dusters. Once he had the can of polish, he applied an even coat to the briefcase surface. Using some elbow grease, he cleaned the outside of the case as best as he could, getting into all those nooks and crannies. He had it glinting in no time. The duster he had used soon bore testament to the amount of dirt he had removed.

It was the same model as the one in the cupboard under the stairs at home. It had the same two, three-wheel combinations, the latches and the keyholes. He opened it and ran the duster around the inside. Once cleaned he needed something to put into it. He had some back copies of newspapers he had used when painting, and some old charts he had found in a cardboard box the previous owner had left. He also had a couple of old rags he had used for mopping up paint. He put them into the case, then he closed the lid, snapped the latches and set the two combinations to one-three-seven. His daughter's date of birth, 13th July.

Now to make the call to the police. He had the business card DCI Winn had given him. There was a landline number, along with an eleven-digit mobile number. He rang the mobile.

Winn answered it within five rings. Relton introduced himself. Winn asked him where he was. Relton told him he was at his houseboat on the Thames, the place where he usually spent Sunday. Winn asked him if he would be so kind as to call into Paddington Green police station at his earliest convenience. There had been a development in the case.

"What development?" Relton asked.

Winn didn't tell him. He just asked him to come into Paddington Green police station on Edgeware Road as soon as possible. He wasn't in any kind of trouble and he wasn't under any kind of caution or suspicion. He was required to help the police with their enquiries. Relton said okay. He didn't have a problem with that.

He was happy to help, after all he didn't have anything to hide or fear. He said he would be there in twenty minutes, thirty at the most. Winn asked him if he still had the case. Relton looked at the briefcase he had buffed up to a shine. "Sure," he replied.

"Please bring it," Winn asked politely.

"Okay," he replied.


Relton had walked through the front door of Paddington Green police station in the last minute. At the counter he told a lady constable that he had an appointment with DCI Peter Winn and DI Devlin. The fact that he was here of his own free will was a testament to the fact that he had nothing to fear and nothing to hide.

It was an archetypical British police station. Nothing much in the way of decoration or colour or welcome. Pretty much bare, cold and uninviting. The tiled floor was clean and tidy. The usual notices and mugshots of some of the United Kingdom's most wanted were blu-tacked onto the walls. The echo of feet on the floor filled the space from the surface to the ceiling. There was a kind of powerful, pungent smell of a cleaning liquid, designed to kill all known germs.

The lady PC got onto the internal telephone and contacted the detective's office. It wasn't long before DCI Winn entered the reception area and fixed his eyes on Relton. DC Devlin was a couple of feet behind his colleague. He looked even more handsome than before. He had an athlete's good looks and swagger. They were dressed in pretty much the same style. Winn was in a sharp cut dark suit, whereas Devlin was in a grey check number. The knot of his tie was loose, the collar was open. He smelled of an aftershave that was as almost as powerful as the smell of cleaning fluid. His teeth were like the finest ivory implants. Winn looked at the case in Relton's hand.

"We'll take that. Thank you."

Relton said nothing. He handed it to Winn. What did Devlin say the other day? 'Put it into lost property. Someone will claim it.' Now they couldn't wait to get their hands on it. Winn handed it to the WPC and asked her to book it in as item of interest connected to the case of the body found in Primrose Hill park.

The constable did as she was asked, took it from him and stepped away. Relton was shown through the door, then taken down a long, narrow corridor, passing a number of closed doors then into an interview room which contained a small table and two chairs, one at either end of the table. There was a single frosted glass window at an angle in the top of the back wall where it met the ceiling, which was closed tight. The light was bright against the opaque pane.

Winn asked Relton to take the seat facing the door. Winn occupied the seat opposite. Devlin closed the solid door and locked it from the inside. He approached the table and stood in-between the seated protagonists. Relton was on edge. He wasn't familiar with the inside of a police station. He had seen plenty of crime dramas on television were the chief suspect was harangued to the point of exhaustion and gave in after a mauling by a skilled detective. To be honest the setting wasn't a lot different from what he had seen on the small screen.

DCI Winn introduced himself. "Thank you for agreeing to come in. You're not under any caution or anything like that." Relton was pleased to hear it. "You may have heard that a body has been found in Primrose Hill park. A male approximately forty years of age."

"I heard something on the radio," replied Relton.

Devlin stepped forward a pace. "It appears from initial investigation that he died due to asphyxiation. You know anything about it?"

Relton looked at him sharply with a mixture of surprise and puzzlement. Surely, they didn't suspect him. He looked at Winn and raised his left hand several inches off the table.

"You don't suspect me, do you?" he asked.

Winn sat back and opened his chest wide. He didn't say a thing.

"Why would we suspect you?" Devlin asked. His words bounced from wall to wall.

"Do you think we suspect you?" Winn asked.

They were doing the old one-two. Playing off each other. One would kick the ball to the other and he would knock it back into play. There was nothing subtle in the way they went about their work.

"I don't know if you suspect me. The truth is I don't care that much. I found the body in the house, with a garrotte round his neck. Just as I told you. I don't know how it got there. I certainly don't know how he ended up in a park."

Devlin put his hands down onto the table, palms flat, to take his weight. "Tell us the story again about how you picked up the guy at the airport."

Relton obliged them. He told them the story for a third time. It didn't deviate one iota from the one he told them on Friday. It was the same from start to finish, almost word for word.

By the time he had finished giving them his version of the events Devlin had backed away from the table a couple of paces. "Why didn't you tell us about the body immediately?" he asked.

"You went home. Didn't you?" Winn asked. "Don't you find that strange?"

"That's how it might look...."

"That's how it looks to us," said Devlin cutting him off in mid-sentence.

"I guess I was scared."

"Of what?"

"Being jumped by the bloke who did him."

Winn sniffed, whilst Devlin turned and took a few paces across the floor then stopped and turned back. "So, you drop off a guy who said he was Doctor Kinden at the hotel. Then he asks you to deliver a briefcase to an address in Primrose Hill? Didn't you find that odd?"

"Of course, I did, but hey I'm a cab driver. I've had a lot of strange requests in the last fifteen years. And he gave me two hundred pounds to deliver it."

"You never mentioned that before," Winn said.

"Guess, I forgot to mention it."

"I guess you've forgotten a lot of things." Devlin said.

"That's not true. I've told you the truth. I've told you everything."

It was Winn's turn. "So, you find a body. It must have been a gruesome sight. I mean someone's being garrotted. Must be a horrible sight. But you act in a rational matter. You go home. Rest for an hour then decide to return the case to the man in the hotel. A complete stranger. Didn't you think he could be implicated in the murder?"

Devlin didn't allow him to answer the question. "That's right. It just doesn't add up," he said. "If it doesn't add up, its bound to be untrue. How about you dropped off the guy at the hotel, then you picked up another passenger from outside the hotel. He wants to go to Primrose Hill. You take him there. He invites you in for whatever reason. You argue over something. How about the fare? You kill him with a garrotte, then steal his briefcase. Then you go back to the hotel and make up some cock and bull story about returning a briefcase." It sounded as if they were trying to hit the bull's-eye with one dart.

Winn raised his eyebrows then gently nodded his head. Almost as if he expected Relton to put his hands up and say: 'It's a fair cop. Yes, it was me. I murdered the man, then dragged his body into the park and left him there.'

They may have been throwing darts at a dartboard but they weren't even getting close to hitting it. They were working on speculation and getting nowhere fast.

Relton didn't respond for a long moment, then he just shook his head from side to side. "No. I grant you that I was foolish even to pick up the guy from the airport and even more foolish to agree to deliver the case. But there is no way I picked up the guy and took him to Primrose Hill, then once there I strangled him. For what? What's the motive?"

Now it was the cops turn to be silent. Devlin moved back a couple of paces. Winn turned to a side and crossed his legs. A raised voice came from outside of the room, followed by the sound of someone being escorted down the corridor. Relton's nose puckered against the sharp scent in the room. Devlin stepped back a pace and rested against the wall. "Did you know the victim?" he asked.

Relton looked up and offered him a half smile. "I've never seen the bloke in my life."

Winn looked at Devlin, then at Relton. Maybe in that instance they had come to the conclusion that Relton was on the level with them. Winn scratched the loose flesh under his chin.

"Did you see anyone in the vicinity of the house?" he asked.

"Which house?

"The house in Primrose Hill"

"On Thursday."

"Yes. On Thursday."

"No. I just wanted to get away from there and quickly."

"Why?"

"In case the killer came for me."

"Killer. What if there was more than one of them?"

"Killer. Killers. I don't know. When I saw the dead guy, I panicked. I suppose a kind of survival instinct kicked in and told me to get out as soon as possible."

There was no consistency to their questioning. Maybe they were never convinced he was involved and this was just an elimination exercise. Or they were fishing for clues. They didn't have a *scooby-do* about who had killed Hank Peterson, or why. Or how he was transported from the house to the place where he was found. After a couple of minutes, Winn thanked Relton for his attendance and advised him he was free to go.


Relton didn't hang around. As soon as he was free to go, he got up from the table and approached the door.

Winn had to have the last word. "Don't go anywhere. Stay close to home in case we need to talk to you. If you think of anything, no matter how trivial it may seem, give me a call." He withdrew another business card from a pocket and passed it to him.

"Fine," replied Relton.

Devlin showed him out of the room, escorted him down the long corridor and out into the reception area where the pretty WPC was sitting at the counter. As Relton stepped out, he breathed in the fresh air.

As Relton was driving home from the police station, the short distance to Harrow, he received a call to his mobile. He took it whilst driving, something he hated doing, but needs must and all that.

Ray Slater introduced himself. "Yeah Ray. What did you discover?" Relton asked.

"Plenty," he said. "It will cost you. It took some doing. It's a good job the girl in the office fancies me something chronic."

"You wish."

Slater chuckled. "Too right."

"What have you got, Ray?"

"The guy who checked in on Thursday night at eight-thirty checked in as Eugene Fewster."

"He told me his name was Peter Kinden."

"Not according to what he said at check-in. He checked in as Eugene Fewster from Binghamton, New York."

"Never heard of it."

"He's probably never heard of Watford, but who gives a shit? His US passport matched his name. The guy in 529 is Doctor Peter Kinden of New York, New York. His passport matched."

Relton was confused. He didn't speak with a New York accent. "Anything else?" he asked.

"Yes. The weird thing is that this Fewster guy hasn't been seen since."

"What do you mean?"

"He's disappeared."

"You don't say."

"I do. And what is odder is that the room hasn't been used. The cleaning team, reported to security that the bed hasn't been slept in and the bathroom hasn't been used. That's unusual, but not entirely unheard of."

"I should say."

"On arrival this Fewster went to his room, and then he may have met up with some people in the hotel bar. They apparently had a couple of drinks then all left together with the guest. But Fewster never returned and never checked out."

Relton took it in. He was struggling to absorb the facts. He waited for a long moment then said. "Thanks Ray. That's very helpful."

"By the way I didn't tell you this."

"No problem Ray. I owe you a score."

"Yeah. See you shortly."

Slater ended the call. Relton carried on to his home. He didn't know what to make of it. He wondered why the guy who told him he was Doctor Peter Kinden was in fact someone else. Eugene Fewster from Binghamton, New York. Why would he do that? Unless he was trying to implicate the other guy in some kind of skulduggery. The guy in the hotel who said he was Kinden didn't speak with a New York accent.

Relton got home for five o'clock. Sonia wanted to know if he had contacted the police. He said he had. She asked him what it was about. He said someone who had got into his cab last week had suddenly died in a hotel. The police had traced him by the receipt he had given the passenger. They wanted to know if the guy was by himself. He had contacted the police and told them he was alone. That was all there was to it. She seemed convinced by his explanation. She made a light meal of one of his favourite dishes – a spaghetti carbonara. How he loved Italian food. And Sonia knew how to get the sauce just right.

It was seven when the landline telephone rang. It was DCI Winn. He wanted to see Relton. He told him there had been a breakthrough in the case. The name of the victim was confirmed. He was Professor Hank Peterson. The very name Relton had given Winn two days before.

Professor Peterson was an American citizen who worked in a laboratory at University College London, Medical Centre, as a visiting scientist who was working on a joint US and British government project to discover a drug that could slow the onset of cancer.

DCI Winn wanted Relton to accompany Devlin and him to the Minerva hotel. They would be at his home in twenty minutes. They wanted him to identify the man who said he was Doctor Kinden. He told Sonia the police were coming to collect him. It had something to do with the guy who had died in his hotel room. He told her not to worry.

DI Devlin collected Relton from his home. DCI Winn was in the car with him. Devlin drove into the city and they soon arrived outside the hotel in the City of London. It was a cold evening; the sunlight had given way to a clear sky. The lights from the building across the narrow street were reflecting in the large glass windows masking the wide hotel reception area behind. A number of people were coming and going from the foyer entrance where the door man on duty was supervising a member of staff who was taking luggage from a black cab. A number of pedestrians ambled by. It was a common scene outside any of the large hotels in the central area of the city.

Relton accompanied by Devlin with Winn a couple of paces behind him went through the glass door and into the warmth of the foyer with its plain pastel coloured walls, tiled floor and mock regency chairs and tables in which a number of people were sitting enjoying a beverage.

Winn approached the check-in counter. He dug a hand into an inside coat pocket, extracted a wallet and flashed his ID badge. The hotel employee behind the counter, resplendent in her crisp uniform, looked at him with a neutral expression on her face. 'I'm Detective Chief Inspector Peter Winn. This is my colleague Detective Inspector Devlin. Can we speak to the hotel security manager please?"

"One moment please," said the young lady. She reached for a telephone, tapped in a number and instantly spoke to someone and asked him to come to the front desk. She listened to the reply, then placed the telephone down. "If you would like to take a seat over there." She pointed in the direction of the seating area. "Our head of hotel security will be here in a moment."

They did as requested and stepped to the seating area and sat at a low table. No sooner had they sat down, then a short, balding chap in his mid-fifties appeared from a door further down the foyer and approached them. He was wearing an ill-fitting blue-grey suit. He aimed straight for the three men sitting at the table, stretching his hand out as he came to DCI Winn.

"Good evening. I'm the hotel security manager. My name is Ivan Leeman. How can I help you gentleman this evening?" he asked in a hushed voice, then immediately looked around the interior at the people sitting there. "Perhaps you'd like to come into my office."

"That's a good suggestion," said Winn.

They followed the security manager through the foyer, into a carpeted area then into a smart office that contained all the equipment the head of hotel security required. The room was encased in teak wood panels. A large desk dominated the floorspace. There were several items on the desk, telephone, pen holder, papers, nothing out of the ordinary. There was a PC and monitor.
Leeman manoeuvred two chairs, which he placed in front of his desk and a third in a corner.

He sat at the desk in a leather chair and leaned forward. "Would it be at all possible to see some identification?" he asked.

"Of course," said Winn. He extracted his ID as did Devlin. He was soon satisfied they were who they said they were. Winn introduced Relton.

"What brings you here to this hotel?" Leeman asked. He ran a hand over his chin.

As the leading investigator, it was Winn who answered the question. "We're investigating the possible murder of an American who was found in Primrose Hill last night. You may have heard something about it?"

"Yes. I did," replied Leeman. "Is this the chap who was found in the park?" He had obviously heard the news through the media.

"Yes. He was found in Primrose Hill park."

"What has it to do with the hotel?" Leeman asked.

Devlin took over from Winn. He told Leeman that there was a theory that someone who had checked into the hotel at eight-thirty on Thursday evening had requested that an item of luggage be delivered to the home of the victim at close to the time he was being murdered.

Leeman listened to what he was being told and nodded his head. Devlin told him that the person in question had been picked up from Heathrow on Thursday night, then dropped off at the hotel at approximately eight-thirty. What the police needed to do was to discover who this person was. What room he was in and where he was now, in order that they could interview him. They would also like to view the CCTV from that time. Leeman made some notes on a pad; then he got onto his PC typed in a few commands and found the page he was looking for.

"On Thursday evening at eight-thirty pm one person checked in to a pre-booked room." He read the details. "A Eugene Fewster of Binghamton, New York. Booked in for two nights. Room 645."

"Who pre-booked the room?" Winn asked.

"It was done through a booking dot.com agent in the US. Paid for at that end." Leeman looked from the screen. "The funny thing is that the guest didn't sleep in the room, and he didn't check out on Saturday. Or in other words he never used the room."

"Is that normal practice?" Devlin asked.

"No, it's far from normal. Guests usually stay for the full duration of their stay with us, but it's not wholly uncommon for a guest to stay for only one night, then for whatever reason check out the next day."

"But this guy didn't stay and he didn't check out?" Devlin asked.

"That's correct," Leeman confirmed.

"Can we see if you have any CCTV of him leaving on Thursday night?" Winn asked.

"Yes, we can. I will arrange for a CD to be made of the tape. Then you can collect it if that suits you best."

"How quickly can we view it?" Winn asked.

"I can arrange for it to be done immediately. Once it's downloaded onto a CD, then I can let you know and you can come back to collect it."

"Thank you," Winn said.

"Another thing is that when the taxi driver asked for this Eugene Fewster for his name, he told him he was a Doctor Kinden." Leeman must have come to the conclusion by now that the guy sitting in the corner of the room and saying nothing was the taxi driver in question.

Winn continued. "He came back to the hotel with the intention of giving him the case and asked to see Mister Kinden, but it wasn't the same man he had dropped off."

Leeman narrowed his eyes in a quizzical look as if he was having difficulty keeping up with the plot.

It was Devlin's turn. "We believe you have a Mister Kinden staying in the hotel. We would like to interview him if possible."

Leeman turned back to the PC and tapped a few keys on the keyboard. It took him twenty seconds to find his name on the lists of guests. "There is a Doctor Kinden staying with us. He checked in on Thursday evening and is staying here for six nights. He is due to check out on Wednesday."

"Who made the booking?" Devlin asked.

"He did. Well, him or someone on his behalf, direct to the hotel front desk by telephone from the States."

"We would like to interview him," said Winn.

"I can't speak for our guests." Leeman said. "If he's willing, then that's fine.

Going by the scope of the conversation, Relton concluded that he was well and truly out of the equation.

Leeman looked at the screen and found the room number for Doctor Kinden. He tapped it into his phone and put it onto open mode rather than a closed line.

It looked as if the guest was out of his suite. But then the ringing call was answered on the sixth ring. "Hello, Doctor Kinden," said the person answering the call.

"Doctor Kinden. Good evening. My name is Ivan Leeman. I'm head of security in the hotel. I'm sorry to bother you but would you be able to give me two minutes of your time."

"What is it?" Kinden asked. He sounded as if he was put out by the request.

"It's a police matter. I have two Metropolitan Police detectives here with me."

"Okay. Why?"

"Rather than discuss it over the phone, would you be able to meet me at the bottom of the elevator in two minutes?"

"Yes. Okay, then."

"Thank you for your assistance. It's most appreciated."

Leeman put the telephone down. "Before I bring him into the office, please let me speak to him in private. If he is happy to talk to you, I shall bring him in here."

Winn agreed to the suggestion. This guy knew his stuff. If the American refused to co-operate then they couldn't do a lot about it, other than ask him to accompany them to the nearest police station and risk upsetting the American embassy.

Leeman left the room to await Doctor Kinden at the bottom of the elevator.

Five minutes passed before he returned with the doctor. It was the same man Relton had spoken to on Thursday night. Then he had been wearing a plush dinner suit. Now he was more casual, in a wool sweater and slacks. He was as polished as he had looked before. He still had the nicely styled hair and the bronze tan. He eyed Relton and must have recalled the scene from the other night when Relton had told him he wasn't Doctor Kinden. That someone else was the real Doctor Kinden. Leeman introduced the two police officers, who rose out of their seats to greet him. They were obliged to show him their identification badges.

"What's this about?" asked the urbane Yank.

"We are conducting some enquiries into a murder here in London," Winn said.

"Do you know a man by the name of Eugene Fewster?" Devlin asked swiftly.

Relton, who was still sitting in the corner, could see the American's feet twitch.

"No. Should I?" he asked with a touch of mild annoyance and impatience in his tone. Relton was no body language expert but he could see a sign that actually he may have recognised the name. If he could see it, surely the two detectives would also see it too.

"Have you any idea why a man called Eugene Fewster would tell this man," … he glanced at Relton… "that he was Doctor Kinden?" Winn asked.

"No," he said. "What's this about?" he asked again.

"As I said we are investigating a murder of a man we believe to be Professor Hank Peterson, an American citizen working and living in London," Winn said.

"Does that name mean anything to you?" Devlin asked.

He shook his head. "No, I don't think so."

Winn and Devlin shared a face. "Well either you do or you don't," said Devlin in slightly raised tone of voice.

"Well I don't," he replied with a snap of belligerency in his voice.

"Why are you in London? Is it a vacation?" Winn asked.

"I'm attending a meeting of the Forum of Medical Scientists in the Queen Elizabeth conference centre in Westminster," he replied.

"What's the event exactly?" Devlin asked.

"A meeting of scientists to discuss advances in medical research and disease prevention."

"You sell medicines?" Devlin asked.

"I'm an employee of Western Industrial Pharmaceutics, and yes, we make and sell such merchandise," he said.

"Where are you based?"

"New York City."

"Where are your headquarters?"

"The Harvard Medical school campus in Boston."

"So, you specialise in drugs?"

"I prefer to call them medical merchandise." He was well schooled in the use of the correct terminology.

"What kind of merchandise?"

"A broad range," he replied.

Winn paused for a moment as if he had quickly become exhausted with the questioning, or he was thinking of a new tactic. "Where were you on Thursday night at seven thirty to ten o'clock in the evening?" he asked.

Kinden looked at Winn. "In the hotel. At a function. Several people who are attending the forum are staying at this hotel and there are fringe events and talks each night."

"So, there are people from all over the world at the event?"

"Yes. From Europe and beyond. So yes, I'd say from all over the world."

"Where, like China? The Middle East? The Far East?"

"Yes. Those areas."

"Do you arrange deals at these types of events?" Winn asked.

"Depends what you mean by deals. Possibly. But it's mainly for scientists to meet and to discuss their work in the field of medical research."

"When does the event finish?"

"It comes to an end tomorrow afternoon with the final key note speeches."

"When are you returning home?" Devlin asked.

"I have one more day to relax and do some sightseeing, then I return home the day after," he stalled for a brief moment. "On Wednesday morning."

"Is this your first trip to London?" Devlin asked.

"No. I've been here several times before."

"Do you know the Primrose Hill area?" Winn asked.

"Not specifically. No," he corrected.

"So, you've never heard of a guy called Eugene Fewster nor someone called Professor Hank Peterson?"

"As I said. No. Those names don't mean anything to me."

Devlin shifted his feet. "Professor Peterson worked in a laboratory in the University College London as a visiting scientist."

"Did he?"

"Yes."

"He was attached to a British-American research project here in London."

Kinden looked at Winn. He didn't respond to this revelation. Instead he went all coy and didn't say another word. A period of silence descended. Winn and Devlin looked at Kinden and he at them. Eyes travelled from one to the other in a triangle of intrigue.

Kinden was the first to snap. "Maybe you should speak to the embassy about this. I think I'm done talking here." He took a step back and he tried to relax his body but his body language displayed a tense, nervous edge.

"Just one more thing," asked Devlin. "Do you recognise anyone here?"

"You mean this guy?" he said and nodded his head towards Relton.

"Might do," said Winn. "Why do you think the man he dropped off at this hotel on Thursday evening would say he was you?"

"You've already asked me that and I said I've no idea."

"And you don't know him or Hank Peterson."

"No."

Winn decided to cut his losses, not before asking Kinden if he had any identification on him.

Kinden produced his US passport which he handed to him.

Winn looked at the passport. "Thank you, Dr Kinden," he said. "And thank you for your assistance. Have a nice stay in London." He handed his passport back to him and they shared a brief handshake.

As all five of them filed out of the office, Leeman said he would accompany Doctor Kinden back to his room.

As they emerged from the room, several men in suits, speaking in a Far East Asian language came by. Relton recognised two of them. They were the same two men he had seen on Thursday night.

# Chapter 12

For the remainder of that Sunday night Relton contemplated his next move. He didn't have a clue what the case contained, but assumed it was something of value, and that was the key word. 'Value'. For the first time in all this confusing mess, he found himself wondering if he could profit.

He had a crazy idea. He knew from the Spanish doctor he had picked up in his cab that tomorrow, Monday, was the final day of the 'Forum of International Medical Scientists' in the Queen Elizabeth conference centre in Westminster. Perhaps, he could make contact with the party of south-east Asians, and put a question to them. Did they want the case? If the answer was yes, were they willing to purchase it from him? Though he would hate himself for thinking on these terms, he had to think long term. He not only needed a cash injection to finish the houseboat, but his daughter would be completing college in a year, and she was hoping to go to university to study Sports Science. That wasn't cheap. With the annual fees touching nine thousand pounds, he had no wish to see her out of pocket for the rest of her early adult life. This could be a way of making some money. He wasn't a Christian. He had few scruples when it came to making money.

Not only did he want to speak to the oriental guys, but he was intrigued about what these people spent four days talking over. The more he thought about it, the more determined he was to see it to the end.

If he could blag his way into the conference centre, he could well come across the guys he saw in the hotel and ask them if they were interested in a trade. Something told him they may hold the key to this episode.

Sonia questioned him on his return home. He had managed to convince her that he was just helping the police with their enquiries. That it was nothing to lose any sleep over and she had nothing to fear. He was home, wasn't he? Sitting in the lounge with his shoes off, watching some God-awful programme on television, with his girls by his side. If he was in any kind of trouble with the police, this would be the last place he would be.

The following morning, he left home at eight and hit the streets looking for business. He stayed out for three hours, then returned home knowing full well that Sonia would have left for her job in the supermarket, and Hailey would be in college. Once home he changed out of his work gear – jeans and t-shirt – and put on a clean shirt and tie, a suit jacket and his best trousers. Ten minutes later he was off, back into the centre of town.

The morning rush hour had died down. The morning was chilly in the shade, but sunny and warm and the light was bright. The sunlight was reflecting in the windows of the office buildings. The prospect of something better to come was on the horizon.

Once in the centre of town he managed to park his cab along Tothill Street in the heart of Westminster, then walked the short distance to the Queen Elizabeth Conference centre. The façade had a kind of stone and glass cubist style in front of a circular grassy area. A banner over the front canopy proudly proclaimed:

'Welcome to the International Forum of Medical Advancement'
Saving lives around the globe.

There was a wide assortment of people, both male and female in their best attire and from every continent, making their way up the steps to the front of the building. He could see that a number of people dressed in security guard uniforms were checking the accreditation of the delegates and looking inside their bags and possessions as they neared the entrance. He managed to get himself in with a group of people approaching the entrance doors. He tapped the arm of a man to his side – a man of close to sixty years of age in a loose-fitting suit. Gold rimmed spectacles over his eyes. The chap looked to him.

"Nice day for it," Relton said and smiled. The man looked at him through his spectacles.

"Pardon me?" he said.

Relton glanced up. "Nice day for it." He thrust his head skywards.

"Yes, it is," the chap replied coolly.

They edged further towards the people checking the tags around the necks of the people about to step inside.

Relton held his hand out. "Doctor Relton," he said.

The guy offered him a strained smile but took his hand. "Doctor David Struthers from the University of Toronto."

Relton looked at his identification card, perched on his upper chest. "Nice to meet you."

The Canadian looked at Relton and seemed to notice that he had no identification tag.

"Left it in the hotel," said Relton. "I keep losing things. The first sign of dementia." He gave a soft chuckle. They stepped onto the top step with only a small group before them at the doors.

"What is your speciality?" the man asked.

Relton coughed. He said the first thing that came into his head. "Renal dysfunction" he said.

The guy looked at him with a puzzled face. "Oh. Good."

As he stepped onto the top of the steps one of the hawkeyed door staff clapped his eyes on Relton. He could see he had no accreditation tag.

"Sir," he asked. "Do you have your identification?"

"Sorry. Left it in my hotel," he said. "I'm Doctor Relton. Renal dysfunction. I'm with Doctor Struthers from the University of Toronto," he said as though that was the only accreditation he required. The guy looked at him quizzically. He could see that he was hardly public enemy number one. He wasn't carrying a bag of any description, so he waved him forward. Anyway, why would anyone in his right mind want to gate-crash a conference to do with medical research? Relton stepped inside the centre. He had blagged his way in.

In the main foyer there were delegates and dignitaries gathered at a number of feeding stations that were providing tea, coffee, or juice, and biscuits. Along the length of the foyer were a number of stalls where a large amount of publications and freebies could be obtained. Pull up stand notices were placed here and there, all advertising medical books that Relton had no knowledge of whatsoever.

The good Doctor Struthers from Canada stepped to him. "I say, did you say renal?" he asked. "At which institutions do you practice?" he asked.

"Oh. Here and there," he replied. Then he noticed the sign for the toilets. "Excuse me please. Just got to go for a leak," he said and stepped away from the inquisitive doctor and entered the male toilets.

A minute later he came out and followed the delegates into a large auditorium. It was a spacious room with around thirty rows of straight-backed chairs set out in a theatre style. At the top end was a stage with all the requisite lighting and a table to one side with microphones perched on it. A lectern was placed in a central spot on the stage. Stringed music was playing over the public address, and the chit-chat coming from the delegates already seated was becoming sharper by the second.

Relton stepped down the central aisle and slipped into a seat halfway down its length. He took a paper that was on the seat. It was to remind the delegates of the date of the next gathering of the forum which would take place in Seoul, South Korea in two years' time. This was an alien place to Relton. The last time he had been in a hall this large was to listen to a comedian. There would be few belly laughs with this lot.

Over the next ten minutes the hall began to fill with delegates taking their seats. Relton read the details on the paper. After a further five minutes the lights dipped. The sound of delegate chit-chat decreased as a party of five men and two women appeared on the stage. Six of them took up positions behind the table, whilst one of the ladies went to the lectern and raised the microphone. She started to address the audience and ran through the programme for the final day. The details were projected onto a large screen, high above the back of the stage.

In keeping with the tradition of the forum the final key-note speech would be given by the chairman of the committee for the next forum. The final act of the conference would be a thirty-minute question and answer session with the panel of leading scientists gathered at the table. After that the chairman of the London committee would give her final remarks and it would be all over until they met again in Seoul.

Once the housekeeping was out of the way, the lady had great pleasure in introducing the chairman of the Seoul organising committee for the final address. Doctor Lei Park of South Korea rose from the table and stepped to the lectern.

When he was centre stage the face of the chap was projected onto the screen. Relton recognised him immediately. He was one of the men he had observed in the hotel when he attempted to return the case to the man he knew as Doctor Kinden. He wasn't Chinese, he was South Korean. Though Relton's geography wasn't great, he knew it was near enough.

Doctor Park began his key note speech by saying that he was delighted to invite all the delegates to meet at the next meeting of the forum. It was the usual pat-drill. He thanked everyone under the sun for the hospitality of the London committee. Then he got into his speech.

He talked in medical terms that completely went over Relton's head. He droned on for ages. If it wasn't for a slick visual presentation on a big screen Relton would have fallen asleep. Forty minutes into his speech Dr Park told the audience that his team of researchers at a pharmaceutical giant in Seoul were working on a drug to treat cases of bowel and liver cancer. He hoped by the next time the forum gathered he would be able to announce a major breakthrough. He received a standing ovation from the delegates. Relton listened with interest. After all, bowel cancer had killed his mother. He warmed to the man. He even stood up and joined in the round of applause. When Doctor Park wrapped up after sixty minutes at the lectern, he was warmly applauded off the stage.

The end of conference plenary was like a bus-man's holiday. All these great minds gathered in one place. Minds of people whose sole desire was to do better for the human race. Relton felt quite emotional. He admired them, though the topics were like rocket science to him, for all he knew about them.

After thirty minutes of questions and answers to the top table, it was just left to the lady chairman of this forum to give her final remarks and to close the event. Everyone stood and applauded her off the stage. Relton followed suit.

When the final curtain came down and the lights came up, he followed the delegates out into the foyer. On his way out of the door he was given a silver fountain pen as a gift, courtesy of the organising committee. In the lobby, the delegates were exchanging handshakes and indulging in small talk. The chairman of the next meeting, the South Korean guy was mingling with his colleagues and doing the rounds.

By the way most of the people gathered here were attired, the industry must have been worth billions of dollars. That got Relton thinking. Was there a connection between Doctor Kinden, Professor Peterson and Doctor Park? Could it be that the South Korean was connected to them? He didn't know any of the answers to the questions.

Dr Park was joined by several of his entourage. Relton wasn't able to get close to him. They stepped out of the exit and onto the top step, as a silver bodied car pulled up at the bottom of the steps. Relton had seen it before. It was the same car that had followed him on Saturday night. The one that nearly crashed into the retractable bollards near to St Pauls. He was now convinced there was a tangible connection.

Just as he was going to step out of the centre the good doctor from Toronto caught his attention. "Which institutions did you say you are at?" the doctor asked.

Relton shook his head. "I didn't. I'm a London black cab driver," he said. The chap opened his mouth ajar and just mouthed the word; 'Oh.'

Relton left the bemused doctor from Toronto on the top step and moved away from the entrance. He set off to walk the short distance through Westminster. He was soon on Tothill Street and next to his cab. He opened the door, jumped into the driver's seat and started the engine. Just as he was close to pulling away, he heard a tap on the passenger side front window. He looked to see a man of south east Asian appearance standing on the pavement looking at him. He hit the button to let the window down.

"You are for hire? No?" The man asked in English with a heavy Asian accent.

"Yes. Sure," said Relton, not knowing if it was a coincidence or if there was something far more sinister and contrived to this. The guy didn't say anything as he stepped to the back door, opened it and climbed into the back of the cab. Relton glanced onto the pavement as a rain cloud suddenly broke and sent people scurrying for cover into the doorways of the buildings along the street.

He looked back to see the guy sit into the middle of the seat. He wasn't old, maybe thirty years of age. South-east Asian facial features. A light-yellow tint to his skin. Black hair flat to his head. Small, slim nose. He smiled. The dark overcoat he was wearing made his shoulders wider than they really were. He didn't look like anyone he had seen before, but he could have been one of the guys in the hotel.

"Where to?" Relton asked.

"Anywhere you want," replied the man.

Relton turned to look at him and gave him a puzzled look. In all his time as a cab driver he couldn't ever recall a passenger saying 'anywhere you want'. London was a big city. Anywhere you want could be twenty miles away.

Before he could utter a word, the man hit him with a question that changed the whole dynamic. "You have the case? No?" he asked. It was either a question or a statement of fact.

"A briefcase?" Relton asked dumb style.

"A silver briefcase."

Relton felt a modicum of intrigue. He checked on the dashboard that the passenger doors were locked. "I don't know what you're talking about," he said and turned to face the steering wheel. "Anyway, where to?" he said all casual.

"You do. You have the case Doctor Kinden give you."

That sealed the deal. Relton turned his head to fix his eyes on the chap who leaned forward in the seat. "It's Steve, isn't it?" He didn't reply. "Steve Relton. We know you." His English vocabulary was good, but he used words sparingly.

"What do you want?" asked Relton as pulled the cab away from the kerbside.

"The case," said the guy. "We are happy to negotiate with you for the case."

Relton glanced back. The guy's face was non-descript but at the same time expectant of a positive reply.

"Negotiate?" he asked.

"We happy to pay you for the case."

Relton's ears pricked up at the word 'pay'. This was a game changer. He recalled the thoughts he had last night; the ones that concerned paying for the work on the houseboat and Hailey's university education. Were his desires about to come true. The guy had a perceptive sense of theatre. It was as if he knew the thoughts and questions in Relton's head. "We give you a lot of money," he said without any prompting whatsoever from Relton.

"How much are we talking?" he asked.

"How much you want?" he asked.

Relton felt a hollow sensation in his throat. Oh, my word, he thought to himself. Was he offering him a blank cheque? He reflected for a moment. He knew that the guy wanted the case. He had seen it in his face. He was as serious as a heart attack. While he was an honest citizen who worked hard and paid his taxes he was also stuck for cash. The thirty thousand he needed to complete the houseboat was at least a year of hard graft away. His daughter's future hung in the balance. Here was his chance to get the money to pay for both. He concentrated on driving for the moment. He was on Whitehall, passing the entrance to Downing Street and heading in the direction of Trafalgar Square.

He looked into the windscreen mirror. Thoughts went through his head. He told himself he was human. He wasn't a saint. He was prone to avarice just like the next guy.

"One hundred thousand pounds for the case," he said.

In the mirror, he could see the man's face turn into a smile. "That is reasonable price," he said. "Agree?" Relton did not reply. "Agree," the man repeated

"Agree," Relton said hardly able to believe it. Then his mind came back to the reality. "Will it be in cash?"

"In cash."

Relton immediately got the idea that he had sold himself short. The man may have been willing to buy it for a lot more. Still a deal was a deal. He wouldn't welch on it.

"Will you put the money in a holdall?" he asked.

"Yes."

"When?"

"You decide."

"Tomorrow?"

"Tomorrow."

"Where?"

"You decide."

He let Relton think about it whilst he sat back into the seat, looked out of the window onto Trafalgar square and crossed his legs. The man from Korea was chilled and relaxed. As the cab went around a corner, he reached up to grip hold of the hand strap at the door.

"Do you know Chelsea Embankment?" Relton asked. He was non-committal for a moment. "The Albert Bridge on the river by the Chelsea embankment."

"I will find it."

"Meet me at the north end of the bridge tomorrow. I'll give you the case. Just you," he demanded, though he was in no position to be demanding.

The man chuckled at the clandestine nature of it all. "Just me," he replied.

"And you'll bring the money."

"Of course."

"At three in the afternoon."

"Of course."

Relton didn't say anything for a few moments. The cab was caught up in heavy traffic going along Charing Cross Road. He felt like asking him if he was the man who had attempted to break into his house, but decided against it, so as not to antagonise him by asking the question.

In the next moment the guy requested to be dropped off at the junction of Oxford Street. As a sign of good faith, he handed Relton a fifty-pound note for the five-minute journey. Relton slipped the cab into the kerb outside of Tottenham Court Road underground station, ironically, close to the spot where he had picked up the guy who had wanted to go to Heathrow last Thursday night. The guy he had cursed, for taking him to meet the American with the case worth one hundred thousand pounds.

The man got out of the cab, closed the door and stepped the ten paces towards the entrance to the underground station. Relton wondered if that exchange had just occurred, or he had dreamt it all.

He felt a sensation in his throat. Then it came to him. One hundred thousand pounds for the case. What was inside it? Despite someone trying to flag him down he drove on for two hundred yards then made a U turn, came back along Tottenham Court Road and glanced into the underground station. There was no sign of the Korean. He had disappeared from view.

Relton decided to keep the 'Hire Sign' off, and go home and change before Sonia came back home. Then he would visit the houseboat. He felt a tear in his eye. He was selling his soul for one hundred thousand pounds. It felt good. It felt more than good, it felt bloody marvellous.

# Chapter 14

The following morning, Tuesday, Relton was up at six, just as dawn was breaking over the city. He hadn't been able to sleep. He was too hyped up for sleep. Sonia asked him if he was okay. He said he was fine. After the episode with the police over the previous couple of days she had refrained from questioning him too much. As the police hadn't contacted him again, she assumed it was over. Their daughter Hailey was planning to travel up to Loughborough in the next couple of days, to have a look around the university campus. She had set her heart on going there to study Sports Science, and also to join the prestigious athletics club based there.

Once she went, their child would have flown the nest. He didn't know if this was a good or a bad thing. It could work one of two ways.

He got up early and made himself some breakfast, then he retrieved the case from the cupboard under the stairs. He was out of the house for seven-thirty. He put the case into the gap in the front cage and placed it out of view by the passenger side door.

He was feeling vulnerable and nervous about later in the day. He just hoped that it would go okay. If all went to plan this would be his biggest ever payday by some margin. One hundred thousand pounds would make a massive difference to his bank balance, to his life and to his family.

In an effort to pump himself up he slipped a CD in the player but played it at low volume. 'Sex on Fire' by 'The Kings of Leon' sounded good, even at low volume. The melodic riffs and the thumping base soon got him up for it.

He made his way to St Pancras International station and joined a queue of cabs at the rank. There were a healthy number of passengers waiting for cabs to take them to their destination, rather than struggle through the rush hour on the underground.

For the next three hours of his life, he kept his wits about him and his concentration on the job. That said, he was surprised that DCI Winn hadn't got back to him about the content of the case he had given him. Surely, he would realise that Relton had given him a replacement. Maybe so – maybe not.

The day was changeable. Dark clouds came over for a few minutes, then cleared to allow sunshine for another five minutes. It was a typical April day in the capital, with a stiff breeze blowing, and a discarded coffee cup rolling along the pavement.

In the morning spell from eight up to noon he had a good number of passengers. He appreciated the two northerners, in London to attend a conference, who got him chatting on last night's football. It took his mind off the events to come. He liked to indulge in football talk but if the truth be told he wasn't particularly knowledgeable. He had an opinion on most things but where football trivia was concerned, he was hopeless. Perhaps he didn't care that much. He had long since ejected the 'Kings of Leon' CD and replaced it with an album of Supertramp's greatest hits.

At one-thirty he turned the 'For Hire' indicator off and made his way towards Chelsea. He headed along the Kings Road from the Sloane Square end. Then a mile or so down he made a left and headed down Oakley Street towards the magnificent Albert Bridge. At the end of Oakley street, he got into the left lane. Instead of going over the bridge he turned left onto the embankment, then another left onto Royal Hospital Road, drove along it for fifty yards then into the kerb and parked the cab. The time was a shade after one forty-five. He elected to try and take a snooze, so he turned off the CD player and relaxed as best as he could.

No matter how hard he tried he couldn't close his eyes. Just after two-thirty he took the case, got out of the cab, locked the door, then walked the short distance across the road to the embankment, then up to the pier where his houseboat was moored.

The body of the Marie-Claire was gleaming in the sunlight. The blue paint job he had given it had the shell looking almost new. The sun was reflecting in the sheen he had applied to the upper structure. The green waters of the Thames were gently bobbing. Across the river the glass in the face of the new apartment block overlooking the river on the south bank was dazzling. The sun had broken through the sky. It was going to be a lovely afternoon and early evening. The red brick buildings on the north bank were set well back from the river, but still gave their residents a superb view over the river and the green line of the edge of Battersea Park in the background.

A chilly wind was blowing along the embankment, whipping up the top of the river into sharp rippled edges. Just ahead was the picturesque Albert Bridge with its ornate bronze topped columns and cables. Relton walked by the gate leading onto the gangway that went onto the platoon in the water and continued along the walkway toward the bridge. A steady line of vehicles was rumbling over the span.

The money man wasn't there. A glance at his watch told him it was only a quarter to three. He put the big silver case in-between his feet and decided to wait. He felt a little conspicuous so after a few minutes he decided on a change of plan. He wanted to get the case out of view. He stepped the ten yards to the gate leading to the gangway, unlocked it and walked down the ramp to the pontoon, turned right and, then onto the jetty where his boat was moored. At the stern end, he stepped up onto the barge, and glanced around at the openness of the river, and across to the other bank a good hundred yards away. He opened the door flap and stepped down into the interior. He put the case down on the floor and slid it under a tarpaulin sheet on the floor. From there he got off the barge, stepped along the jetty to the pontoon, went up the ramp and out onto the embankment. The time was eight minutes to three. Once through the gate he looked onto the embankment at the traffic. There was no evidence of anyone standing near to the bridge. He walked the ten yards back to the start of the structure. He felt a little jittery and nervy. After all, there had already been one victim in this. He recalled the sight of the dead man in the chair. The aghast look of surprise on his face bounced back into his mind.

He wondered if he was getting in too deep. Too late for second thoughts. As he looked onto the embankment a long silver bodied car with smoked glass windows came rolling along the road. It glided into the kerb and came to a halt twenty yards from the left turn onto the bridge.

The back door opened and the man who had got into his cab in Westminster yesterday emerged. He was wearing a black zip-up jacket, closed to the neck, brown pants and black shoes. He had a pair of large, mirror lens shades over his eyes. He turned to the back door where someone hidden from view passed a holdall to him. Once he had the holdall, he walked towards Relton at a relaxed pace. He was tall for an oriental fellow, at least a couple of inches taller than Relton. For some strange reason he was wearing black gloves on his hands.

Relton stepped forward a few paces to meet him. The guy looked to see where the case was, then he glanced back to the car which was still stationary. On nearing Relton he raised his hand. "Where is the case?" he asked.

"Where's the money?" Relton replied

He eyed Relton through the shades. The white of his eyes was just visible behind the mirrored lenses. He waited for a few moments then lifted the holdall in his grip. Relton looked at him. In that instant, something told him there was a chance that this might end badly.

"In here," the man replied.

The car hadn't moved. As the windows were blacked out it wasn't possible to see inside. It was all too sinister for words. Relton felt vulnerable but decided to gamble.

"Where is the case?" the Korean asked again.

"On my houseboat," he replied. Before the Korean could say anything. He told him to follow him. Relton walked a few yards to the gate. The other guy waited for a few seconds. Relton saw him glance towards the car, then he took a step towards him. Relton carried on, went to the gate, unlocked it and led him down the gangway to the pontoon. The ramp was gently bouncing under the weight of two people.

Relton glanced behind him. The Korean was a few paces from him. He followed Relton down the gangway, onto the pontoon, across it, then onto the pier where houseboats were secured to the jetty. A breeze was whipping along the top of the river to ripple the water. Above them, in the bright light the structure of the suspension bridge looked magnificent. Relton stayed a pace ahead of the Korean. They stepped onto the jetty passing the first pair of boats tethered to large pillars of wood embedded into the river-bed. Buoys over the sides of the vessels were there to stop them from colliding with the jetty. Ahead the Marie-Clare was on the left hand, the river side of the jetty. The name was stencilled into the bow of the barge. It was his pride and joy. He had put in many hours over the previous eighteen months. It needed many more hours. With the money he could complete the job in a few weeks.

"Where we go?" the Korean asked. They were not far from the end of the jetty.

"Here," said Relton. He stepped up the narrow plank resting on the jetty, lifted his leg onto the top of the ledge of the side and jumped down onto the deck of the barge. The guy with the holdall in his hand stepped onto the vessel; though it was hardly a vessel in the conventional sense of the word. It was only twelve feet wide from side to side at its widest point and fifty feet long from bow to stern.

Relton took hold of a brass topped handle grab rail to steady himself, then he opened the door flap. The Korean was right behind him. "Where the case?" he asked.

"Where is the money?" retorted Relton.

The guy followed him through the flap, then down a step, lowered his head under the roof and stepped into the interior of the boat. He inspected the surroundings. "Where is the case?" he asked again.

Relton took a couple of steps forward, lifted the tarpaulin sheet on the floor, reached down and took hold of the case. "The money," he said.

The Korean eyed the shiny metal case. There was a whisper of a smile on his face. He was happy. He opened the bag in his grip, pulled a flap open and there inside were the piles of cash.

"Open the case," asked the Korean.

"What?"

"Open it," he repeated.

"I can't. It's locked."

Relton was the first to hear a noise outside. It sounded like the feet of someone running along the jetty. The sound became louder. It was immediately followed by the impact of someone or something hitting the top of the deck above their heads. The Korean was aware of the sound at the same time as Relton. He looked at the Englishman. His face was startled. "You do this?" he asked.

"What?" Relton replied. He was just as baffled as to what the noise could be.

Before he could utter another word, the flap came open and the dark legs of a figure appeared in the opening. It took Relton a moment to notice the barrel of a gun in his hand. The Korean opened the zip of his jacket, dug his hand inside and withdrew a long barrelled black handgun which he pointed at the stranger.

"Drop it. You're surrounded," shouted the person on the top deck. There was evidence of a second or third person on the deck, and the sound of someone running along the roof towards the bow of the vessel.

The Korean swivelled ninety degrees and let off a shot. The guy at the door dived for cover. Then there were shouts and evidence of a general fracas from above. The barge gently swayed from side to side. The guy who had dived for cover came back and poked the end of his gun through the gap and returned fire. Instinctively, Relton dived to the floor and covered his head with the tarpaulin sheet. A gun battle was about to kick off. The Korean guy went down to the floor, then crouched behind the end of the galley. As he bobbed down, he let off a second shot which splintered the wood at the opening but also took out the guy standing there, hitting him in the thigh. Then there were shouts and screams from people on the jetty, in a language that wasn't English, followed by the crack of another shot. The Korean was still crouched by the opening. He returned fire. Relton chanced the opportunity to raise his head to see what was going on. He was just in time to see the Korean take the holdall containing the money and throw it at the opening in an attempt to hit one of the guys crouched at the opening. He partially succeeded.

Someone on the outside shouted "drop it," but to no avail. The Korean pointed his firearm and let off a third shot. Relton was petrified by the sudden turn of events. The next sound he heard was the sound of glass smashing as someone on the outside sought to get a shot at the man with the firearm through a porthole.

"Come out with your hands up," someone shouted. His English was without fault though the accent wasn't local or common to this country. Several more shots came from outside in rapid succession. It sounded as if a gun battle was raging on the jetty with maybe as many as half a dozen combatants involved. Relton could only pray it would end soon. No chance, two more shots followed. These were accompanied by more shouts. The door flap at the bow end of the boat flew open. A man with the agility of a trained commando jumped in and let off a shot in the same movement. Relton who had his head down heard the sound of the bullet hitting the Korean. He groaned loudly and fell to the ground. The gun which had been in his grip fell to the floor with a solid clatter. There were several more rapid pop-pop-pops from outside. Then a catastrophe happened. A stray bullet hit one of the gas canisters on the floor. There was an almighty bang as it went up. Flames exploded upward. All this had occurred in a less than fifteen seconds.

Relton could see that the Korean had taken a direct hit to the chest. It didn't look good for him. The flames propelled by the leaking gas soon took hold and ripped into the roof in less than a couple of seconds. There was a smell of escaping gas. Relton knew he had to get out before the fire took hold and got him. One more shot came from outside, followed by the sound of something heavy going into the water. Relton twisted as best as he could and managed to get by the Korean who was still alive, but losing a lot of blood from a chest wound. His skin was already turning grey and his eyes were glassy. His hand was on his chest in a vain attempt to stop the blood. The flames were now licking along the roof. The resulting smoke was becoming thicker by the second. Relton managed to squeeze by the Korean, get to the top of the step and poke his head out into the open. On the roof a guy was stretched out flat with a gun in his hand. It took Relton a few seconds to see it was the man who called himself Doctor Kinden. There were a couple of other Caucasian men who were both dressed in a similar style to Kinden at two points on the top of the barge. Both had guns in their hands. Meanwhile on the pontoon several men were running up the gangway towards the embankment in an effort to escape and get away from the gun fight.

As Relton glanced back into the living space. A second canister of gas went up and a sea of blue tipped flames ripped along the ceiling. The barge wouldn't be saved. The smoke now swilling throughout was as thick as fog. The smell of burning wood and the sound of fire consuming the vessel were overwhelming.

Relton got out on to the deck and looked back to see that the flames were now on the outside and the vessel was being eaten by the fire that was burning the wood with ease. The man called Kinden got up from off the deck, ran along for a few yards, then jumped down onto the deck. "Where is the case?" he demanded to know.

"In there," replied Relton.

Kinden went to go inside. He opened the door, looked at the fire, but thought better of it. "Too late," he said. "But we need to get him out," he said referring to the Korean. He stepped down into the interior, Relton followed him. Between them they were able to grab hold of the Korean, pull him and manoeuvre him out of the opening and out onto the deck. They laid him down flat. He didn't make a sound or move a muscle. He was possibly dead. Kinden looked at the flames. "We'll have to leave him. He's gone," he said.

As the wind got up the flames shifted in direction and took a hold of the portside where the ropes attaching the vessel to the jetty were. The flames quickly spread to the ropes. There was a thick, toxic black pall of smoke swirling overhead, the colour of soot. The structure would be lost. There was nothing anybody could do. Then there was an almighty creak and crack as the ropes snapped and the barge swayed from side to side, then moved away from the jetty. Such was the strength of the current that the barge was soon adrift from its mooring. Kinden and the other two took a running jump and leapt onto the jetty.

Relton looked back along the top of the deck to see that the flames were now spiralling and dancing along the roof like an out of control spinning cauldron. The heat was intense. He knew he had to get off or else the flames would soon engulf him. He looked to see that the jetty was now ten feet away. He had no alternative but to jump into the water and swim for it.

The shock of hitting the water took the breath out of his body. Nevertheless, he swam as best as he could and aimed for one of the supporting poles holding up the jetty. Unfortunately, the jetty floor was at least six feet above him. He took in a mouth full of foul-tasting water and felt it going down into his stomach. He spluttered and coughed out. He was out of shape and gasping for breath. It took him a good ten seconds to make it to the jetty by swimming in a kind of overhand crawl. Above he could make out the shape of a figure kneeling on the jetty with his hand reaching out to him. The guy reached down and was able to get a firm grip of his shirt and secure a hold. Meanwhile, the sound of wood splintering and the barge being destroyed by a torrent of fire was overtaken by the sound of a siren and the sound of shouts.

"Grab my hand," said the voice of the man from above. Another guy came to assist him. Between them they were able to get hold of Relton, grab him around the shoulders and haul him up and out of the water. As his legs came out of the water, he was able to pull himself up and literally roll onto the jetty. He turned to look at the barge. It had drifted out some thirty feet towards the centre of the river. It was hardly visible against the pall of smoke that surrounded it. Flames were leaping twenty feet into the air. A police launch was coming towards the vessel from the direction of Chelsea Wharf. The cracking sound of fire destroying a wooden structure was overpowering. The upper section would be gone in a matter of minutes.

As he watched it die, he couldn't do anything, but cry real tears. He cried for the first time since his mother had passed away five years ago. There were shouts from the embankment and the sound of a fire engine arriving on the scene.

Relton was drenched. He had lost his shoes and socks in the water. He reeked of smoke. He was covered in what felt like a film of oil. He was cold. He was numb, but those were the least of his worries. He was still alive, unlike the Korean whose body was being cremated by the flames.

Within ten minutes of the end of the gun battle, the pier was swarming with a dozen or more uniformed cops, plus several men in plain clothes. The houseboat was now a third of the way across the river, drifting across the surface. It was little more than a burnt-out shell. The raised top deck had all but gone. All that remained was the hull. A floating fire hydrant had just arrived on the scene. It was pouring water into the vessel at a rate of one hundred litres a second in an effort to save what remained and to prevent it from drifting towards the bridge and damaging the structure. Luckily the fire barge had so far prevented it from threatening the bridge. One of the men who had pulled Relton out of the water had given him a gabardine jacket to put around his shoulders. An ambulance was on the embankment. The first responder gave him a silver sheath blanket to wrap around his body to fight off hypothermia.

He knew he was in deep trouble. The case which contained whatever the Korean was desperate to get his hands on had probably melted in the flames; the same could be said for the holdall containing the money. The body of the Korean would have been burnt to little more than a blackened corpse.

Several of the uniformed cops came down the gangway to the pontoon then onto the jetty and descended on Relton. The other protagonists in the gun fight must have long since scarpered. The silver car containing the Koreans had long since left the scene. Relton was escorted up the gangplank to the embankment. He was holding the silver cape close at his chest. Half a dozen or so men in civvies were standing on the pavement chatting in hushed conversation. The accents were American and British. No one appeared to give Relton a second glance. One of the men was the man who called himself Kinden. He was no doctor. He was a taker of life. He had shot the Korean guy. He was a special something or other? Relton had no idea.

An unmarked car came racing along the embankment, and pulled up behind the ambulance. It was a sleek black shiny car. It was the car that had been following the cab on Thursday night. There was no doubt about it. The doors opened and several more men arrived on the scene.

Relton was placed in the back of a police car. From the embankment he could see onto the river and what remained of the barge. Now it wasn't flames coming out of the vessel, but a cloud of steam. Someone on the police rig was attempting to secure a line to the bow. After a couple of minutes, the police car, containing Relton, pulled away from the kerb and joined the traffic along the embankment.

Relton was taken to a police station in central London. Once in the station, he was taken into the custody suite and into a room. He was ordered to strip naked. The custody officer provided him with a towel to dry himself off and a paper overall to hide his embarrassment. They said they would get a doctor to check him out. He said he was okay. Once they were satisfied, he wouldn't succumb to hypothermia or required a doctor, he was placed into a cell and locked up.

They left him in the cell to stew, and to think over the predicament he had got himself into. He felt grim and literally gutted. All he could do was sit at a table and rest his arms on the surface. He wondered what the police were doing. Maybe they had raced around to his house to search his possessions. Oh my God, what would Sonia say? He feared her wrath more than the police. He tried to get his story right and get his ducks in a line.

As there was no clock in the cell and his watch had gone, he had no idea of time. Fading light was coming into the room through a high sealed window with frosted glass.

After a period of forty minutes the door of the cell opened and two plain clothes officers stepped in. They took Relton out of the room, along a corridor, opened a locked door, down another corridor and into an interview room. Three men, two of whom he had seen on the embankment were waiting for him. The man who said he was Doctor Kinden was one of them.

Relton was seated at the table, while the others remained standing nearby in a close-knit group. Once Relton was seated they split and approached the table. One of them who he didn't know took the chair at the other end of the table and sat down. He was wearing a dark casual jacket and plain denim jeans. He looked to be in mid-thirties. A kind of everyday looking guy. Dark hair, thinning on top. He rested his forearms on the table.

"Steve, tell me what happened out there?" he asked. Relton looked at him and pursed his lips. He took a deep breath then he told him. He told him everything. How he was planning to swap the case for a lot of money.

They asked him how much. He told him. The man asked him if he knew what was in the case. He said he didn't have a clue.

The guy turned to look at one of the others. He looked at Relton, and nodded his head in a solemn way.

"What if I told you it contained the technical data for a drug developed in an American laboratory, that any other manufacturer would be keen to get their hands on."

Relton didn't respond. They were looking for a reaction, like an admission that he had something to do with it. He wasn't involved in anything like industrial espionage. It was way out of his league. He was a cab driver, for crying out loud. They must have known that from the outset. He was just a London Hackney carriage driver who had got himself caught up in something that was way over his head. He shrugged his shoulders. "I had no idea what was in the case," he said.

"Who gave you the case?" the man asked.

"The guy I picked up from Heathrow. The guy who called himself Doctor Kinden." He described him as best he could.

"What happened in the taxi?" was the next question.

He told them the precise sequence of events. How he had picked up the fare from outside of Terminal Four and driven him into London along the M4. How the passenger told him they were being followed. How he had managed to shake off the car. How Kinden said he would reward him with a large tip. Then how the passenger had asked him to take the case to a house in Primrose Hill and how it would earn him another two hundred pounds. What was he to say? No? This is how he made his living. He was a taxi driver for Pete's sake.

"You desperate for money?" one of them asked.

It was a strange sort of question, thought Relton. "Aren't we all," he said, then explained that it was his intention to renovate the barge in order that he could sell it to pay for his daughter's university education. He needed somewhere in the region of twenty thousand pounds to finish the project. The promise of one hundred thousand pounds was way too much of a temptation to turn down.

They asked him what he planned to do with the remainder of the money. "Pay for a holiday for me and my wife to celebrate our twentieth wedding anniversary next year," he replied.

He was sorry for what had happened. He didn't know what was in the case. All he knew was the predicament he was in.

The lead interviewer said that was all for the time being. They ended the interview and left the interview room.


Two minutes later a member of the custody team entered the room and gave him a lukewarm mug of tea. He asked him if he wanted something to eat. He turned down the offer. He was left alone. He couldn't think straight. He was in a puzzle and a jigsaw rolled into one. He didn't have the answers or the pieces to solve it.

A further ten minutes passed before the door opened and who should enter but DCI Winn and his able sidekick DI Devlin.

"Oh dear. You've got yourself into a right fix here," Winn said.

"Only you could get yourself involved in a war between big players in the pharmaceutical business." Devlin said in a jocular tone of voice. Relton gave him a blank face.

"What you say?" Winn asked. He put one of his polished brogues on to the seat opposite and remained standing.

Relton didn't reply. He put his hands to his face, propped his elbows on the table and lowered his head. He wanted it to be a bad dream, but it wasn't. It was all too real.

The two detectives backed out of the room to leave him with his head in his hands and left him to contemplate and try to collect his thoughts as best as he could. He just sat there, forlorn with his head buried in a portrait of despair, and self-pity.

# Chapter 17

At the end of the day the police could speculate anyway they wanted to. Their theory was just as plausible as anyone else's. My theory and I shall stress the word 'theory' is that the Doctor Kinden in the taxi was exactly who he said he was. For a reason, probably to do with not wishing to be easily traced, he had checked into the hotel in a different name, Eugene Fewster would do for the job. Fewster could be the name of a genuine person. The guy who he met in the hotel and said he was Kinden, was in fact a US government agent, possibly working for the Drug Enforcement Agency. He did produce a passport but that was no guarantee that he was Dr Kinden. A passport in the hands of an agent of some description means nothing. For reasons that will never be fully explained the man in the taxi was involved in a plot to sell intellectual property – in the form of drug research – to a foreign competitor – thereby breaking US trade and copyright law. The case he was carrying contained intellectual property in terms of manufacturing details and full trial data, such as: codes, recipes, specifications and so on. Other parties were keen to get their hands on this property because it could be worth millions and millions of dollars in the competitive drug market.

The Doctor Kinden who Relton picked up at Heathrow was already suspicious that he was being trailed by US agents from a government agency, and not by Koreans or anyone else. Therefore, the car that Relton managed to shake off on the way into the city from the airport may have been manned by US government agents, from the Drugs Enforcement Agency, or some other alphabet soup offshoot.

When they couldn't snatch him on the way to the hotel, they decided to do it in the hotel. When he checked-in, he didn't have the case containing the intellectual property. On arrival in the hotel he checked in as Fewster, but they already knew he was heading there and took him into their custody.

As for Hank Peterson, I guess he was also involved with Kinden to sell the property to the Koreans. He possibly had some more papers that when paired with the papers Kinden was carrying provided the full set of the codes and what have you.

It wasn't the Americans who got to Peterson first, but the Korean. He killed Peterson for the details he held. Maybe Peterson had decided to call off the deal. The Koreans stole the plans and murdered him with a garrotte. They came back later to the house probably at the dead of night to clear up, take the body and dump it in the park which was only a couple of hundred yards from the house.

Kinden believed that he was close to being captured by his countrymen so decided to give the plans to Peterson, but for whatever reason the Korean guy had already killed him. With his set of papers and plans and construction of the drug, all they required were Kinden's material to complete the set. All this was taking place against the Forum in London which gave Doctor Kinden the ideal reason to travel to Europe. In London he would meet up with the Koreans who were also attending the forum.

After Kinden was taken from the hotel, he was replaced by an agent acting as him, possibly to try to persuade the Koreans that he was no longer interested in selling the property.

When Relton came to the hotel after finding Peterson dead, the agent had to act out a scenario that he knew nothing about it. Two of the Koreans had witnessed the stand-off and must have been confused by the episode, assuming that the taxi driver had made a mistake, or he was working for the Americans in an attempt to creative a clever smokescreen to put them off the scent.

No one knows for certain who attempted to break into Relton's home to try and get the case, whether it was the Americans or the Koreans. Due to the police getting involved then I guess whoever it was decided not to try that particular move again.

The discovery of Professor Peterson's body put the cat amongst the pigeons. It revealed that the Koreans had no scruples about killing anyone. I suspect that the Koreans had followed Relton the second time around, maybe in an effort to force him into an uncompromising position. Little did they know that he had a device to open the retractable bollards and therefore he was able to lose them. Once they had established that Relton did have the case, they decided to entice him with the offer of money. Relton fell for it. There is little doubt in my mind that the killer of Peterson would have killed Relton as well. If he had succeeded in getting the second set of materials, there was nothing to stop them from stealing the intellectual property. If I was a betting man, I would say that the Koreans had first approached Peterson, who was working in London,

145

with a huge offer to buy the material. After all, once they had it and could manufacturer the product, no one could say they hadn't developed it in their own laboratories. Maybe Peterson was working as a double agent to draw out a mole in the US Company, and the Koreans killed him for that reason.

The Americans, with help from their British colleagues, may have kept track of Relton, and discovered that he was planning to profit from the stroke of luck that had presented itself. He was only human. They had to stop him delivering the case to the Koreans at all costs. They were determined to stop their property from getting into the hands of a competitor. The opportunity to make a substantial amount of money from a drug that had the potential to end the scourge of cancer was enormous.

That is my theory. I could be wrong on one or more factors. Who knows? What I do know is that Relton had got himself – through no fault of his own – into deep water. No pun intended.

The media soon got wind of the gun fight near to Albert Bridge. The authorities attempted to put a lid on it, by saying it was a fight between two sets of criminal gangs. The British government had no desire to see London become a battle ground for rival pharmaceutical giants. Behind the scenes, the South Korean ambassador was summoned to the foreign office for a dressing down.

Steve Relton spent six hours in custody. He was arrested and charged with criminal damage. He was released on police bail at ten o'clock that evening, and allowed to go home. A few weeks after it

146

had all blown over the Crown Prosecution Service dropped the charges against him. He went back onto the road to earn a living.

What remained of the houseboat was towed to a pier. The body of the Korean was recovered. Ironically, no trace of the metal case was found. Maybe it survived the fire. Maybe it's still in the Thames, floating down river towards the open sea. Maybe it became trapped in a grid over a sewer pipe somewhere. Maybe some kids found it floating in the river, took it out and kicked it around on a rough piece of ground.

The official reason for the fire was marked down as an accident. The crazy thing is that months later, Relton was able to claim insurance. He was awarded fifty thousand pounds. Now that the houseboat had gone, he would have plenty of time to tackle the garden and take Sonia on holiday.

Today, Steve Relton still drives a black cab. He would never forget the night he picked up the American from Heathrow. Of course, as part of the deal that saw the charges dropped, he agreed never to talk to anyone about the events of that night. The only person he told was me. I told him I would sharpen my pencil, grab a writing pad, and put it down in fiction. The only things I've changed are the names. And this story will linger in my mind for a long time. And therein lies the tale of a black cab driver.

**The End**

# 'Firestarter'

# Chapter 1

**Friday, 18<sup>th</sup> August.**

In the shimmering heat of the day, the group of bare-chested youths tossing a cigar shaped football to each other, was partially lost in the haze rippling across the open fields. The previous evening, the weather girl on the national news had advised viewers not to stay out too long in the open, because todays UV rays could hit a record high for this time of the year. Suffice to say, some of the sun-bathers laid out on the grass had either not heard the warning, or had failed to heed the advice. It was a common scene in London's Regent's Park at the height of the summer.

Two days before, a warm front, with a sweat-inducing rise in temperature, had descended over the city. It wasn't unusual for the middle of August.

Metropolitan Police Detective Inspector Stephen Taylor, and Reece Lister, entered the park from the York Gate side. They were sauntering side-by-side, along a pathway, close to the edge of the Serpentine Lake. They were chatting like a couple of workmates escaping from the heat of the office for their lunch-break. Lister was carrying a document holder in his right hand. On the lake, people in rowing boats were drifting across the flat, calm surface.

In the background, the gentle hum of the traffic provided a kind of urban symphony, and reminded the two that they were in the heart of a big city. After a further one hundred yards they were in an area shaded by the branches and foliage of overhanging trees.

The pathway was lined with benches where several people were sitting. Some were eating lunch, others reading newspapers or paperbacks, others just enjoying the open vista and the sunshine.

DI Taylor gestured towards a vacant park bench, and suggested they sit there. They sat down, relaxed, and breathed in the scene. The scenery was magnificent, the colourful flowers and the tall trees thick with leaves. There were several rowing boats on the lake. In the branches of the tree, birds twittered gently. The time was a shade after three o'clock.

Lister opened the black leather document holder, extracted a thick manila envelope, and handed it to DI Taylor. Taylor opened the envelope and extracted three documents of varying thickness. He looked at the front of the largest of the documents. It had the following words embossed on the cover:

*1-3. The Israeli connection?*
*Author: Reece Lister.*

As a freelance journalist, Reece Lister had written numerous articles for several red-top newspapers and glossy magazines, both here in the UK and further afield. During his time, he had written for prestigious newspapers like the Sunday Telegraph, the London

Times, the Sunday Observer, and a boat load of other international publications, such as Time Magazine and several US based journals. His report represented the findings of the research he had carried out over the previous eleven weeks.

His priorities were to ensure that the report wasn't only well written, but that the content was timely, and had relevance and truth, which was something every journalist didn't adhere to.

His speciality was terrorism, specifically the rise of Islamic terrorism throughout Europe and the western world, and how the nations of the industrialised world were, or were not, meeting the challenges they faced.

In the past day, he had completed the final draft of a report which he planned to pitch to his market in the next few weeks or so. It was a twenty-thousand-word article that had taken him six weeks to research and two weeks to write. To complete the article, he had undertaken many hours, including desk research and several face-to-face interviews.

Lister was pleased with the finished piece, though the subject matter wasn't an easy one to work with. It was a report reviewing an event, in London, that had occurred just over five months before. An act of terrorism had resulted in the deaths of ten school-aged children, in the age range of seven years to fifteen years of age, who were killed when a bomb exploded outside a Jewish school on the streets of north London. The article was an exposé of the truth, what had really occurred, before, during and after the event, and who was responsible for the atrocity that had shaken the nation to its core.

The event of 'one-three', as it had become known, had been the worst terrorist event in London since the 7th July 2005 when four Islamic extremists had detonated three bombs in quick succession onboard London underground trains, and later, a fourth on a double-decker bus in Tavistock Square. Fifty-two people were killed on that day, and over seven hundred were injured in the attacks, making it Britain's worst terrorist incident since the 1988 downing of Pan Am flight 103 over Lockerbie, Scotland.

Like the date of Thursday 7th July, Wednesday 1st March had become ingrained into the memories of people throughout the country. The first official report into the findings had been released three months later in June. The authors of the 'official' report laid the blame for the atrocity at the door of a Palestinian man, who had links to Islamic Jihad and some other shadowy groups affiliated to Islamic State.

Reece Lister had no need to doubt the findings in the 'official' report, or who was responsible for the deaths of ten children. The report concluded that a lone-wolf terrorist had sneaked into the country in the back of a wagon. He was helped by a British national of Pakistani heritage, called Asim Malik, who had purchased the components for making a crude bomb, from several DIY stores. The bomber had succeeded in making the bomb using an everyday pressure cooker crammed with fertiliser, nitrate and ball bearings, and in setting it off, using a mobile phone, and killing the children outside the school.

Reece Lister had read the official version of the events from a leaked report. Two days before the report was to be made public, he was contacted by someone who told him the report was a whitewash, and what he knew about the event cast huge doubt on the findings of the 'official' verdict. That man was Metropolitan Police Detective Inspector Steve Taylor.

Taylor said he wanted to remain anonymous, but would be happy to meet with Lister and tell him what he knew. In response to the telephone call, Reece Lister agreed to meet DI Taylor the next day in Regent's Park, at a spot close to Serpentine Lake.

## Chapter 2

**Two and a half months earlier.**

Thursday 8th June, was a damp and overcast day. Reece Lister had walked along the same path they took before. He caught sight of a man sitting on the bench with his back pressed into the rails and his legs stretched out. He had a rolled-up newspaper in his hands and a black umbrella at his side. Although he was seated in a somewhat languid posture it was clear to see that he was of average physique and height.

DI Steve Taylor was wearing a light-coloured suit, and shiny black brogues shoes on his feet. He had a head of nicely groomed dark hair. He was a decent looking guy, perhaps in his mid-thirties.

Lister approached the man, and sat down on the bench several feet from him. Lister was dressed in a more relaxed style when compared to the man sitting at the bench. He was in a casual jacket, a plain polo shirt, blue jeans, and walking shoes on his feet.

The chap sat up, unrolled the newspaper, and ran his eyes over the headline. Then he scanned his eyes along the path. A young mother was pushing a stroller with a crying child inside. There was an elderly couple further back, ambling along at a leisurely pace. The sun was trying to poke through the grey sky.

DI Taylor kept his eyes away from Lister. "Are you Reece Lister?" he asked, without looking at him.

"Yes. I'm Reece Lister. You must be Detective Inspector Steve Taylor," he replied.

It was all cloak and dagger stuff, with laconic secretive characters going about their business in a shifty, clandestine manner. Taylor shifted in his seat, crossed his legs and continued to run his eyes over the tip of his shoes. "Be careful. We might be listened to."

"You sure?" asked Lister.

"It's possible," replied Taylor.

"By whom?"

"Take your choice."

Lister glanced around his surroundings for the second time in quick succession. "I can't see anyone nearby. Let's keep this distance. I understand you've got some knowledge about one-three," he said.

Taylor closed the newspaper and propped himself up. "Let's walk and talk," he suggested.

"Okay."

Taylor got up from the bench and set off to walk away. Lister did likewise and came level to the other man.

Taylor had his umbrella in his right hand and the rolled up his newspaper wedged under his arm. The pair of them set off together along a semi-circular path in a northerly direction towards the seats outside a bustling café where half a dozen people were sitting.

They walked for fifty yards in silence along the path before coming out into a wide-open area of parkland that was dissected by walkways. The lush green grass was giving off a dewy, aromatic fragrance. The trees, shrubs and bushes were plentiful and in full bloom. Several people were walking dogs.

"It's good to walk. Sort of keeps me fit and fulfils my wish to exercise as often as I can," DI Taylor said.

"What have you got to tell me about one-three?" Lister asked.

"Plenty," replied Taylor.

"All right. Just one question before we get started. Why did you choose me? You could have gone to anyone. Why me?" Lister asked.

"Good question. I recall reading your piece on the July 2007 bombing in 'The Observer' I thought you'd be the kind of journalist who'd like to investigate this, and take it to the next level."

"Which is?" asked Lister.

"Going public."

"What's your link to the 1st March bombing?"

"I was assigned to the case as a detective." Lister didn't reply. Taylor continued. "The evidence in the official report points to a lone-wolf terrorist, working with a British-born sympathiser. But I've got my doubts about the findings. They're too convenient. To easy…"

"What're you saying. A rush to judgement?" asked Lister.

"Yeah. That's one way you could put it," said Taylor.

Lister looked at him. "The evidence points to a plot orchestrated by a shadowy group based in Gaza. A kind of splinter group of Hamas and Islamic Jihad."

"That's what we're led to believe," said Taylor. "But the evidence I've got points in a different direction."

"Which direction?"

"That the plot to bomb the Jewish school and a synagogue were actually created by the Israeli secret service with the latent support of MI5."

"You serious?" Lister asked.

"Yeah. I'm serious."

"That's one hell of an accusation. Why would Israelis want to kill Jewish schoolkids in London?"

"To discredit a senior member of the British government who had sympathy with the Palestinian cause. If what I think really happened it will cause a mini earthquake not only in London, but in Tel-Aviv and even in Washington DC."

"You want me to investigate?" Lister asked.

"If what I think did happen, you'll be exposing the truth and righting a wrong."

"Why have you waited almost three months to reveal this to anyone?"

"Because I didn't know what the final report would conclude. I've only seen a leaked copy of the report, and the conclusion it came to."

"Which is?"

"That a lone wolf Palestinian called Hashem Abbas killed those ten children and injured the others."

"That's my understanding. I've read the leaked report," said Lister.

"What I know about the real connections will scupper that theory."

"Why don't you go public with what you know?" Lister asked.

"Because I can't be one hundred percent sure."

"So, you want me to investigate?"

"I'm in no position to carry out the investigation. I signed the *Official Secrets Act*. You've got the connections. I don't."

Lister didn't respond for a few moments. He pondered on DI Taylor's words. The man sounded genuine. He did know something about the event and was keen to share it so the truth could be known. He paused, turned and looked into Taylor's eyes.

"Okay. Why don't you tell me everything you know," Lister asked.

Taylor turned his head away from Lister and eyed the unoccupied bench seat just a few yards ahead. "Let's sit here."

They approached the bench and sat down with a gap of only two feet between them. In the branches of an overhanging tree, two blackbirds were having a spat. The sound of voices of people in rowing boats on the Serpentine, just beyond them, reached their ears.

Taylor turned to face Lister. "I'll tell you everything I know. Right from the very beginning. Do you recall the six arson attacks on the homes of Muslim families in north London?"

"Sure, I do. Six fires over a period of five months in north London. They resulted in the deaths of nine and serious injuries to others."

"Let me take you back eight months or so. The third fire has just occurred. It's Friday 18th November. I'm sitting at my desk in the office in Paddington Green Police station. It's a couple of days after the third fire which resulted in the death of two adults and two children. My desk is covered with files. I was assigned by the lead detective to try and establish a pattern. I'll take you back to a time just after the third fire."

Reece Lister pictured himself in a room. DI Taylor was sitting at a desk with files and papers across it, plus all the other items you would expect to see on the desk of a Detective Inspector of the London Metropolitan Police service.

# Chapter 3

**November, the previous year**.


DI Taylor sat back in his swivel leather armchair, stretched his legs underneath his desk, and put his fingers to his mouth. He was in a squad room in Paddington Green Police station. It was a room he shared with two colleagues. Two other Detective Inspectors: Peter Hamilton and Rebecca Hindley, who were also assigned to finding the north London arsonist.

He was deep in thought. He put his eyes on the front of the coloured hardbacked file. The case file had remained un-opened for the past thirty-six hours. The case number was written in the top left-hand corner in a thick, black felt-tip pen. He disliked the insipid olive-green cover, with a disdain that boarded on hatred. It was cheap. Inside it, papers and cuttings had been threaded into plastic covers inserted into a securing strip that made it look like some school kid's homework, not the contents of a file that contained information about a series of arson attacks on several homes throughout north London. Each member of the team also had a similar file. The information was also lodged in electronic format. DI Taylor was old school, he liked the physical feel of a hardbacked file. It felt malleable, like something that could be battered but still retain its shape. He had a pet name for the case and the clippings that recorded the fires. He referred to it as the 'Firestarter' file. Because that is what it was all about. A Firestarter was on the loose.

The third and most recent arson attack had occurred days before. On a chilly, misty morning in north London an arsonist had broken into the home of an Asian family in Friern Barnet, and set fire to the house. The file contained the report, the London Fire Services investigation team had provided. He had sprayed a paraffin-like substance onto the hallway carpet, on the curtains and onto the sofa in the living room. The fire began near to the front door. With the aid of the flammable accelerant, the flames had quickly spread along the hallway and into the living room, where the fire took hold. From there the flames spread throughout the rest of the house and up the stairs where the family were sleeping.

Four members of the family, two children and both the father and mother of the mother of the two children, succumbed to the smoke and the flames. Four other people who survived were all still in hospital, two of them, the parents of the children were suffering from smoke inhalation, and were fighting for their lives.

The fire had been the third blaze to be started by the same arsonist. The culprit had used the same method to start this blaze. The first blaze had been in September, two months previously. The second occurred almost exactly one month after the first, and now there had been a third incident, which was almost one month after the second. It was clear to all that a serial arsonist was reaping havoc on the streets of north London. All three fires were all within one mile of each other.

The number of deaths was six. Two in the first fire, and four from the third. Ten people were in hospital, with a combination of burns and smoke inhalation. All the victims were of British-Asian heritage, from a Pakistani, Bangladeshi, or Iranian background. None of them were known to the police or any of the security agencies. They were all law-abiding citizens who paid their taxes and didn't cause anyone any grief.

DI Taylor and the team of three other detectives had been assigned to the case full-time. They were working on the assumption that the fires were hate related. None of the families knew each other. They had no connection whatsoever, therefore the conclusion was that the arsonist was targeting Asian homes at random.

DI Taylor sat forward, took the hardbacked file, and browsed through the reports, clippings and the results obtained from door-to-door enquiries. Despite several hundred-man hours of arduous investigation, they were no closer to finding the Firestarter. The reports provided by the London Fire Service investigation team, led by a very likeable, experienced, and amiable guy called John Leyton, were an interesting read. He had attempted to profile the mind of the Firestarter. He had concluded that this guy wasn't likely to stop any time soon.

Commander Leyton said all three blazes had been started in the exact same way, using the same break in and enter method and the same type of accelerant, a paraffin-based substance. The blazes appeared to be the work of someone who knew what he was doing. The three fires had been started in the early hours of the day, in a twenty-minute timeframe between two-thirty to ten-to-three.

None of the survivors had heard the arsonist breaking into the house. In the second fire, the arsonist had even gone to the bother of removing the battery from a smoke detector, such was his disregard for human life, but on that occasion, no one had died. It was believed that all of those who died in the first and third blazes were killed by a combination of smoke inhalation, and toxic fumes spewing out of everyday household furniture.

DI Taylor closed the file and reassumed his languid posture in the seat. He sat back, put his hands behind his head, and took in a deep breath. Outside the window, the dull light of the day had hardly enough strength to register. On a scale of one-to-ten with ten being bright and sunny, it was at best a one-and-a-half. It was one of those horrible dull days that made people hanker for the warmth and vitality of the spring and the summer to come, but those seasons were still a long way off. It was nearer to Christmas than spring. As the father of two school age children he looked forward to enjoying some quality time over the festive period with his wife Susan and children. They lived in a nice area in a three-bedroomed detached house on the southern fringe of Welwyn Garden City. A distance of twenty miles from Paddington Green and a world away in terms of surroundings of north-west London.

Taylor had been handed a role in the case by the Senior Investigating Officer - DCI Sarah Lake. Several other detectives had been assigned to the case with DI Taylor. The other key members of the team were DI Peter Hamilton, and DI Rebecca Hindley. Taylor wasn't sure why he had been brought in. As far as he was aware, he hadn't upset anyone upstairs.

The first of the fires was in Whetstone, the second in Finchley, and the third in Friern Barnet. They had occurred within one mile of each other. This seemed to point to the fact that the arsonist was local to the area. Whoever the Firestarter was he was savvy, because he never left a clue to his identity, nor had he been spotted on CCTV. Video taken by the fire service at the scene of the fires had been examined by members of the investigation team. The same person hadn't been spotted in the crowd of rubbernecks observing the aftermath. All other potential Firestarters known to the Met police had been eliminated from their enquiries. Therefore, they were looking at a new Firestarter. He was a clean-skin, a new kid on the block. The only real snippet of evidence was that the fires appeared to be in a triangular shape, consequently there was a pattern in terms of location and chronology.

The Firestarter case had been aired on local TV in the London area, and on the BBC's nationwide 'Crimewatch' programme. Sadly, it hadn't resulted in much useful information. No one had rung in to give the name of the arsonist. What information they did receive was at best the public trying to guess who was behind the blazes, but without actual names. The trail had – not to put a pun on it – gone cold. The local police had conducted extensive door-to-door enquiries, but nothing much had been gleaned. The results of all forms of investigation had been extremely disappointing.

# Chapter 4

**10<sup>th</sup> December**

The sound of his bedside landline telephone awoke DI Taylor from sleep. He opened his bleary eyes and looked at the clock on the bedside table. His wife, Sue, turned over and let out a sigh. The luminous handles on the clock were just visible. The time was a few minutes after five on this a dank, dark, and rainy December morning. Outside, a gale was blowing and raindrops were beating a rhythm against the windows.

Reluctantly he put the receiver to his ear. "Yeah," he said, half asleep.

"It's Sarah Lake," came a muffled voice on the other end of the line.

Taylor came wide awake and propped himself up. His wife muttered something under her breath. She was used to these early morning calls.

"What have we got?" Taylor asked his boss.

"We've had another blaze this morning," said Lake with an air inevitability in her voice.

"Oh, shit. Where now?"

"In the Whetstone and Finchley area. Right on the border between the two," she said.

"Close to the other fires then?" Taylor said.

"Yeah. About half a mile away from both the first and second," Lake said.

"How bad?"

"Bad enough. Three confirmed dead. Two critical," she said.

"It's another Muslim family I assume?"

"A family of British-Indians this time," Lake replied.

Taylor swung his legs out of bed and sat on the edge of the mattress. He still had the telephone to his ear. "I'd better get over there. Any clues?" he asked.

"Nothing obvious according to the uniformed guys who got the call. Just that it looks like the others. Fire started near to the back door this time. Someone broke in at around three. Poured paraffin all over the place. The usual MO."

"Who's there now?" Taylor asked.

"The Fire Service are mopping up. A police uniform crew have just arrived on the scene."

"I'll alert the team and…" said Taylor, as he paused to rub his eyes, "I'll get there in the next thirty minutes."

He ended the call, remained sitting on the edge of the bed, and let his head clear. He dressed in a hurry and went downstairs into the warmth of the lounge. He took his mobile phone and contacted DI Peter Hamilton and DI Rebecca Hindley to inform them of another arson attack. He asked them to meet him at the address in one hour from now.

Before the clock reached five-thirty DI Taylor left his home on the edge of Welwyn Garden City, to drive into the city and to the location of the fourth fire.

He arrived at the scene precisely thirty minutes after he left his home. At six in the morning the streets of north London were relatively quiet. The rain was still beating down and the roads were glistening in the streetlights. As Christmas was only a few weeks away, many of the houses along the street were draped in lights and festive displays. A paper-tape cordon had been put across the road to prevent vehicles or anyone on foot from getting close to the house.

Taylor put his side window down and approached the uniformed police officer manning the exclusion zone. He could smell the pungent aroma of smoke, mixed with the damp, dull scent of the morning.

There were still a good number of emergency service personnel milling around the front of the house. Two fire brigade engines were in attendance. Several firemen were standing close to the open front door, no doubt talking shop. A reporter from a local radio station was speaking into a hand-held microphone, making a recording for a piece that would probably go out as the lead item on the first news broadcast of the day. The fourth major house fire in the past four months was bound to be the lead item.

Taylor climbed out of his car, stepped over several water hoses, and approached the house. The fire had ripped through the interior, blackening the front walls, and blowing out the windows on both the ground and upper floor. Steam was still rising from the roof and the smouldering embers. The acrid smell of burnt wood and plastic was strong.

He stepped through the opening in the bordering wall, down a short path and into the house. The hallway was an inch deep in black, soot-filled water. Two firemen were standing on what remained of the staircase. The fire had been so hot it had melted the plaster off the walls, to such an extent that in several places the bare brick underneath was exposed. There was no sound except for the drip,drip,drip of water seeping through the roof. It seemed as if the rage of the fire had expelled all other noises with its savagery.

In a back room, one of the Fire Service investigation team was using a fancy three-hundred and sixty-degree swivel camera to film the inside of the house. The damage to the house was incongruous. It was hard to believe that it had been a family home. Now it was a scene of utter devastation. A child's doll lay in the water. Most of the plastic from its head had been melted so half of its face was missing.

Although he wasn't a fire expert, Taylor knew that the flames must have taken hold very quickly and spread through the house, with a whirlwind effect that ignited everything in its path. He stepped into the kitchen, then out of the backdoor, and into a courtyard at the back of the house.

Commander John Leyton of the London Fire Service investigation team was standing in the back garden, with DI Peter Hamilton and DI Rebecca Hindley by his side.

The scale of the destruction was even more apparent at the back of the house than it was at the front. Leyton stepped forward to meet Taylor. He was wearing a thick black jacket. His dark hair was matted to his head. For someone in his early fifties it looked as if he kept himself lean and fit.

He greeted Taylor with a glum face, as well he might. After all, three people had died and two were in hospital on the critical list. The arsonist now had a record of seven dead and a dozen badly injured.

"What have you got for me?" Taylor asked Leyton.

John Leyton looked at him with a blank face. "The same MO," he muttered mournfully. He turned and took a step into the kitchen. Taylor followed him inside. "Looks as if he got in through the back door. Forced it open. Then he set about burning the place down. He sprayed paraffin in this room, then into the hallway. The trail of damage would indicate that it started at the back door."

"That makes a change," said Taylor. "He usually comes in the front way."

"Not this time," Leyton confirmed. "He must have decided that it was too dangerous to come through the front, so he decided on the back instead."

Taylor had no reason to disagree with him. This man had many years of fire investigation experience.

"Is there any clear indication of timing?" Taylor asked him.

"Difficult to be precise, but I'd say it was approximately two-thirty. We got a call from a neighbour at two forty-five who said he heard windows cracking. He got out of bed, looked across and could see flames coming out of the back of the house. The first engine was here at two minutes to three. By that time the house was well and truly alight. Those who died where in the front upstairs bedroom."

DI Hamilton and DI Hindley came inside the room, gingerly stepping through the black water.

DI Taylor looked at his colleagues. "As soon as it gets light, let's go down the street and knock on the doors. Someone might have heard something or saw someone. This guy has to make a mistake some time. Let's redouble our efforts and revisit all the hardware stores in the area, and see if anyone has been buying jemmies, and things that could be used to break into houses," he said. He looked at Leyton. "How soon can I have your report?" he asked.

"I'll get back to the station and write my report. I'll email it to you by noon at the earliest," Leyton said.

"Thanks," said Taylor. He sighed aloud. "This arsonist is really beginning to worry me. How many more fires are we going to have before we get him?" he asked.

Leyton couldn't do anything, but shrug his shoulders.

# Chapter 5

**The same day**


Later that morning coverage of fire number four was aired on all the local TV and radio stations. It was now coming to the attention of a lot of the Met Police brass that a serial Firestarter was out there. The pattern was the same. He had burned down a house at the same time of the month for the past four months. The target houses were the homes of Asian families. None of them were in any way connected to terrorism or any kind of criminal activity whatsoever. So why were they targeted by a madman? DI Taylor and his team were determined to find an answer to that question and in doing so find the arsonist. The pressure was mounting on the detectives to find the killer. Several local politicians were beginning to voice their concern. The Mayor of London had commented on the fires in an address to a full meeting of the council in City Hall. The story was now prominent in several local papers. The Evening Standard had run with a front-page piece that provided the reader with all the true facts and some others that could be classified as gross exaggeration.

Later that day in Paddington Green Police station a case review took place. The conference room on the ground floor of the building was packed with near to thirty detectives and some of the senior brass, including a Deputy Chief Constable of the Met. The senior investigating officer DCI Lake, DI Taylor and DI Hamilton, were sitting at the top table. Each of the officers in attendance had been given a copy of the case file, which contained all the relevant information about the fires.

On an overhead projector screen, a large map showed the locations of each fire. DCI Sarah Lake led the review. Lake was a veteran senior detective with many years of experience at the cutting edge of serious crime. She was in some way a bit of a throwback to a bygone age, and someone who didn't necessarily gel with some of the younger members of the team. In truth she was good at what she did. She was due to retire in eight months' time. This would probably be her last major investigation. She would want to go out on top. Taylor admired her immensely. After all, Sarah Lake, had given him his first big case, and had shown him the best methods of managing complex cases and using scarce resources – both human and other – to the full. She was a detective's detective, who had a reputation as being as straight as a brickie's plumb line.

Lake asked each detective to redouble their efforts, to keep their ears to the ground, to speak to their contacts and to keep their eyes open. Someone out there had to know who this arsonist was, or had their suspicion as to his identity. There had to be some information filtering out of the grapevine. The lack of solid information confirmed to everyone at the meeting that the identity of the Firestarter was a complete mystery. If the arsonist was like some of his contemporaries, there was a good chance that he wouldn't be able to resist the urge to brag about his work to someone. It was an element of human nature to want to tell someone what he had done.

Almost like someone who wanted to boast and brag about his or her sexual conquests. If this was the case, then hopefully someone would deem it credible enough to report it to the police. Privately, DI Taylor thought that this Firestarter was too careful and too clever by half to let anything slip. He didn't want to be caught, and he didn't want the notoriety and the kudos that would follow his capture.

The review meeting lasted for a few minutes over the hour. At the close, as the majority of the detectives dispersed, DI Taylor and several other colleagues stayed back to consider their next plan of action. DI Taylor was joined by DI Peter Hamilton and DI Hindley on the top table.

DI Peter Hamilton was a young man for a detective. He was only in his early thirties. Taylor had taken a shine to him, and asked DCI Lake to put him on his team. He was a handsome guy. Tall and slim and well turned out. He spoke with a south London accent, Bromley way. He was an all-round good guy. Almost too nice to be a detective. DI Rebecca Hindley had graduated from detective school and, make no mistake, she was as good as her male colleagues. She wasn't anything to write home about in the attractive stakes, but she more than made up for that in her intellect and ability to think like a criminal.

Each of the three detectives studied the map with the locations of the fires clearly marked. The demographic of the area was a mix of people and faiths. Nothing new in multicultural north

London. The area had previously been dominated by people from a Jewish background. There was still a sizable Jewish presence, though now people from an Asian background were moving into the area in increasing numbers. Several of the old established Jewish businesses were moving out to the fringes of suburban north London, to New Barnet and the like.

This got DI Taylor thinking. As he looked at the map on the overhead screen, something occurred to him. He asked Hamilton and Hindley if they could see some form of a shape developing. In order to clarify what he was saying he took a pencil and a ruler and proceeded to connect the dots showing the location of the first three fires by drawing a line to link them. The shape was triangular. The location of the fourth blaze was to the north of the second fire and north-west to the first fire so it in effect cut across the shape of the triangle.

"There's a pattern here," said Taylor. "I predict the fifth fire will take place to the east of fire four and north-east to the location of fire one." He took a marker pen and placed a dot on the map where he predicted the fifth fire would take place. "A sixth fire will occur well to the south of fire one but in a direct line underneath it."

He placed another dot onto the map. Then taking a pencil, he connected the dots between the location of the four fires, to the predicted locations of fires five and six. The lines made a shape of two inverted triangles.

DI Hamilton gulped. "Incredible," he said. "A Star of David shape."

"Oh, my good Lord. The arsonist is drawing a Star of David shape over the area," said DI Hindley.

"You've got something here," said Hamilton to Taylor.

Taylor kept his reaction closed. He refrained from smiling, but something told him he had established a concrete grasp of what the Firestarter was trying to do.

He looked at his colleagues. "I think the arsonist is targeting the homes of Muslims in an area that was once nearly all Jewish. The pattern tells us the likely location of the next target."

Hamilton nodded his head. "The guy is in effective scrawling a Jewish symbol over the area. The location of the fires are the six points of the two triangles."

"You've got it," said Taylor. "He's seeking to do exactly that," he added.

Taylor went to a telephone on the end of the table, picked it up and punched in a four-digit number into the keypad. He put in a call to the Senior Investigating Officer DCI Lake. He suggested to her that she reconvene the meeting of detectives at the first available opportunity. He advised her that he thought the arsonist was likely to be someone from the Jewish community or from a Jewish background. The motive was hatred against Muslims who had moved into the area. The arsonist was in effect sending out a message. He didn't want Muslim people in the area. In scratching a Star of David shape into the map he was also sending out a clue as to the location of the fifth and sixth fires.

DCI Lake did as Taylor recommended. She reconvened a second team meeting in one hour after the first meeting had ended. Most of the detectives who had attended that meeting returned for the second time. At the second gathering DI Taylor revealed the six-point pattern of the fires to all his colleagues. DCI Lake informed her boss, a Deputy Chief Constable, who informed her boss: The Commissioner of the Metropolitan Police.

The Commissioner requested a total news blackout. He didn't want a word of this leaking to the press, in case there was a backlash against the Jewish community. This was a very delicate situation that required careful management and tact. The last thing the Met police wanted was increasing racial tension in a two-mile square section of north London, with hotheads from other areas being drafted in to start a protest and begin a potential tit-for-tat response.

In the meantime, DI Taylor received the full report from Commander Leyton's office into the circumstances of the fourth fire.

It was much like the previous three reports. Just that the location had changed. All four houses had been in similar locations, along busy urban streets or roads leading to and from main arterial roads. Not exactly the homes of the rich, but not exactly at the other end of the scale either. On each occasion the Firestarter had targeted houses without security devices like CCTV, alarm boxes, intruder lights at the back of the property and perhaps the best security device a house could have – a large dog that had a powerful, loud bark and a nasty bite. None of the houses had any of these, therefore they were easy targets. This seemed to imply that the arsonist, had done his homework, rather than target the houses at random, which further suggested that he was local to the area. The developing profile of the Firestarter was that he was shrewd, lived locally and was from a Jewish background, though this may be a massive red herring. It was speculation at best.

Chapter 6

**27ᵗʰ December**


The Christmas festive period in the Taylor household had been a bit of a damp squib. Stephen and Susan's five-year-old daughter Samantha had gone down with a heavy cold on Christmas Eve. This took the shine off the festive period. They all tried to enjoy the holiday as best as they could, but other external pressures were pressing down on Taylor. After all, he was one of the team leading the search for the arsonist, and no matter how he tried to push it to the back of his mind, it kept coming back to the forefront. If the Firestarter stayed to form, he would attempt his fifth blaze in mid-January.


Because the head of London police had insisted on a news blackout and a softly-softly approach, none of the people in the area knew of the likely location of the fifth attack or the timing. None of the print media or TV news agencies had picked up on the links, and nothing had been leaked to the press. Therefore, the good ship SS Met Police was as tight as a rock drummer's bass drum. At the end of the day there was no guarantee that the arsonist would stick to the script. He may be wise enough to realise that the police would by now have discovered the Star of David shape pattern, consequently he may choose to change some aspect of his routine. Maybe he might decide to end the campaign of terror as it hadn't had the desired effect. Whatever, the police still had to work on the theory that he would soon strike again. If the aim of the exercise was to inflame the local population to begin a tit-for-tat exchange that would result in heightened tension between the Jewish and Muslim communities, then it had failed. Or maybe the Firestarter was attempting to pitch Muslim against Muslim, to divide the Shia and Sunni faiths.

The decision of the commissioner to insist on a news black-out may well have been a very shrewd one. The head of police in the capital had called for increased covert surveillance in an area of north London three miles square. More cops had been drafted into the zone and new CCTV units had been swiftly and surreptitiously installed, literally overnight.


## 8th January


In a move described by DCI Lake as Sod's Law, the arsonist changed his routine. The fifth fire came far earlier in the month. The eighth of January to be precise. Not in the middle of the month. But this time he had been sloppy and lazy. The fire had caused little damage to the property.

DI Taylor received a call at five-thirty in the morning to attend the scene. The fire wasn't in the location he had predicted. It wasn't in the fifth point of the star but the sixth. At the bottom end of the second inverted triangle. This time someone in the target house, a man in his forties, had heard the sound of someone breaking into his home. He got out of bed to investigate and had gone down stairs.

As he went towards the back of the house, he caught sight of a figure – dressed all in black – standing in the narrow galley kitchen. The arsonist had ignited a pool of liquid on a worktop. Luckily for the householder he had shouted out in a loud booming voice, which caused the intruder to turn tail and get out of the back door. Before the flames had chance to take hold the man managed to get to the sink, grab a towel, run it under a tap and throw it over the flames.

When he arrived at the scene at seven o'clock with DI Hamilton, DI Taylor interviewed the man. He was an Iraqi refugee. The chap spoke reasonably good English.

Taylor asked him if he had got a good look at the man's face. The chap described him as being medium height and build, but he had a hood over his head and a scarf across his lower face, so it wasn't possible to get a good look at his features, plus the fact that it had been very dark at three in the morning.

In his haste to get out of the house the intruder had left a vital piece of kit, a transparent plastic spray bottle. It was still half full of a pink paraffin liquid. It certainly smelled like paraffin.

This was the first item to be recovered from any of the break-ins. It could be a vital clue. The Scene of Crime team put it into a clear plastic bag and took it away for further examination.

The house was occupied by a family of six. All refugees who had fled from Iraq and had been granted asylum in the UK. Two adults and their four children. The children were in the age range of six to sixteen years of age. If it wasn't for the fact that their father hadn't been able to sleep and had heard the Firestarter breaking into the house, then this house may have gone up like the others and resulted in even more deaths.

When talking to his colleagues back in Paddington Green, DI Taylor concluded that the arsonist was becoming even more brazen, but, at the same time, lazy and sloppy. He had been lucky on this occasion. Maybe he wouldn't be so lucky the next time. If he had left his fingerprints on the spray bottle, then they had got the breakthrough they needed to identify the culprit.

The team were planning to return to the scene of the fire in the next hour to interview the rest of the family members. None of the other five people in the house spoke English well enough for the detectives to carry out a formal interview, therefore they had requested an interpreter be at the location to assist in the task of taking witness statements.

One and a half hours after leaving the house DI Taylor, DI Hamilton, and DI Hindley returned to the scene. An Arabic interpreter, a young lady called Fatima, was at the house to help them with their questions.

Taylor and the other detectives entered the house where the head of the family greeted them. All six occupants were crammed into a small lounge. Four were sitting on a dilapidated sofa, whilst the two youngest children were sitting on the floor. The house still reeked of smoke. Taylor stepped into the back room with the head of the family and went into the tiny kitchen area. Scorch marks had burnt paint off the storage cupboards, and blackened the cheap granite work surfaces, which frankly had seen better days long before someone tried to set them on fire. The head of the family had attempted to clean up as best as he could. Despite what he had been through he still smiled and said 'thank you' to DI Taylor several times. Taylor felt incredibly sorry for them. They had escaped from their home land, sought protection in a faraway land, only for an arsonist to break into their home in the dead of night and attempt to burn the house down to the ground.

From the kitchen, they returned to the lounge. The mother of the children wore a black hijab over her head. The four children were still, silent, and attentive.

The lounge was dark and dingy. The carpet felt as if it had been down for many years. The furniture was cheap and ancient. No doubt the landlord charged the local council a king's ransom to put up these unfortunate people who, through no fault of their own, had to escape from their homeland to this hovel in a cold and miserable place called England.


DI Taylor took charge of the proceedings. He looked to Fatima. "Can you ask the boys if they saw anything from out of the windows?" he asked. She asked the question in Arabic.

The elder of the boys, who looked to be sixteen years of age replied in Arabic.

Fatima translated his words into English. "Aman said he sleeps in the upstairs back room. He looked out of the window and saw someone climbing over the fence at the bottom of the garden."

"Can he describe him?" asked DI Hamilton.

Fatima asked the question and listened to his reply. "He wasn't a white man. He is more Arab than white, said the boy."

DI Taylor was surprised but not stunned by this revelation. He kept his emotions and thoughts under tight control. "Is he certain?" he asked. "How can he be so sure?" he asked.

Again, she asked the question and listened to the reply.

"He said his hood of his coat fell down. In the light from the building across the way he could see him as clear as day. He is a dark-skinned man, not negro, but middle-east looking. He had dark hair."

DI Taylor looked at Hamilton and Hindley and they each shared a face. If the boy was correct, then clearly, they were not looking for a white person, though it didn't mean to say the arsonist couldn't have been from the Jewish community.

DI Taylor thought long and hard about the next question, but he had to ask it. "If he had to put a nationality on him how would he describe him?" he asked.

She translated his question into Arabic, then the boy's answer to English. "Maybe Pakistani, or Bengali," she replied.

If the indications coming from the boy were correct, then there was a possibility – albeit a possibility – that the Firestarter was of East Asian descent, rather than Middle-East Arab or Jewish. But

184

of course, it wasn't a scientific exercise by any stretch of the imagination, though the boy did seem pretty much clued up. The family had lived in London for the past four years; therefore, the boy wasn't a newcomer to the country. Plus, he would have no need to make up such a story.

As soon as the interviews were over DI Taylor, Hamilton and Hindley stepped out of the house and loitered on the path outside, talking for a couple of minutes. Then Taylor got onto his mobile phone and called DCI Lake.

Lake answered the call within five rings and introduced herself in a laconic, deadpan style. "Lake," she said.

"DI Taylor."

"What have you got for me?" she asked.

"We may have reason to reassess the ID of the Firestarter," he replied.

"Fill me in." This was her unconventional invitation to tell him what he had learned.

"One of the occupants in the house, a boy of sixteen, said he got a look at our man."

"And?"

"He said he saw him climbing over a fence at the bottom of the garden. He said our man's hood fell and he got a look at him."

"But it's pitch black in north London at two-forty in the morning," she said.

"Not if there's a bright light attached to the building across the way."

"Go on," she encouraged.

"The kid said he saw the guy's head and face. He's one hundred percent certain that he's Asian and not a Caucasian or Arab."

Lake didn't say anything for a moment has she considered the significance of his words. "That's interesting," she said. "Why would an Asian be setting fire to the homes of fellow Muslims?" she asked.

"Maybe he's not Asian."

"Yeah, it's possible. A recent convert to Christianity attacking the homes of Muslims he thinks are involved in terrorism," she said.

"I doubt that."

"I tend to agree. When you get back here send out an email to the detective group informing them of this development, but ensure it comes with a caveat."

"Such has?" he asked.

"To be aware that we are not looking for a Caucasian male, but maybe it's a copy-cat arsonist."

"Can't be," said Taylor.

"Why?" Lake asked.

"He left a spray bottle full of a paraffin spirit. The same MO has the previous four. The SOCO team will be dusting it down for prints as we speak."

"If we've got a fingerprint, we could have him," she said without any excitement in her voice.

"Exactly."

"Keep me posted," asked Lake, before she ended the conversation.

The significance of finding the bottle wasn't lost on any of the team. It could be the breakthrough they had been seeking. If the Firestarter had been through the criminal system, they would have a fingerprint match, but that was assuming he had been arrested on some other misdemeanour, and that wasn't always the case. He could be a pair of clean hands.

Chapter 7

**28th January**

It was now the back end of January with the start of February a couple of days away. As the fifth attack had come in the first week of the new year, there was no guessing when a sixth attack would come, if at all.

The news from the forensic team hadn't been what they had hoped for. They had examined the spray bottle under ultra-violet light and dusted it down. Alas, it didn't give up a full fingerprint.

Nevertheless, Taylor thought that the noose was tightening around the arsonists neck. Five points of the Star of David had been completed. A sixth would complete the two triangles. There was a distinct chance that the Firestarter may have concluded that it was too dangerous to attempt to finish the job. He had nearly been caught in the act. Perhaps he may conclude it was becoming too risky. Maybe next time he wouldn't get so lucky. The team couldn't guess his state of mind.

**13th February**

It was five o'clock on the morning of the thirteenth of February that Taylor was awaken from his sleep by the sound of a bedside telephone. He took the receiver and put it to his ear. It was DCI Lake, yet again.

The content of the following conversation informed him that the arsonist had attempted to complete the sixth and final point of the double triangle. The Star of David was complete. But the key word was 'attempted'. The attempt had failed. This wasn't the only good news to come down the line on this frosty February morning. The arsonist had broken into the target house only for the occupant to tackle him coming through the back door. The bark of a neighbour's dog had alerted the householder to a presence in his house at two-forty in the morning. He went downstairs. As he stepped into the kitchen the intruder was coming in through the back door. Not knowing what the hell was happening, the occupant made a grab for him. The intruder dropped the spray bottle and a glove. He also left a jemmy wedged in the doorframe and a foot print in the frost. As he attempted to get away, he inadvertently put his hand through a pane of glass in the door. In doing so he left a sample of his blood on the glass.

The man chased the intruder down the path, but wasn't able to hold onto him as the burglar climbed over the wall and escaped into the alley running parallel to the back of the house. The man had called the police immediately. The police arrived at the location within twelve minutes of the 999 call. Knowing that an arsonist was on the loose, the police had secured the crime scene and called in a forensic team. The team would be at the house in the next couple of hours to collect the blood. It would be analysed for a DNA link.

On receiving the news of the sixth attack, DI Taylor went through the usual procedure. He contacted his colleagues, DIs Hamilton and Hindley on the telephone. He requested they meet him at the scene within the hour. Hamilton said he was surprised that the Firestarter had attempted a sixth B&E so quickly after the failure at the fifth address. Then it crossed Taylor's mind that there were maybe two arsonists working in tandem, but the evidence only pointed to a lone wolf, so he quickly dismissed the notion.

Taylor left his home in Welwyn Garden at six. There was now a hint of light in the sky at this time of the morning.

The scene of the sixth B&E was within the range of the others. It was just a matter of a quarter of a mile or so from the location of the first and third blazes. It was typical of the other locations A house on an everyday street in an everyday part of urban north London.

It was on a long road of middle-of-the-range properties. A police car was parked outside. Lights in the nearby houses were on and several neighbours were gathered on the street to observe what was going on outside. Word had gotten out that something had occurred here that morning. The sight of a police car never failed to fuel a thousand theories. Overhead, the first crack of dawn was appearing between the gaps in the dark sky.

As he emerged out of his car, Taylor pulled his coat collar up and sunk his hands into the deep recesses of his coat pockets. The cold nip in the air wasn't as potent as it had been along the open roads of Welwyn Garden City. In the tight streets around here, the temperature was up a few degrees. The air was laced with the smell of frost.

Taylor met a uniformed officer outside the house who filled him in on the details. The house was occupied by two families of Syrian refugees who were crammed into a three-bed house. Eight occupants in total.

After a few minutes chatting to the officer, DI Hamilton and DI Hindley arrived on the scene in Hamilton's car. They met with DI Taylor on the pavement outside the house. All three of them looked haggard and tired. This wasn't the first time they had been called out in the small hours. Sunrise was still thirty minutes away.

All three of them entered the house and made their way into the back where a second uniformed officer was standing at the back door, guarding the broken panes and the smudge of the intruder's blood.

The interior was filled with the aroma of spicy food. The decor was minimal, the fixtures and furniture functional. The families had decorated the interior with reminders of home like aerial views of the Syrian city of Aleppo, before it was devastated by the civil war. The eight occupants were in a lounge room sitting at a dining table. The officer pointed out the guy who had confronted the intruder.

He looked like a colossus. They knew that the intruder was average height and build, therefore one look at this guy coming towards him must have persuaded him to back off and to get the hell out of there. In his haste to get out, he had put his hand straight through a pane of glass, leaving blood and a sample of cloth fibres and skin. The forensic team would have enough material to do a DNA comparison.

DI Taylor elected to stay in the house until the SOCO team arrived. DIs Hamilton and Hindley interviewed the man who had confronted the intruder, then they left the house to knock on the doors of the neighbours and conduct house-to-house enquiries.

It was quarter to nine when a police investigation unit van containing the SOCO team arrived on the scene. The team of four immediately got down to the task of collecting the blood and the skin deposits left on the broken glass. They also bagged the iron bar he had used as a jemmy to prise the back door open, and the dropped glove. Taylor spoke to the leading investigator, DCI Lake. The good news was that the intruder had left enough blood to give them an adequate sample for a DNA test. A positive match against the records of anyone on the database represented a one in ten million chance that the DNA didn't belong to the Firestarter. If they had the intruder's DNA on the database, then they had the identity of the arsonist. It was that simple.

As soon as DIs Hamilton and Hindley had conducted a brief door-to-door knock along the street, they came back into the house to speak to Mr Hassan, the tenant. The other seven occupants of the house were still sitting at the dining table, looking less than animated by the attention they were receiving. The four children were still and silent. The two wives were dressed in long gowns with headscarves covering their hair.

Mister Hassan proved to be a nice guy. He said he had been a doctor in an Aleppo hospital for the previous ten years, before the civil war had driven him out of his country. Because he couldn't provide evidence of his background, and his English language skills were not great, he hadn't been successful in obtaining a similar position with the NHS. He worked part-time for a local door-to-door leaflet distribution firm on a temporary basis. That was the only employment he had been able to find in the time he had been in the UK.

DI Taylor engaged him in a conversation about the incident that morning. He wanted to hear the details from him first hand. He told Taylor exactly what he had told the first police officer to arrive at his home. He had been woken at approximately two-thirty by the sound of a neighbour's dog barking. Then he had heard someone breaking into his home. He had gotten out of bed, crept downstairs and confronted the intruder at the back door in the kitchen. His first response was to shout out loud, partly to warn the intruder, but also to alert the people inside the house.

As he was a beefy-looking guy, the intruder had backed off and got out of there as soon as possible. In doing so he had dropped not just another plastic bottle, but also the iron bar. Mister Hassan had made a grab for him, and got hold of his jacket. The arsonist had reached out to get hold of the door, but misjudged the distance and only succeeded in putting his hand through the glass. The collision must have pushed the sleeve of his jacket up to expose his flesh. As he pulled his hand out, he sustained a cut against the sharp edge of the broken glass and in doing so, left his blood at the scene. Hassan had chased him down the path, but he wasn't able to hold onto him when he jumped onto the wall. The arsonist had succeeded in climbing over and escaping down the adjacent alleyway.

By the time the three detectives had concluded their investigation at the house it was getting on for ten forty-five. The forensic team had left ten minutes ago.

After completing their business at the house DIs Taylor, Hamilton and Hindley went to Paddington Green police station to complete their report and to update the case file. Hamilton added the final dot to the Star of David pattern on the map. If Taylor was correct this would be the end of the fire campaign. The two overlapping triangles were complete. However, there was no guarantee that the arsonist had stopped his burning spree.

DI Taylor sent another email to the detective group to inform them of the latest development. In his own mind, he thought they were close to identifying the Firestarter.

# Chapter 8

**15th February**


The breakthrough came forty-eight hours following the sixth break-in, via the forensic team based at New Scotland Yard. They had analysed the sample of blood taken from the latest crime scene. They had managed to extract the DNA profile and run it against the records kept on the national database. It had come up with a hit. The DNA profile matched that of a twenty-eight-year-old British man of Pakistani heritage. A man by the name of Asim Malik.


Asim Malik had been arrested several years ago on a charge of racially aggravated incitement, when he had verbally abused several members of the orthodox Jewish community outside a synagogue in central London. He was a borderline *wannabee* bad-arse Islamic extremist. He didn't do any jail time but had been fined, given a six-month suspended sentence and placed on a 'watch-list'. In the time between his arrest and now he hadn't come to the attention of the security services. His last known abode was at an address in Tottenham Hale, north London.

Why Malik would want to burn down the homes of refugees was a complete mystery. It just didn't seem logical.


Within an hour of receiving the report from the team at New Scotland Yard, DCI Lake convened a meeting of all available detectives in Paddington Green Police Station. As a matter of protocol, two members of the Met counter terrorism unit were invited to attend, but at this stage there was nothing concrete to suggest that the fires were related to terrorism.

Fifteen detectives attended the meeting. The conference room was only half full, but the atmosphere was feverish. News had spread that the identity of the Firestarter was known.

The overhead lights were on and a dozen eager faces greeted DCI Lake and DI Taylor as they entered the conference room. Two officers from the Met Counter Terrorism Unit were in attendance. They were Officers Malcolm Storey and his colleague John Winn. They were two ex-members of the Serious Crime Squad who had moved over to Counter Terrorism in the wake of the recent activity and the perceived notion of increasing terrorist activity to come. DI Taylor knew both of them. They were solid, reliable guys, so he didn't have any problem, whatsoever, with them being in attendance.

The chatter in the room ceased as DCI Lake and DI Taylor sat at the top table and pulled the microphones close to them. It was Lake who kicked off the meeting.

"Colleagues," she said. "The forensic team at the Yard have identified the name of the arsonist. He is twenty-eight-year-old Asim Malik. His last known address is 83, Devenish Road in Tottenham. He's known to be a supporter of some Islamic Jihad groups. He was arrested two years ago, for a verbal attack on several orthodox Jews outside a synagogue in Central London. He was arrested for incitement. He's a follower rather than a player. Since the time of his arrest until now, he has not moved up the list of names to watch."

The officers listened in silence and remained attentive throughout the introduction. Lake continued. "We've concluded that the fires have been placed at six points to make the pattern of the points of a Star of David over the area. We can only think that this is an effort to inflame the local Muslim population to retaliate against members of the Jewish community, but so far, we've avoided that. Still, it may be only a matter of time before the media make the connections and report it. We must find Malik before that happens. Any questions?" she asked.

"Is there any indication that he's working with anyone?" one of the detectives asked.

"Not that we're aware of," replied Lake.

"But we're not sure," injected Taylor.

"That's why we need to find him and bring him in fast," said Lake. "I want a team of six officers, led by DI Taylor and DI Hamilton to go to the address to see if he's there. If he is then we'll bring him in for questioning. We'll be supported by a backup of uniformed officers. Can I ask for volunteers?" she asked.

All the detectives put their hands up.

"That's great. Thank you," she said. She swiftly chose six detectives to accompany Taylor and Hamilton. "We'll go to the last known address in three cars. Uniformed backup will follow us. At this stage, I'd like to ask our colleagues from Counter Terrorism to fill you in on what they know about Malik."

Malcom Storey got to his feet. He was a large man with hard features, and a shaved bald head. He looked like a cross between an all-in wrestler and a weather-beaten cowboy. He was unsmiling and serious. "Thanks," he said. "What we know about him is that following his arrest, a search of his home took place. We found some anti-Semitic material and some Jihad pamphlets asking true believers to avenge the deaths of Palestinians by the Israelis. We also examined his PC and found evidence that he'd been watching and listening to sermons delivered by a few hothead imams. The usual suspects. He appears to be a follower rather than someone who would be likely to carry out an act, but we don't know for sure. He may have been further radicalised in the intervening period from his arrest to now. We don't think he's armed, but we're taking no chances, both myself and DI Winn are carrying standard issue, loaded firearms. If he does kick off, we'll take him down if we must, but of course we'd rather not." He looked over to DCI Lake. "Thanks. Over to you," he added.

"Any questions?" asked Lake.

"Do we have a description of who we're looking for?" someone asked.

"DI Taylor will provide you with his mug-shot on your way out," she said. "We know that he's five-eight tall, medium build. Light brown skin. Dark hair. Dark eyes," she added.

She looked out over the spread of detectives. "If there are no more questions, let's go."

All fifteen detectives got to their feet. Six of them came to the front table to take an A4 size photograph of Asim Malik from DI Taylor.

Once outside in the courtyard the officers climbed into three different unmarked cars. Several uniformed cops were waiting in a police wagon. Once each vehicle was ready, they left in a convoy and drove onto the streets of central London.

The day had turned chilly with an icy-edged breeze blowing along the streets. Maybe warmer weather was waiting in the wings.

The four vehicles were in range of Malik's last known address within twenty-five minutes of setting out from Paddington Green. Nobody knew if they would find him in the family home or if he had shipped out some time ago. He had kept his nose clean for the past two years, though that didn't mean to say he had mellowed. It could be he hadn't been caught doing anything or connected to any plot. It was believed that four other members of the Malik family lived at the house.

Devenish Road in Tottenham was a compact road of tightly clustered, terraced houses, in a post-war development of residential homes. It was par for the course around here. Council rubbish bins were lined up outside most of the homes as the weekly collection was today. Some of the homes looked nice, other less than nice. The area was racially tolerant and mixed amongst the full range of multi-cultural Britain at the start of the second millennium. Once, it had been an up and coming area, and much sought after. Many of the original, white-British residents had move out to the northern fringes of the city and into bordering Essex. Members of the Caribbean and British-Asian community filled the void, and increasing numbers of Eastern European immigrants were moving in to give it a cosmopolitan melting pot feel.

The house at number eighty-three was an inconsequential looking home with net curtains over the windows and a rather down at heel frontage. The UPVC window frames looked in need of a rub down with a cleaning solution.

The cars driven by DI Hamilton and DI Taylor were the first to arrive at the address. The two following vehicles were not far behind. Once all three cars and the wagon containing the uniformed officers were at the location, all the detectives got out. Three of the uniformed cops were asked to go to the back of the house to ensure Malik didn't escape over a garden fence. As Malik seemed to be adept at going over walls and fences of the homes he had attacked, there was no desire to let him escape from here.

# Chapter 9

**The same day**

The sudden appearance of three cars discharging a group of men on the road hadn't appeared to create any kind of alarm amongst the tenants living in the vicinity. Officers Storey and Winn were both armed with concealed handguns perched in holsters under their heavy car coats.

DI Taylor and Hamilton were leading the way. They stepped through a wrought iron gate and approached the front door. The front area was a concrete surface behind a brick wall in which the mortar was crumbling and weeds were growing. A large bow shape window to the right looked out onto the front.

DI Taylor knocked on the front door. He noticed the fast food leaflet stuffed in the letter box which would suggest that no one was at home. However, within twenty seconds of knocking the blurred configuration of someone appeared behind an opaque glass pane. The door opened, and a man close to sixty years of age with dark Asian features appeared. He greeted the arrival of DI Taylor and DI Hamilton with a scowl on his face, as if to say 'I know who you are but what do you want here?'

Taylor withdrew his ID badge from an inside jacket pocket and showed it to him. The chap looked at it fleetingly and once again offered a none too happy expression.

"I'm DI Stephen Taylor from Paddington Green. This is my colleague DI Peter Hamilton. We need to speak to Asim. Is he home?" Taylor asked.

The man looked at him, then over his shoulder at the other men gathered on the pavement. By the fact that several officers were in attendance he must have known it was serious. He put his eyes back on DI Taylor.

"I'm his father. He's not here," he said. "I not see him for a year. He go and not come back."

"Go where?" asked Taylor.

"I not know."

"You don't know where he is?"

"No. I not see him for one year. At least," he added.

"Do you have any idea where he could be?" DI Hamilton asked.

"No. Why do you want to talk to him. Is he in trouble?" he asked.

"We'd like him to help us with our enquiries into a series of fires in the north-west London area."

"Fires?" he asked if he didn't understand the word. His expression changed from one of petulance to one that was neutral and slightly more at ease. It seemed as if he had experience of talking to the police regarding his son. Asim did have a sheet that contained arrests going back to his teenage years. Therefore, this was nothing new. But arson was a whole new ballgame. By the number of plain-clothed police outside his home, he knew this was serious.

"Yes. Fires," said DI Hamilton. "Have you any idea where he might be?" he asked.

"No."

"Can you contact him?" DI Taylor asked.

"I not speak to him for over one year. I have no idea where he is," he said.

"How about any other members of your family? Have they seen him?" DI Hamilton asked.

"No one sees him. No one know where he is." By the tone of his answers he seemed pretty adamant that this was the case.

"Do you mind if we come in and have a look?" DI Taylor asked.

In truth, he didn't have much wriggle room to say no. He thought about the question for a few brief moments. "Who is here?" asked DI Hamilton.

"Me and my wife," he replied.

"Can we come in and check he's not here?"

Mister Malik turned his head to look down the hallway. If he wasn't here, he had nothing to worry about. Perhaps it was better to get it over and done with and get the officers off the street before they began to attract too much attention.

"You come in," he said in a resigned tone of voice. He turned into the hallway and led both DI Taylor and DI Hamilton into his house. Several other officers followed them inside. It was an ordinary house in terms of décor and furniture. Nothing special, but definitely not the worse. A strong aroma of curry lingered along with the smell of spicy food.

"How many people live here?" asked DI Taylor.

"Me, my wife and daughter," he replied.

Taylor glanced into the main sitting room. There were no religious paintings or symbols. Just photographs of long-gone members of the wider family on a mantelpiece above a fireplace in which an old gas fire sat. On the walls were several street scenes from the nineteen-fifties. They could have been streets in Karachi or Lahore. There was no immediate obvious indication that Asim was here.

Mr Malik took both Taylor and Hamilton upstairs and showed them the three bedrooms and inside the bathroom. Taylor noticed the hatch that led into the loft space was covered in cobwebs which suggested that it hadn't been opened any time recently. Two of the bedrooms were in use, but the third was being used as a room to store luggage, clothes and items of furniture. "Whose stuff is it?" Taylor asked, thrusting his chin at the items.

"My son," he said.

"Why didn't he take it with him?" DI Hamilton asked.

"I've no idea. For all I know he may have gone abroad."

"To where?" Taylor asked.

"To Pakistan."

"How about Syria?"

"No. He never said he wanted to go to Syria."

"Not to join IS?" Hamilton asked.

"No."

Taylor looked to Hamilton. He was peering out through the back window to the garden where two colleagues were in the garden, and two others were searching in a brick shed for Asim. He wasn't in there.

Taylor turned to Mr Malik. "If Asim gets in touch with you. You'll be sure to let us know, won't you?"

Mr Malik looked at him with a glum face that displayed displeasure at the implied tone in his voice. He remained non-committal. Taylor dipped a hand into a pocket and withdrew a business card. He handed it to Mr Malik. He took it without saying a word. "My contact details are on the card. Please call me if he gets in touch. We need to speak to him urgently."

"I not speak to him for over one year," he repeated.

"But if he does, my contact details are on there."

"All right," he said in a reluctant tone. Perhaps he was in denial about the whole thing. If he had heard news on the recent arson attacks in the north London area, and if his son was involved in them, then he was in serious trouble with the police. Little wonder he wasn't exactly co-operative with the detectives.

He took Taylor and Hamilton down the stairs and back to the front door. The search of the house was over. They hadn't found Asim Malik, or learnt where he was holding out. Taylor was still a little suspicious and suspected that his father may have known his whereabouts. It may be a smart move to keep eyes on him in case he suddenly left the house to visit his son.

The two detectives stepped out of the house and joined their colleagues on the path outside. They all climbed into the three unmarked vehicles and took off back to Paddington Green Police station. En-route Taylor put in a call to DCI Lake to update her on the progress so far. According to his father, Asim Malik had gone walkabout. He told them he hadn't seen him or spoken to him for over a year.

In that case DCI Lake suggested that they put some eyes on Mr Malik, and put out a media call to ask for information leading to the arrest of Asim Malik. Lake said she would clear it with her superiors. If they agreed she would contact the Met's communication team and ask them to action it immediately. She would also organise a watch on the house, in case Asim returned, or his father left in a hurry.

# Chapter 10

**The same day**

The request for information from the Met communication team went out, within two hours of receiving the agreement from those further up the chain of command. Both the BBC and ITV and other news media organisations were asked to broadcast a bulletin about the search for twenty-eight-year-old Asim Malik, wanted for questioning about the arson attacks in north London over the past few months. He wasn't to be approached. It was thought he wasn't dangerous, but might turn violent if cornered.

The bulletins began going out at four o'clock on all BBC platforms. Independent radio stations were also asked to put out requests for information. Anyone who knew where Asim Malik was staying was encouraged to contact the police right away. Newspaper news rooms were also informed, and asked to put a message on their websites with a photograph of the wanted man. ITV news said they would feature the request in their main national news beginning at six-thirty. With the assistance of the media, DI Taylor was optimistic they would have Malik in the next few days.

The Met knew that he hadn't skipped out of the country as the Border Agency had been asked to check if anyone with that name had passed through the border. The British transport police in all London rail terminals were also asked to keep a look out for

Malik, should he attempt to get out of the capital. His photograph was now plastered over not only television, but the internet as well.

When all said and done, the response from the public was very good. There were reported sightings of Malik in such faraway places as Glasgow in the north, to Plymouth in the south-west. And as far west as Blackpool, and as far east as Scarborough.

## 16th February

The big breakthrough came, the following day, at just after three o'clock in the afternoon. A man who said he had rented a house to someone who resembled Asim Malik called Scotland Yard. The content of the call was relayed to DI Taylor. The man was called Afonso Figueiro. He said he had rented a two-bedroomed house in north Wembley to Malik.

DI Taylor called Mister Figueiro. He was a Portuguese national, who had bought the house six months before, then moved out to share a house with his partner. The house in north Wembley became vacant so he had advertised it for rent in a local free paper and on the internet. A man calling himself Eshan Butt had contacted him. He looked exactly like the man in the photo on the TV. They met at the house the following day. Figueiro had shown him the house and the man said he wanted to rent it for a maximum of six months.

Taylor asked Figueiro to describe the man he had spoken to. His description fitted the description of Malik. Taylor asked Figueiro if he would meet him outside the address in one hour from now. Figueiro said okay, he would be there.

DI Taylor left the police station with his colleagues DI Hamilton and DI Hindley and made their way the relatively short distance into north Wembley. They also arranged for uniformed officers to be at the house for back-up.


The house in north Wembley was on a pleasant tree-lined thoroughfare, close to the boundary where it merged into Harrow-on-the-Hill. At five in the evening the area was busy with cars and people in abundance. DI Hamilton was driving the unmarked police vehicle, Taylor and beside him and DI Rebecca Hindley was in the back. Hamilton pulled up outside the address.

It was a semi-detached house with a bow frontage and a pebble dash finish. Typical of the area. A recently constructed wall formed the boundary around the property. There was a side drive leading to a single garage.

It was several notches up on the house in Tottenham Hale. Pastel coloured blinds were down over the windows, so it had a vacant look. The stout gloss painted front door had gold metal numerals attached to it.

Several minutes passed before an old-style Jaguar pulled in behind them. This must have been the landlord. The door of the Jag opened and a short plump guy with an olive complexion got out and stepped onto the pavement in front of the house. DI Hamilton put the side window down. He withdrew his warrant badge, put his hand out and flashed his ID.

"Are you Mister Figueiro?" he asked.

The man confirmed he was. He had a Mediterranean appearance. Neatly groomed dark hair, dark eyes and an oily skin. He stepped towards the police car.

"Jump into the back for a moment, will you please?" Hamilton asked. The man eyed the people in the car, then opened the back door and slid onto the seat next to DI Hindley.

Taylor and Hamilton turned to him. "When did Mister Malik rent the house from you?" Taylor asked.

"Five months ago," he replied. His accent was similar to that of a famous Portuguese football manager who had made his name in London. Not that that was of any importance or of great significance to the case. It just confirmed he was from that part of the world.

"How does he pay you?" Hamilton asked him.

"He doesn't," replied Figueiro.

"What do you mean?" asked Taylor.

"He paid six month rent at the beginning of the agreement."

"Straight off?" Hamilton asked.

"Yes. He pay full six-month rent, plus a security bond of one thousand pounds."

"How much is the rent for a place like this?" Taylor asked.

"I charge one thousand and eight hundred pounds each month."

Taylor did the calculation in his head. "That's nearly eleven thousand up front," he said.

"Plus, the thousand pounds security deposit," added DI Hindley. "That's nearly twelve thousand." She was spot on the money.

Both Taylor and Hindley looked at each other. The question going through their heads was how had Asim Malik got his hands on that kind of money? They knew Malik didn't have a job, and according to the latest account he was in receipt of state-paid benefits.

"How did he pay you?" asked DI Hamilton.

"In cash," he replied.

"Jeez," said Taylor under his breath. "How did he get his hands on that kind of money?" he asked. Mister Figueiro didn't answer the question. Both DI Hamilton and Hindley pondered on it, but didn't offer an answer or speculate. In the next few moments a police car arrived outside the address and pulled up directly opposite the driveway. In effective blocking it. Four burly officers emerged. Several of the near neighbours observed the activity on the street. The curtains were already twitching. Taylor thought it was time to go into the house to discover if anyone was home.

"Do you have a spare set of keys?" DI Hamilton asked Figueiro. "If not, the boys might have to break in," he added.

"I have keys here," he said quickly and eagerly withdrew a set which he gave to Taylor. With that all four of them got out of the car, joined their uniformed colleagues on the path, entered via a gate in a low wall and approached the front door.

DI Hamilton asked two of the uniformed guys to go to the rear of the house to ensure that no one attempted to escape through the back garden. Two of them did as requested. The three detectives and two of the other uniformed cops stepped towards the front door which was under an arched porch.

The letter box was at waist height so DI Taylor got down on his haunches, opened it and looked inside just in case someone was standing there. There wasn't. He could see straight into the hallway to the rear of the house and an open door that looked as if it led into a kitchen. Sunlight was streaming in to illuminate the interior. There was no shadow and no evidence of any movement or presence inside. What he did notice was a strong chemical smell.

He tried the door in case it was open. It wasn't so he took the bunch of keys, found the front door key and inserted it into the lock, turned it cautiously, and pushed the door open.

"Police officers," he shouted at the top of his voice as he stepped over the threshold. The other police officers were right behind him. "Anyone at home?" shouted DI Hindley.
There didn't appear to be anyone in. There was a cold silence, and a sense that the house may have been vacant for some time.

Taylor stepped forward and came level with the banister rail of a staircase on the right-hand side. There was a closed door to the left. The corridor on the ground floor led into a spacious kitchen. The coat pegs attached to the outer wall were empty. There were no shoes in the shoe-rack. A closed umbrella was propped up against the staircase support. The house was almost too clean, as if someone had recently gone through it with a bucket of bleach filled detergent to wipe down the surfaces and collected every scrap of fallen food or litter.

The sharp chemical smell was very evident. It was so strong that it left a raw feeling at the back of the throat.

"What's that smell?" asked DI Hamilton.

"Smells a bit like bitter almonds," said DI Hindley.

"It seems to be coming from up the stairs," said Taylor. He looked to his colleagues and the two uniformed guys. "Would you guys look downstairs. We'll go upstairs and see what we can find." One of the uniformed cops elected to stay close to the front door in case anyone tried to get in. It was becoming increasingly obvious that the house was unoccupied.

DI Taylor and DI Hamilton ascended the stairs to the first floor. On the landing, they turned back on themselves and went towards a closed door that must have led into a bedroom at the front. Again, the floor was spotless. The chemical smell wasn't that strong up here but there was a secondary more disturbing aroma.

Taylor took the door knob. "Anyone at home?" he shouted. No reply, so he took the handle, turned it, and pushed the door inward. As soon as the gap was wide enough, he looked inside the room and got the shock of his life.

The body of a man lay across the carpeted surface. Head to the right, feet to the left, back turned towards the door. He was laid on his side with his head down. The top half of his torso was covered in blood. He was dressed in a white vest and a pair of black underpants. The white of the vest had been almost obscured by the volume of blood that had come out of his abdomen. A bloodied knife was laid a metre or so from his feet.

"We've got a dead body," Taylor said to Hamilton.

He opened the door wide and they both stepped gingerly inside the room. There was an unmade bed on the right-hand side. The sheets had been pulled back. There was a pungent aroma of death and dried blood. There was a pile of clothes strung over the mattress. The top drawer in a chest of three drawers was open. Some clothes were hanging, half in, half out. The two of them stepped carefully across the floor and approached the body.

The victim was of Asian appearance. Dark hair, light brown skin and a familiar face. There was little doubt that it was Asim Malik. Taylor got down on his haunches and looked closely at the body. Meanwhile, DI Hamilton was putting in a call to colleagues in Paddington Green to report the discovery of a body.

What Taylor could see were several stab wounds on the victim's upper torso. By the look of his flesh and the smell, he could have been dead for several days.

It looked as if whoever had killed him had stabbed him from close range a number of times. There were cuts on Malik's fingers and hands and slash marks on both lower arms. It looked as if he had raised his hands to try and defend himself against his attacker. He may, at one stage, have been able to grab the blade of the knife. The amount of blood on his hands would suggest that he had placed his hands on his chest and tried to stem the flow of blood, but it was no use. The blows had gone deep into his chest and probably cut into his heart and ruptured the vital valves and veins. He had died of shock and the result of catastrophic blood loss. There were a couple of graze marks on his face. His attacker might have punched him in the face or kicked him in the head.

As soon as he had completed the telephone call DI Hamilton joined Taylor and examined the body at close quarters. "How long do we think he's been dead?" he asked.

"By the dried blood and by the marks on his face and the smell I'd say about two to three days, maybe longer." Taylor gently took Malik's left hand and felt it. "Rigour is evident."

"What's your first assessment?" Hamilton asked him.

"Maybe he's been in bed. He gets up. Puts on his vest and underpants. Goes to the chest there. Opens the drawer, throws some clothes onto the bed. His attacker comes into the room. They struggle. There's a graze across his right-hand knuckles. Maybe he punched his killer. The guy pulls the knife on him. He tried to grab the knife and gets the cuts and the slashes in the process, but his killer is more powerful than him."

Hamilton took in his assessment. He waited for a few moments. "I agree," he said. Taylor continued. "He put his hands up to defend himself. There are slash marks. He must have grabbed the knife and tried to wrestle it out of his hand, but the blows got through to the centre of his chest."

Taylor pulled himself up off his knees, stepped towards the chest of drawers and opened the second drawer. It was stuffed with clothing. He turned to look back at the body and Hamilton who was still on his knees bending over the body to look closely at the marks to his face.

"Do you agree?" Taylor asked him.

Hamilton thought about it for a few brief moments. "I'd say your assessment is pretty conclusive," he replied. "An alternative is that Malik is in bed, already dressed in the vest and his underwear. He's asleep. His attacker comes in, either to wake him or to attack him in the bed. He pulls him out of bed. They argue. The guy pulls the knife. Lunges at him. He tries to fight him off. The other guy soon gets the upper hand. Stabs him. Several times. He falls here."

"How do you account for the open drawer?" Taylor asked.

"Killer's looking for something. Opens the drawer. Throws the items onto the bed. Finds what he's looking for, or he doesn't. Decides to get out of the house."

Taylor nodded his head. "Could be," he said. "Either way we know he didn't stab himself."

Just then there was a shout from below. It was DI Hindley.

Taylor stepped out of the bedroom and went to the top of the stairs. DI Hindley was standing at the bottom. "What you got?" he asked.

"Better come down and see what we found," she said.

216

"Like what?" Taylor asked.

"A lot of empty chemical containers. A couple of empty packets of fertiliser. Some discarded electrical components. Looks as if someone's been making a bomb."

The sound of the word 'bomb' seemed to echo up the stairs in triplicate. Taylor mouthed the words. 'Oh shit' under his breath.

"What about you guys up there?" she asked.

"Malik. Stabbed to death. Seal the house. Pete's called HQ. The team will be here P.D.Q. Oh and we'd better call in the bomb squad and the counter terrorism unit as well," he added as an afterthought.

DI Hindley took her mobile phone and began to make a series of urgent calls.

Taylor went back into the bedroom. Hamilton was on his feet looking out of the front window. He turned as Taylor came back in.

"I wonder where all this is going to end?" Hamilton asked.

"I've got a nasty feeling that it will get a whole lot worse before it gets better. Finding him dead is something I didn't expect. The possibility that he's involved in making bombs is something else," he added.


After a further minute, they stepped along the landing and down the stairs to the ground floor. DI Hindley then showed them into a back room that looked as if it was used as a second bathroom and a laundry room. There was a large bath. Stacked up against a wall were at least ten empty grey plastic containers with sealed tops.

There was a pungent smell of a substance that had an acrid component. There were several used face masks littering the floor.

"Look at this," she said and pointed to the base of the bath which looked as if a tool of some description had scoured the surface. The enamel was partially melted. There was a tidemark around the bath at least two inches wide. "Someone's used the bath to mix chemicals and fertiliser together to make the substance for a bomb," she said. There was no doubt about it. No doubt at all.

"If Malik's the bomb maker, he's dead," said Hamilton.

"The question we need an answer to is who murdered him, and why," said Taylor.

"That's two questions," DI Hindley remarked.

"You're not wrong," Taylor sighed.

# Chapter 11

**The same day**


The house in north Wembley was soon swarming with about twenty-five police officers. Some in uniform, others in plain clothes. Several officers from the counter terrorism unit, including Mal Storey and John Winn were also on the scene.

They were in the downstairs laundry room securing the empty containers and the other items that had been left behind. Before he was allowed to go, the landlord was questioned by several officers for a long period of time. They asked him if Asim Malik had really given him nearly twelve thousand pounds in cash. He was adamant that was the case. The tenancy agreement was due to end at the end of February, which was just a couple of weeks away. This was significant because it pointed to the possibility of some event happening around that time. Figueiro told them he had never had any need to visit the house. He hadn't received any complaints about the tenant from the neighbours, so he had never had any need to contact Malik. He had no way of knowing if Malik had sublet a room to anyone else, or if he was sharing the house with others.

During a search of a shed the police found a large plastic container filled with several litres of paraffin, along with plastic spray bottles. They looked like those found in the last two houses he had tried to firebomb.

DCI Lake was on the scene leading all the Paddington Green-based detectives. She had allocated several colleagues to make door-to-door enquiries in the immediate area to ask neighbours if they had seen anyone coming or going from the house.

The outcome of the door-to-door enquiries proved to be very useful. Several neighbours said that the house looked as if it was being shared by two men, Asim Malik and another man, who came and went on a regular basis. The second man had a middle-eastern appearance. In the period they had been renting the house, they tended to keep themselves to themselves, and were said to be neighbours who never caused anyone a problem. They seemed to be a pair of students, perhaps studying at a local college or at a university in central London. None of the neighbours had seen any vehicles at the house. They seemed to come and go on foot and use public transport, though one of the neighbours did mention he had seen taxis at the house every now and again.

The question was: Who was the other man? Was this the person who had killed Malik. Was he a bomb maker? Whoever he was it looked as if he had left in a hurry, leaving the empty chemical containers, the empty bags of fertiliser, and the electrical components.

Investigations to find the identity of the second man went into overdrive. A team of detectives were directed to look at Malik's finances, under legislation established in the Proceeds of Crime Act 2002. The police request opened his bank account. They found Malik had just over twenty-five thousand pounds in a single account.

Further enquiries revealed that he was no longer claiming state benefits, but he wasn't working, so he had to be receiving money from someone. Forty thousand pounds had been transferred into his bank account, of which twenty-five thousand remained. His credit card transactions were accessed by order of the High Court. He shopped at a local supermarket on a regular basis, sometimes spending up to four hundred pounds a month on food and other items. Other transactions revealed the purchase of the chemicals from several different DIY stores on several different occasions, along with the electrical components. The items required to make one large bomb or a number of smaller bombs.

Knowing what they knew now, the police stepped up the pace of their investigation. A second door-to-door exercise took place. The aim was to create an identikit of the second man. CCTV cameras in the area were trawled for hours to find images of the two men together. After searching through hours of film the police got lucky. They spotted a man who looked like Malik with a second man who fitted the description given by the neighbours. Working tirelessly and using the image from the CCTV film, and the description given by the public, the police created a photo-fit of the second man.

Three days after the discovery of Malik's body, the Met police issued an image of the man they wanted to speak to in relation to the body found in the house in north Wembley. Nothing was mentioned about the discovery of materials that suggested that a crude explosive device had been assembled.

Interpol and other security intelligence services throughout Europe were contacted and asked for help. After several hours, it was counter terrorism officials in Rome who provided their colleagues in the Met with some valuable information.

The man in the picture was believed to be a Palestinian man called Hashem Abbas. A man of the same name and fitting the description had claimed to be a refugee from Gaza. He had travelled into Egypt then took a boat from Alexandria to Italy. The Italians had admitted him as a refugee. He had been living in a refugee centre in Rome until late August last year when he went missing and disappeared off the face of the planet. He had been on an Italian watch-list, but he had given them the slip.

If this was the case, then he had managed to travel halfway across Europe and slip into the UK, possibly in the back of a lorry. Why? What was his intention? Then the French authorities gave the Met some information. Hashem Abbas was a terrorist aligned to the militant wing of Hamas. Worse still he was a skilled bomb maker. This revelation was very disturbing. A bombmaker was in London, but what was the target or targets? No one knew the answer to that question.

Within hours of receiving the information from both the Italians and the French authorities, a full meeting of the Met Counter

Terrorism unit took place. Members of MI5 were in attendance, along with a government junior minister who was reporting direct to the office of the Home Secretary and to the Prime Minister. All the information was laid on the table. The priority was to find Abbas before he had chance to plant a device, therefore a game of find the bomb maker began. No one had any idea of what the target could be. Abbas's two brothers had died fighting the Israelis in the 2015 Gaza conflict. Abbas had vowed bloody revenge against the Israelis and their interests throughout the world.

If he had a thing against Israel and the Jewish people, and if he had put a bomb together, the question was: Where was it? It was a very worrying time for all in the security service and all in the government. The Commissioner of the Met Police in consultation with the Home Secretary insisted on a news blackout. No one wanted any of this to get out.

# Chapter 12

**20th February**

It was now four days since DI Taylor and DI Hamilton had found the body of Asim Malik in the house in north Wembley.

They were sitting at their desks in their Paddington Green room. DI Rebecca Hindley was out on another case. The telephone in front of Taylor rang. He picked it up.

"DI Taylor," he said.

"It's the main switchboard. I've a gentleman wanting to speak to you. He said his name is Doctor Farid Moussa. I think that's how he pronounced his name."

Taylor didn't know anyone of that name. "What's his business?" he asked.

"Said he wants to talk to a detective about Hashem Abbas."

"Put him through, please." The line went quiet for several brief moments, "DI Taylor. How may I assist you?"

The caller waited for a moment before answering the question, then he responded in a deep, guttural voice. "My name is Doctor Farid Moussa. I am the London representative of the Palestinian National Authority," he said precisely.

"How can I be of assistance to you Doctor Moussa?" asked Taylor.

"I'd like to meet with an officer in charge of the enquiry."

"You can speak to me," said Taylor. He looked up at Hamilton and flicked his fingers to try to get his attention. Hamilton looked up. Taylor gestured for him to pick up the phone and listen into the conversation. Hamilton picked up the handle and put it to his ear.

The caller seemed reluctant to speak, therefore there was a further brief period of silence. "I have some information, but I don't wish to speak over the telephone."

"Information about what?" Taylor asked.

"Hashem Abbas."

"If you don't wish to talk on the telephone, I can meet you anywhere you wish."

"Do you know the outside of the British museum on Great Russell Street?"

"Yes."

"It's near to my office. I can see you there in forty minutes from now."

"Fine. We'll meet you there."

"We?" said the man.

"Me and my colleague. DI Peter Hamilton."

The doctor appeared to be apprehensive. He stalled in his response, then said: "All right. I'll be there." The telephone conversation ended at that juncture.


DIs Taylor and Hamilton left Paddington Green twenty minutes after the telephone call and made their way into town. The day had turned bright though the now familiar stiff breeze was blowing through the streets of the city. Most people were wearing sensible warm clothing and few were prepared to linger unless it was absolutely necessary.

DI Hamilton drove his car the short distance to the meeting place. He managed to find a parking spot near to Gower Street. He displayed his police car parking permit, therefore paying for the privilege of parking wasn't required. From there the pair of detectives walked to Great Russell Street, and were soon near to the wrought iron gates beside the entrance to the museum.

The air was filled with the sound of a siren as an ambulance came by the end of the street adjacent to nearby Oxford Street. The breeze picked up and ruffled the leaves on the roadside trees. Overhead the silver underbelly of an aircraft cut across the opal sky. Someone outside a pub across the street was putting out chairs across the pavement. Sunlight was glinting in the windows of the galleries and book shops along this stretch of Russell Street.

They had five minutes to wait before the forty minutes were up. As they stepped to the gates, they clapped their eyes on a tall, polished, imposing looking chap in a long dark overcoat. He had a middle-east appearance. He was holding a rolled-up man's umbrella by his side. He was alone. He had a large head under a dark flat-cap. He wore round, black- rimmed spectacles over his eyes.

DI Taylor approached the man while DI Hamilton stayed back a few paces. The chap had his hands firmly planted into the warmth of his coat pockets. He looked up as Taylor came closer to him. His face was serious and unsmiling.

"DI Taylor?" he asked.

"Doctor Moussa, I assume," replied Taylor.

The chap nodded his head. Taylor noticed his thick lips and the brown liver spots close to his eyes. He had a Palestinian flag pin-badge in the lapel of his coat.

DI Taylor dipped his hand into an inside jacket pocket, extracted his ID badge and flashed his identification in front of the man's eyes. He turned to glance over his shoulder at DI Hamilton. "This is my colleague DI Peter Hamilton." Hamilton was just out of earshot. Just twenty yards ahead a long line of people were standing by the gates waiting for them to open so they could enter the museum. The sound of the traffic on the nearby streets, provided a vibrant soundtrack.

"You said you have some information about Hashem Abbas," said Taylor.

He nodded his head stiffly. "I'm Doctor Farid Moussa. I'm the representative of the Palestinian National Authority here in London," he said.

He had a soft educated accent with the trace of a North American edge. He must have spent some time in the US or Canada. Taylor knew it was the same person he spoke to on the telephone.

Moussa continued: "I've been talking to my colleagues in Rome. We have some information that concerns the person you are looking for." Taylor didn't say a word. He wanted him to keep talking. Moussa could sense this. "We believe that Hashem Abbas was recruited by agents of the Israeli state."

Taylor narrowed his eyes. "To do what?" he asked, trying not to display his surprise.

"To carry out an attack in London against a Jewish target."

Taylor kept his expression closed. "Have you got any evidence of this?" he asked.

"Abbas said he had been in contact with some sympathisers in Rome. He told them he'd been recruited by a group linked to Islamic Jihad in Gaza, to attack a chosen target in London. But we know they have no such people in Rome. They were agents of Mossad, the Israeli secret service, posing as members of an extremist group," he revealed.

"Do you know what the target is?" asked Taylor.

"Sadly not. It could be a synagogue here in London."

Taylor was trying to get his head around this. He had no idea if there was any truth in what Moussa said. The most obvious question popped into his head. "Why would the Israelis wish to attack a place of Jewish worship in London?" he asked.

"To discredit a senior member of the British government."

Taylor was even more surprised. "Who?" he enquired.

"The Home Secretary. Sonia Masterson."

It was a well-known fact that the current British Home Secretary held negative views on the actions taken by Israel, in claiming disputed land as their own, and building settlements. Taylor wasn't aware that she had expressed any pro-Palestinian views.

Moussa continued. "Your Home Secretary has recently voiced her concern at the Israeli government's plans, to steal Palestinian land to build further settlements close to Jerusalem. She has influence in your government," he said. "The British Prime Minister is under increasing pressure to reflect the views held by some of his colleagues. The Home Secretary included. And your Prime Minister has the ear of the President of the United States, and some influence in other western Europe capitals."

Taylor glanced towards DI Hamilton and let out a sigh. This was way out of his league. He was just a detective, not a political academic. "This is serious stuff," he said. He didn't know if the word 'stuff' was the appropriate one to use but he said it all the same.

"If this is true, and of course I've no way of knowing if it is the case, I still can't understand why the Israelis would see the sense of hurting their own people," Taylor said.

Dr Moussa adjusted his eye glasses. "Believe me, they are capable of anything. Mossad has a task, and that is to weaken the position of Sonia Masterson. The only way to do that is to carry out a terrorist act on British soil, that will kill members of the British Jewish community with a Palestinian getting the blame. This way, any sympathy for the Palestinian cause will be reduced."

"Who have you told about this?" asked Taylor.

Dr Moussa leant on his umbrella and steadied himself. "No one at all," he said. "Only you."

"Where do you think Abbas could be?" asked Taylor.

"He may already be dead. He may have already given a device, a bomb, to his handlers. The bomb will have his signature on it, and this way the British will put the blame on the Palestinians," said Moussa.

"Are the recent fires at the homes of Muslims in London connected to this?" Taylor asked.

"This is the excuse for carrying out a terrorist attack. It will be seen as revenge for the deaths of those people who perished. It will be seen as an 'eye for an eye' and a 'tooth for a tooth'," Moussa said.

Taylor processed Moussa's words. If he was correct, then an attack may have been imminent with the likely target to be a Jewish place of worship. It didn't seem plausible that the Israelis would attempt to carry out an attack against a synagogue to discredit a British politician, but maybe Moussa had something. Maybe it was something they would do.

"When do you think an attack could come?" Taylor asked.

"I've no idea," replied the doctor. "It may be soon. It may be days away."

"How do you think Abbas got into the country?" Taylor asked.

"The Israelis may have given him a false passport and the money to get here. Or he may have been smuggled into England across the channel in a boat. How do other people get into the country?" he asked with a kind of sarcastic twist in his voice. The more DI Taylor thought about it, the more he considered that Doctor

Moussa was telling the truth. Moussa shifted his feet. "And what about Asim Malik?" he asked.

"What about him?" Taylor asked.

"Mossad probably recruited him as well. Said they were Palestinians or Hezbollah. They told him of the plot to punish the Jews. They gave him money, and the means to do the task."

Taylor nodded his head. "This would account for the money he had in his bank account," he said, then wondered if the doctor had evidence that the Israelis had given him the money. There was little time to act or think. He knew he had no alternative but to report the content of this conversation to his superiors. He didn't know if there was any veracity in what Dr Moussa was saying, but he seemed pretty clued up on things. On the other hand, maybe, it was a clever tactic to take the blame off Islamic extremist terrorism. He looked at the doctor.

"I'll need to contact my S.I.O and tell her of our meeting. If we can stop any chance of a terrorist incident then we will do all in our power. I can assure you of that," he said.

Moussa retained a serious, glum face. He nodded his head.

"Of course. I wish you the best of good luck," he said. He looked up as an old-style black Mercedes saloon car, with diplomatic plates, came trundling down the street. He didn't say another word. He looked at Taylor and Hamilton, bowed his head then stepped across to the edge of the pavement as the car came to a halt. He opened the back door and slid onto the long seat without saying another word.

The detectives watched the car drive away up Russell Street, turn down a side street and go out of view.

Taylor took a moment to recap on the conversation he had just had with the eminent doctor. He told Hamilton this was a watershed moment. What had been a devastating series of arson attacks was now a wider conspiracy that could have been teetering on the edge of disaster. If there was any truth in what Moussa had told him, then it took on a whole new dynamic and direction that was way above his level. He had to first contact DCI Lake and inform her that he had met the doctor who had told him that things might be going to get a whole lot worse.

He took his mobile phone out of his pocket. He found the contact for DCI Lake and called her. She answered the call within a couple of rings.

"DCI Sarah Lake," she said.

"It's DI Taylor. I've just had a conversation with a Doctor Farid Moussa from the Palestinian National Authority. He tells me that operatives from Israeli intelligence are involved in Abbas being in the country."

Lake didn't reply for a few long moments. "I think we'd better meet face to face, immediately. Come straight back to the station as soon as possible. I'll put a call to Counter Terrorism and ask them to meet with us straight away."

Taylor agreed to the suggestion.

Taylor and Hamilton drove straight back to Paddington Green. On arrival, they met with DCI Lake in her office. Lake revealed that she had spoken to the head of the Met Counter Terrorism Unit based in New Scotland Yard, Commander John Stanley.

Stanley requested that a meeting take place within the hour to discuss everything to do with the case. Lake said that Commander Stanley had spoken directly to the Home Secretary to update her. It would be up to Commander Stanley and the Home Secretary to plan going forward.

DCI Lake, DI Taylor and DI Hamilton then left Paddington Green to travel across central London to meet with Stanley and his team in New Scotland Yard.

# Chapter 13

**The same day**

The meeting in New Scotland Yard took place around a walnut-topped table in a conference room on the top floor of the building. There were nine people in attendance. Commander Stanley had his deputy at his side and a man in uniform bedecked with silver epaulets on the shoulders, on the other. A female member of the civilian staff was preparing to take the minutes. Members of the Met Counter Terrorism Team, Officers Mal Storey and John Winn were there. DCI Lake, DI Taylor and DI Hamilton made up the list of attendees.

Through the tall windows there was a splendid panoramic view across the rooftops of Westminster towards Whitehall.

Commander Stanley had been the Head of the Counter Terrorism Unit for the past five years. His team of officers had had numerous successes in stopping terrorist plots from reaching their zenith. He was well respected throughout the security community but had a reputation for someone who didn't take criticism or complaint well. He had been in the Met seemingly forever. He was a tall angular man, in his mid-fifties, with the physique of someone several years his junior. He had neatly-chopped grey hair and a rapidly developing bald patch. In the pyramid at the top of the Met, he sat under a Deputy Commissioner. His priorities were wide and varied but, in a nutshell, his job was to keep the public safe and to disrupt all terrorist plots and activity right across the UK. He was an old Etonian, and very adroit, and wasn't at all condescending.

There was a drinks flask on a silver metal tray, and coffee cups on china saucers. A wisp of steam was winding out of the flask along with the aroma of fresh ground coffee. The secretary in attendance opened a pad of paper and held a pen in between the fingers of her left hand. Commander Stanley introduced his two male colleagues at his side as Tom Armfield and Deputy Commissioner Nigel Foster. Foster was the one in the uniform.

Stanley gave a light cough to signal the start of the discussion. "Let's get down to business," he said. He looked at DCI Lake. "I understand that you've been in conversation with Farid Moussa. We know him to be the London representative of the Palestinian National Authority."

"That's correct," said Lake. "DI Taylor and DI Hamilton met him this morning outside the British Museum."

Stanley looked at Taylor. "Just describe him for the record, will you?"

"Approximately fifty-five years of age. Tall, distinguished looking I suppose you'd say. Round-rimmed spectacles. Approximately fifteen stones at a guess. Speaks with a kind of watered-down American accent."

"That figures" said Stanley, off-the-cuff. "His previous posting was to Canada, in Toronto. Please tell us what he told you," he asked Taylor directly.

"He told me that the Israeli secret service, Mossad, is involved in a plot to discredit a member of Her Majesty's Government," replied Taylor.

"Who might that be?" said Stanley. He looked to his female assistant. "Not for the minutes," he added.

"The Home Secretary," Taylor replied.

Stanley glanced at both the people on his side. He smiled. "The Home Secretary?" he asked.

"Yes."

"Reason?"

"Her pro-Palestinian views," Taylor replied.

Stanley clasped his hands on the table and held them tight. He pursed his lips. "It's no secret. The Home Secretary does harbour pro-Palestinian views. Not for the minutes. Did he indicate what the plot consists of?" he asked.

"To attack a symbol of the Jewish faith, such as a place of worship here in London, or some other place of interest."

"Let me get this correct. The Israeli secret service would arrange for an attack on a synagogue?"

"That's what he suggested."

"I find that hard to believe. But it's possible of course. What is the reasoning behind it?"

"To cause consternation and outrage and in doing so, harm the Home Secretary and reduce her influence on the Prime Minister."

"Shit," said Stanley under his breath, but so everyone heard him. "Let's go from the top, shall we? DCI Lake, perhaps you'd like to provide a summary?"

Sarah Lake adjusted her position and sat forward. "We have reason to believe that the recent arson attacks in north London over the past six months are a prelude to the plot. We know that a man of Pakistani heritage, called Asim Malik, was the arsonist. The pattern of the attacks draws a Star of David over that area of the city."

Stanley listened carefully and intently. He didn't say a word and neither did his two colleagues. Lake continued to provide them with a summary. "We think the blazes were an attempt to create friction between the Muslim and the Jewish communities. Thankfully that hasn't occurred. However, we believe it's only a matter of time before there is an attack."

Commander Stanley considered her words. He didn't say anything for a few seconds. He shifted his posture. His body language was one that told of stress and apprehension. If the summary was correct, an attack was imminent. It was perhaps too late at this stage to prevent it. Going public, and telling a city of ten million people that a bombing was imminent, could cause mass panic. If the target was a synagogue or a Jewish business, then they might just be able to carry out security checks on those places.

Stanley decided to kick the matter upstairs to his boss the Commissioner, for his advice and a plan of action. If the Commissioner's office believed it to be a credible threat then he would take it to the Home Secretary. If the Home Secretary deemed it necessary then a meeting of the Cabinet Office Briefing Rooms, or COBRA for short, would be arranged. COBRA was a committee chaired by the Prime Minister in the event of a national crisis or a potential major incident. If members of COBRA believed that the threat level was to be increased, then it was likely that a warning of an imminent bomb attack would be issued to the people of London, and throughout the rest of the UK.

# Chapter 14

## 1st March

Nine days later, on the 1st March, the bomb went off at precisely two minutes past four in the afternoon. The target wasn't a Jewish place of worship, but a Jewish school in St John's Wood, in central north London. The device turned out to be similar to the pressure cooker bombs that had exploded close to the finishing line at the Boston Marathon, in April 2013. Explosives and ball bearings had been crammed into a colander-like pot, which was placed into a holdall. The holdall had been placed aside a brick column on one side of the metal iron gate that led into the school. The triggering mechanism was a mobile phone connected to a circuit board.

When the bomber rang the mobile phone, the ignition device was activated, and the bomb – a mixture of chemical nitrate and common garden fertiliser – exploded.

Eight children, ranging in age from nine years to twelve years of age were instantly killed. A further thirty were injured, several of them seriously. The number of the dead would have been much higher, if it wasn't for the fact that it had been raining heavily at four o'clock, and several children had decided to stay back in the school to wait for their parents to collect them.

Several people walking on the other side of the road at the time were also injured, but their wounds were not life threatening. Ironically, the brick column against which the holdall had been placed, absorbed some of the blast and had prevented a greater loss of life. The sound of the explosion had been so loud it was heard up to a quarter of a mile away in central London. Before the day was out, two of the injured children succumbed to their injuries. The death toll would reach ten.

DI Taylor had received word of the explosion at four-twenty. His initial reaction was one of anger that a warning hadn't been issued. He felt incredibly sad and partially guilty, that he hadn't been able to stop the atrocity.


That evening, reports of the incident dominated the TV and radio news. The next morning the Prime Minister made a statement in the House of Commons. The Queen sent her condolences to the families of those who had been killed and injured.

It was one of those 'where-were-you-when-you-heard' moments, when an incident becomes ingrained into the memory. Whilst the incident showed the worst side of human nature it also showed the best side of human kind. The hospitals to which the injured children were taken were inundated with people wanting to give their blood to help others survive. A fund was set up for the victim's families, which reached several million pounds within the first twenty-four hours.

DI Taylor, DI Hamilton and others in their department were placed on the investigation team, which was led by Commander Stanley and his team.

The morning after the attack, DIs Taylor and Hamilton visited the scene of the explosion. The location was cordoned off by uniformed officers. A one-hundred-yard exclusion zone was established around the scene. Forensic officers were still collecting fragments of the bomb, and as much material as possible.

That afternoon the Prime Minister gave a news conference from 10 Downing Street. He asked everyone to remain calm. The Home Secretary echoed the Prime Minister's views and said that no stone would be left unturned until they had the perpetrator or perpetrators in custody. They would face the full justice of the state.

Within forty-eight hours of the blast, the blame was put fairly and squarely on the shoulders of radical Islamic terrorism. The bomber was named as a twenty-eight-year-old Palestinian called Hashem Abbas. If the objective of the attack was to further increase Islamophobia in the UK, then it had the desired effect. The number of attacks and threats, both verbal and physical, against members of the Muslim community, increased ten-fold overnight.

Right-wing hotheads used social media to demand that the government end its links with the Palestinian National Authority. There was even a call for Palestinian diplomats to be expelled from the country. If the Home Secretary was feeling the heat, she didn't show it, but make no mistake, her influence in the government had been severely weakened.

Then something happened that greatly alarmed DI Taylor. Four days after the bomb had killed ten children and injured scores more, he was called into New Scotland Yard for a meeting with Commander John Stanley and DCI Lake.

When Taylor arrived on the top floor of the building, he was led into a room in which four people were sitting at a table. One was Commander Stanley, the other two were his sidekick Officer Tom Armfield and Deputy Commissioner Nigel Foster, plus DCI Lake.

Stanley was smiling and looked incredibly cheerful. Despite the death of ten children not ninety-six hours before, there was a rather strange surreal atmosphere in the room. None of them hid their emotions. Whilst they were not exactly popping champagne bottles, they didn't seem downbeat about the whole episode. Instead of being racked with sadness, Stanley was in a relaxed mood.

Taylor sat at the other side of the table and looked across the shiny surface that reflected the light of the day to the three men and DCI Lake at the other side. Out of the window the rooftops of the buildings in Whitehall were visible in between the gaps dividing the surrounding buildings.

Stanley welcomed Taylor. He smiled at him, then cleared his throat.

"We're continuing our enquiries into the explosion that killed those poor unfortunate children. Our hearts and thoughts go out to the families of those involved. Now, with regard to your meeting with Doctor Moussa, we'd like you to forget all about it. We don't believe there is any mileage in what he said about Israeli involvement. It just doesn't make sense."

Taylor felt that a metal barrier was being pulled down and he was going to be placed into an iron suit from which there was no escape.

This move shouldn't have surprised him. Those in the corridors of power were closing rank and were dismissing the theory provided by Dr Moussa. It didn't make political sense to blame Israel even if the theory was plausible. They would dismiss the information provided by Moussa as an attempt to shift the blame from the Palestinian Authority to Mossad. The real culprit was a Palestinian terrorist who had sneaked into the country and who was linked to the militant wing of Hamas or some other shadowy extremist Islamic outfit. The real message was that Taylor was to forget what Dr Moussa had told him. Taylor decided to go along with it. He sensed that any complaint or questioning would create severe problems for him.

He looked Commander Stanley, then DCI Lake, in the eye. "I'll delete all records of my meeting with the doctor," he said.

"Good," said Stanley. "Can you tell DI Hamilton to forget the meeting?"

"Of course," he replied.

"Those responsible for the deaths of those children were Islamic extremists. We don't want it any other way," said Stanley.

"I understand," said Taylor.

That day he left the meeting feeling incensed and betrayed, but not devastated or surprised. It was politics. He was big enough to take it on the chin. He wasn't an amateur cutting his teeth on his first case. He was an experienced Detective Inspector in the largest police force in the land. For the first time, he realised that the Counter Terrorism Unit may have been working with their Israeli counterparts to dampen any Israeli connection. Now he felt more than ever that Doctor Moussa had been telling him the truth.

It was at this point that he knew that he had to do something. But not just yet. He would wait for a while to tell someone what he knew about the 1st March attack.

# Chapter 15

## 8th March

One week had passed since the bomb exploded. DI Taylor was feeling increasingly marginalised, down, and depressed. He had argued with his wife for the first time in years. It concerned something incredibly trivial. It unsettled the pair of them. They made up within a short space of time and Taylor vowed not to bring his work home. His marriage was still strong after ten years; therefore, it would take something far more serious than a little spat to damage it beyond repair, but he thought he could be heading in that direction if he didn't find the underlying cause of what had really happened.

The Met were still combing the streets of the capital looking for Hashem Abbas. The bomb, and the deaths of those ten school children, were continuing to dominate the headlines, though people in the capital were coming out of the initial shock phase. There was a growing wave of anger and increasing Islamophobia.

The city was still moving at a pace and the transport system in and around the centre of the capital was still packed with commuters despite a fear that the bomber may attack the network at any time. Armed police were seen in the main transport hubs in increasing numbers and Londoners were assured that the Met was doing everything in its power to make the city safe. No one knew where Abbas could be hiding. Speculation tended to drift between rumours that he was being protected by sympathisers to he had left the country in the hours between planting the device and it exploding. The Counter-Terrorism Unit acting on a tip-off and led by Officer Mal Storey had raided several homes in south London, but they didn't find him. The operation to locate Abbas and bring him to justice was giving the code name 'Operation Determined Response.'

## 9th March

The following day everything changed. Eight days after the event, DI Taylor and DI Hamilton were called out to check a report that the body of a man with middle-eastern features had been found by a tube line track in north London. It was just a mile or so from the house in north Wembley where Asim Malik had died.

When DI Taylor and Hamilton arrived at the scene there were already a dozen police officers in attendance. Some were in uniform, others in plain clothes. Several members from Counter Terrorism were there. A senior uniformed cop gave DI Taylor and DI Hamilton an update. The body of a man had been spotted laying against the concrete panels that line the side of the rails. It was directly below a six-foot-high chain-link fence that separated the track from a narrow service road that ran parallel to the line. There was a row of small business units on the other side of the road. Someone must have driven a vehicle along the road, stopped, took out the body then pushed it over the fence. The body had fallen into a slight dip therefore it wasn't easy to spot from a train or the road. It had been noticed by someone who worked in a business premises at the other side of the tracks. The person assumed it was a tailor's dummy or a caricature of some kind. It had lain there for three days before the person decided to call the police.


The cop led Taylor and Hamilton through a padlocked metal gate in the fence, and escorted them along the track to the spot. The cop said the body had been found lying face down. One of the first officers to arrive on the scene had turned the victim onto his back.

As the party of three came to the body a tube train not ten feet away from them went by. By the smell coming from him, the dried blood on his shirt, and the moisture on his clothes, the victim must have been dead for longer than three days. He was a man of Arab appearance. There was a single stab wound to his chest. There was little doubt in Taylor's mind that the victim was Hashem Abbas.

Taylor called DCI Lake in Paddington Green to update her. They had found the suspected bomber, but he wouldn't be providing them with a statement any time soon. He was dead.

A team from the forensics arm of the Met police were soon on the scene. They erected a tent over the body and began the task of looking for any scrap of evidence of who had murdered him. The cause of death was a single stab wound to the heart. There were abrasions on his face, but these could have been caused by the fall onto the concrete. There was also a gash to the top of his head. It resembled the attack on Asim Malik, though not as frenzied. Abbas hadn't been given a chance to fight back. It looked as if he had been hit on the top of the head with a heavy blunt instrument then stabbed through the heart. The killer or killers had been clinical. Unlike Malik, they hadn't had to stab him multiple times.

DI Taylor and DI Hamilton discussed the likely scenario. They assumed that the killers had killed him in another location, several days before. Then they had driven to this spot. Two or even three men had hoisted him over the fence and dropped him on the siding. Abbas wasn't the biggest of men, but some effort had to have been exerted to get him over the fence.

The body was removed from the side of the track ten hours after it had been discovered. It was taken to a police mortuary for examination. The team of forensic officers estimated that the time of death was sixty to seventy hours before. The bomb maker had been silenced two days after the attack on the school. Residues found on his hands were consistent with the chemical found in the house in north Wembley. There were traces of fertiliser on his clothes and on his skin and in his hair.

A meeting of detectives led by DCI Lake took place in Paddington Green station. Various theories were considered. A theory doing the rounds was that the killers had panicked when they left him by the side of the track. Alternatively, they had meant to leave him there all along, so he would be seen by people in the trains going by. As the body had fallen into a gully, and the trains had been going by at speed, no one had spotted the body. It had also been dark and murky for the previous few days. No matter, the killer or killers had tied up the loose ends and disposed of the only person who could have exposed them.

Taylor was now convinced more than ever that operatives from an intelligence service had murdered Abbas and, in doing so, eliminated one of the chief protagonists. He was now more certain than ever that Dr Moussa was on the right lines. He had to tell someone of the things he knew. He had to tell his story to someone who would be prepared to dig further, and reveal the truth to the public.

Chapter 16

**8<sup>th</sup> June**

When Taylor and Reece Lister first met in Regent's Park it was three months and one week after the bomb had exploded outside of the school in St John's Wood. Two days later the government released the official report into the public domain. It was published with much fanfare. Taylor was correct in what he had told Lister. The outcome of the report was that a single Palestinian terrorist working with a British-born sympathiser had been responsible for the attack. Both Malik and the bomb maker had been slain by an unknown person or persons. The publication of the report brought the event of 1<sup>st</sup> March back to the public's attention.

Reece Lister began his investigation by de-constructing the series of arson attacks carried out by Asim Malik. There was little doubt that Malik had been responsible for those fires.

The first thing Lister did was to contact the Malik family in their Tottenham home and asked to speak to Mr Malik. After several failed attempts, it took him one week to secure an interview with Asim's father.

**15<sup>th</sup> June**

The meeting took place in a library on Tottenham High Street. Malik senior was still finding it hard to grasp that his son was dead. It was as if he expected him to walk through the front door of the house at any time. Sadly, that wasn't going to happen.

He still didn't accept that his son may have been partly responsible for the deaths of those ten school children.

Lister found Malik's father to be a reserved chap. He didn't reveal anything stunning or anything that cast doubt on his son's involvement. He said that his son had often raised the plight of the Palestinian people and voiced his disgust at what he said were western governments' double standards when considering the Palestinian issue.

Asim had attended a mosque in Tottenham and in Finsbury Park where he had become increasingly radicalised by a firebrand Imam. He had been arrested outside a central London synagogue for the verbal tongue lashing he had given a group of orthodox Jewish men going about their business. He had narrowly escaped jail on that occasion. His father said he wasn't a bad person. He had just got in with some bad people. He had drifted aimlessly for a year, then one year ago he had left the family home, never to return. His father had no idea how he had as much as thirty thousand pounds in a bank account.


Lister knew that his first task was to try and trace the money trail. Who had given Malik the money in the first place? If he could trace the money, that might be a good start.

He asked a friend to look into this for him. Her name was Helen Potter-Smith. They had been friends for the past twenty years.

251

They knew each other from the University of Liverpool where they had been on the same Political Science undergraduate course. She now worked for a finance company in the City of London. Although it wasn't strictly *kosher*, she could use their systems to try and uncover the money trail. He didn't ask her what methods she would use, that was none of his business. All he knew was that she was good at what she did. He arranged to meet her the following day in an Earls Court public house.

He told her of the assignment over a beer and a bite to eat. He told her that a grave injustice may have taken place. As she was an old Trotskyist, from her university days, and no friend of the Zionists, she agreed to look into the matter for him.

It was getting on for three weeks after the meeting in Earls Court pub that Potter-Smith called Lister and told him she had some information for him.

"What have you got?" he asked.

"The money was transferred from a bank in Rome, in one lump sum of forty thousand pounds," she said.

"Do you know the name of the person or company who transferred the money to Malik?" Lister asked.

"The account holder is someone called Andrea Beletti." She spelled out the name. "A-N-D-R-E-A  B-E-L-E-T-T-I"

"Not a company account then?"

"It would appear not," she said.

Lister thanked her for her quick work and rang off. It was known that Hashem Abbas had been in the Italian capital for a period of time. Lister's next task was to discover just who Andrea Beletti was. Maybe it was a pseudonym. He wondered what his next course of action should be. He did know a Rome-based journalist called Luca Zola who occasionally wrote articles for the Rome daily newspaper 'La Stampa' and several left-of-centre publications. He had met Luca at a conference several years ago and they had kept in touch ever since.

Lister emailed him and asked Luca if he could do some research for him.

Zola responded and asked him what the assignment was. Lister told him he was trying to trace a man called Andrea Beletti. Zola asked him why. Lister told him. He didn't bullshit him with a lie. His request for information had something to do with the recent terrorist attack in London that had claimed the lives of the ten school children. There was a possibility that it was a Mossad-led operation. Zola said he would try and help him all he could.

**14th July**

One-week passed before Zola got back in contact with Lister. What he told him was nothing short of sensational. Andrea Beletti was the finance manager in the Rome office of El-Al airline, Israel's national airline. Lister could hardly believe it. It was so blatant, so out there in the open, it was hardly believable.

253

The official government report looking at the events of 1<sup>st</sup> March tended to concentrate solely on the events of the day and didn't go into a lot of details regarding potential connections and the lead up to the attack. Therefore, there was no mention of the possible link to Israel.

Lister wondered if he should travel to Rome to try and interview this Andrea Beletti fellow. It was a risky strategy and perhaps this chap would refuse to speak to him. Other than going to Rome to visit Luca Zola it would be a total waste of time and money. After careful consideration, he decided not to risk it. Zola may have already revealed to other people that a British freelance researcher called Reece Lister was asking questions about an official in the Rome office of El-Al.

The following day Lister contacted Asim Malik's father by telephone and asked him if he knew if his son had recently travelled to Rome. Mister Malik said he had no idea. He had had minimal communication with his son for a year, but he did reveal something of interest. He knew that Asim had been in Amsterdam in the previous two months before his death.

"How do you know that?" asked Lister. "If you had no contact with him in the past year, how do you know he was in Amsterdam?" he asked.

His answer was unequivocally. "Simple," he said. "A friend of the family had seen him walking close to the central railway station."

"Was he with anyone?" Lister asked.

Mister Malik considered the question for a few long moments. It seemed as if he was reluctant to give an answer. "It's very important," Lister said with the nuance of a plead in the tone.

"They said he was Spanish or maybe he was from North Africa," replied his father.

"Can you give me the name of the person who saw your son in Amsterdam?" he asked. Mister Malik didn't want to give him the name, so Lister went for the jugular.

"This will help me," he said. "I don't believe that your son had any knowledge of the attack on the Jewish school. I need to find who is behind the attack because I don't think your son was involved in it. There is little doubt that he was behind the arson attacks, but not the school attack. If we discover who is responsible then I think we can clear your son's name."

Mister Malik took in his words. He thought about it long and hard, then he gave him the name of Yasser Siddiqi, a man of British-Pakistani heritage who lived in the Enfield area. He even provided him with an address. Lister couldn't believe his luck.

As soon as Lister had the address, he thanked Mister Malik and told him he would keep him up-to-date with any developments. He went on-line and found the telephone number for the London office of the Palestinian National Authority. He called the number and asked to speak to the Head of the Office, Doctor Farid Moussa. He got through to the doctor's gatekeeper, a lady who gave her name as Ludmila.

She asked him why he wanted to speak to Doctor Moussa. He referred to the meeting Doctor Moussa had with DI Steve Taylor from the Met police. He instantly regretted doing this, because he had dropped his name into the mix, but there was no other alternative. The line went quiet for a few long moments, then a new voice came over the line. It was the guttural deep voice of Doctor Moussa introducing himself.

"Who do I have the pleasure of talking to?" Moussa asked.

"My name is Reece Lister. I'm an independent freelance journalist doing some research into the 1st March bombing outside of the Jewish school in St John's Wood. DI Steve Taylor of the Met Police has confided in me and…"

"Will he confirm this?" injected Dr Moussa.

"Who? DI Taylor?" Lister asked.

"Yes."

"Yes. He will," replied Lister. "We met several weeks ago, and he gave me some information which included a reference to a meeting outside of the British Museum on Great Russell Street."

"What is your interest?" asked the doctor, after a few seconds hesitation.

"I'm writing an article which I intend to seek publication in a journal or a newspaper. I believe that there are a series of questions to ask about the conclusions in the official British government report."

"In what sense?" Moussa asked, slowly.

"That there was what I would term as 'a rush to judgement' Also, that a foreign power may have been involved in the planning and the execution of the act."

Doctor Moussa didn't reply for a few long moments as he considered Lister's words and his own response.

"Which foreign government would that be?" he asked.

Lister took in a shallow breath. "The Israeli government or elements, or rather its intelligence and security apparatus," he replied.

"Who did you say you are?" asked Moussa.

"Reece Lister. If you 'Google' my name. You will see a photograph of me and see a bibliography of the articles I've written for newspapers and journals all over Europe and in the United States."

"I see. Would you like to interview me as part of your investigation?" Moussa asked.

"Absolutely," said Lister.

"I *must* stress that any information will be given to you in the strictest confidence, and anything I say *must* first be approved by my colleagues in Ramallah."

"Of course," said Lister.

"I will not reveal my source unless I have absolute authority to do so."

"I understand. I shall be pleased to meet with you for an introductory meeting."

"That is acceptable," Moussa said.

"Where shall we meet? It's entirely at your discretion."

Moussa pondered for a brief moment. "Do you know a Turkish café called 'Ankara' on the Edgware Road?" Moussa asked.

"I can find it."

"Meet me there at two-thirty this afternoon. I'll be waiting for you."

"Thank you," said Lister. "I look forward to meeting with you," he added.

"Likewise," said Moussa before he terminated the conversation.

# Chapter 17

**15<sup>th</sup> July**

The Ankara café was situated along Edgware Road close to the junction with Sussex Gardens and Old Marylebone Road. There was a green and yellow striped awning protruding out over the pavement to shield the silver aluminium chairs and tables set out across the pavement. This area of Edgware Road was perhaps one of the most cosmopolitan areas in the whole of central London.

The café was nothing special. It had a narrow front. The words 'Ankara Café' were displayed on the plate glass window in stick-on letters, several of which were peeling off. Lister made his way towards the door where a small, lithe chap was standing in the doorway in a black and white chequered chef's apron, smoking a cigarette. He eyed Lister has he stepped into the entrance.

"I'm here to meet Doctor Moussa," he said.

The chap said nothing and just stepped aside to allow him to enter.

The interior was in shadow. There were a dozen tables each covered with a shiny plastic red and white pattern tablecloth. The décor was simple and easy on the eye. The colour scheme was a crimson shade of red. There was a smell and the sound of spicy kebabs sizzling on an open spit under fluorescent heaters, adjacent to a line of buffet trays full of various foods. Music with a heavy Turkish influence was playing over the airwaves.

Lister glanced around the interior. Only two of the dozen tables were occupied. A single man was sitting in the top right-hand corner by a water fountain feature. It looked like Doctor Farid Moussa from the description Taylor had given him. He had a shaven head the shade of light walnut and the physique of a bulky man over six feet tall.

Lister stepped across the floor and approached the man. The man looked up from the I-pad in his hand and put his eyes on Reece Lister.

"Mister Lister, I assume?" he said. "I am Dr Moussa. It's nice to meet you."

Lister looked into the face of the Oxford-educated Palestinian diplomat, with thick lips and round-rimmed spectacles.

"Likewise," said Lister.

He took the back of a chair, across the table from Doctor Moussa and pulled it out. The table was bare, but for an unlit candle in a glazed decorative glass pot. "Please take a seat," said Moussa, but didn't put his hand out for a handshake.

Lister glanced at the narrow plate window just as a red London bus went by. He put his eyes back on Moussa. "Thank you for agreeing to meet with me," he said.

Moussa didn't smile. He retained a serious face and a certain coolness. "How may I assist you?" he asked.

"By telling me what you told DI Steve Taylor," he replied.

"Is DI Taylor a colleague of yours?" he asked.

"I wouldn't term him as a colleague. No. He contacted me several weeks ago and told me of his concerns about the likely outcome of the report into the 1st March event. He told me what you had told him of the involvement of the Israelis. Please feel free to contact him."

Moussa pursed his lips and nodded his head. He leaned forward in his seat ever so slightly. "That is what we believe happened." The 'we' he referred to must have included his colleagues higher up in the Authority.

"Do you have any evidence?" Lister asked.

"Do we need evidence?" he replied. "We know that Hashem Abbas was in Rome for a period last year. We believe that several Mossad agents posing as Hamas officials, or some other group, recruited him to carry out a terrorist act here in London, against a Jewish target."

"Why?" Lister asked.

"If you understand the whys then you will know that we are correct," said Moussa.

"Perhaps you would tell me what you told DI Taylor?" asked Lister.

"The whole operation was to discredit the British Home Secretary."

"Why?"

"To end her support of the Palestinian cause."

"So, agents of Israel created a plan to disrupt the British government?"

Moussa gave him a steely look. "Of course," he said in an unequivocal manner.

"How do you know?" Lister asked.

"We know that the Israeli's have agents in all European capital cities. They frequently pose as militant Palestinians to recruit young headstrong Arab men to unwittingly help them spread terror and misinformation about Islam and Palestinians throughout Europe. It's a game they play. Spread the perception of terror to weaken the standing of the cause, and in doing so reduce our support."

"To unwittingly help the Zionists," Lister said as a statement, rather than a question.

"They are adept at doing that kind of thing. They've been doing it for a long time."

In the next moment, a waiter, dressed in a white shirt and dark trousers, approached the table. Moussa asked him for a pot of Turkish coffee and biscuits. The door to the café opened and several people came in and sat at a table at the other side of the room. A soulful Turkish pop ballad drifted out of the sound system.

Lister took a few moments to reflect on the content of the conversation thus far, then he decided to move it on a pace. "Did you know that there was as much as thirty thousand pounds in Asim Malik's bank account?" he asked.

"I wasn't aware of that," said Moussa. "But why would I have been?" he asked.

"The money trail leads back to a man who works in the Rome office of El-Al. Are you aware of him?"

"Not at all," said Moussa.

"A man called Andrea Beletti works in the Rome office as their finance officer. The money came from an account he holds."

"That is a most interesting development," said Moussa.

"Are you aware of anyone of that name?"

"Me?"

"Yes."

"No. Why should I?"

"No reason at all."

"None of this is in the report."

"It won't be."

Moussa gave a light-hearted smile that was close to a grin. "There are probably a lot of things that are not in the report," he remarked.

"It barely touches the surface," said Lister agreeing with him. "What I know is a man called Andrea Beletti transferred the sum of money into Asim Malik's bank account. Why would he do this?" he asked.

"To fund the attack," said Moussa.

"Probably. Can you do something for me?"

"What is it?"

"Do you have an office in Rome?"

"Yes."

"Would someone be able to find this Andrea Beletti and take a photograph of him?"

Moussa looked at Lister. He must have been wondering why he wanted a photograph of this man.

Before he could ask why, Lister beat it to him. "I have it on the word of Asim Malik's father that his son was recently in Amsterdam. I wonder if the person he was meeting there is this Andrea Beletti. If it was this man, then there is a definite link between Asim Malik, Israeli intelligence and Hashem Abbas."

"I will see what I can do," said Moussa.

The waiter came back to the table with a silver tray, on which sat a small silver pot, an ibrik, full of piping hot coffee, and some wafer-thin mint biscuits. Moussa waited for him to move away. The newcomers on the next table were indulging in animated conversation in Arabic or Turkish. Moussa eyed them for a second then concentrated again on Lister.

"I can ask my colleagues in Rome if they can find this man, and take a photograph of him."

"Perfect," said Lister, though he didn't know if this was the most appropriate word to use. He continued. "Then at least I can ask the person who saw Asim Malik in Amsterdam if he recognises the man."

Dr Moussa took in his words for a few moments, then he took hold of the ibrik and proceeded to pour some of the coffee into a cup. It was a strong, thick Turkish coffee that almost came out of the pot with the thickness of gravy granules. He looked to Lister and offered him the pot. He graciously declined the offer. He disliked coffee at the best of times. The aroma of the liquid was so strong it drifted up his nostrils and knocked his head back.

Moussa took one of the biscuits.

Lister looked at him. "Perhaps you could answer me this question. Why do the Israelis consider the opinions and mutterings of a British politician to be worthy of creating a plot to explode a bomb outside the gates of a London school?" he asked.

"They feel under threat. That their friends in the west are abandoning them and turning against them as public opinion begins to question the Zionist policy towards the Palestinian people." He took a nimble of the biscuit. "The British Home Secretary has the ear of the Prime Minister, who in turn has influence over the President of the United States. The possibility of losing influence in western capitals scares them, to the point of irrationality."

Lister took a biscuit and popped it into his mouth. He liked the taste of mint. "How quickly can your people in Rome find this chap?" he asked.

"I will call them as soon as I return to my office."

Lister nodded his head. He didn't want to push it too much at this stage.

The meeting ended five minutes later. Lister gave Moussa his telephone number and an email address. He hoped the doctor would get back in touch with him. Maybe he would. Maybe he wouldn't. Lister knew it could take days if not weeks to find the man.

# Chapter 18

**21ˢᵗ July**

It was six days before Dr Moussa got back in touch with Lister. Moussa called him on the telephone. His colleagues in Rome had been able to find Andrea Beletti. He said they had gotten an up-to-date photograph and more. Just what the 'more' referred to he refused to say over the telephone. He asked Lister to meet him in the Ankara Café the next day at eleven in the morning.

**22ⁿᵈ July**

The following day, Wednesday, was cool and drab. The tables outside the cafe were unoccupied at eleven o'clock in the morning. Lister was feeling tired after a sleepless night. It was as if the weight of the investigation was weighing down on his shoulders. He was intrigued to find out what Moussa had been able to obtain from his colleagues in Rome, but apprehensive at the same time. He knew he was getting in deep into the murky world of the Jewish-Palestinian dispute, and becoming involved with some unscrupulous characters. It wasn't an easy feeling to cast off as an irrelevancy. To discover the truth you had, at times, to liaise with some hard-bitten people. These people weren't boy scouts. They were zoned into, and focused by, what they believed to be the truth, and what they believed was true was right. In this line of work, you had to take some dubious people into your confidence. That meant people who in normal circumstances you would avoid. He had to take a few hits now and again. After all, he was investigating an incident that had shaken many people to the core.

Inside the café it was quiet. The sound system wasn't playing. The only sound was the 'hiss' of steam escaping from a coffee maker. The doctor was sitting at the same table he had occupied previously. He was wearing the same or a similar coat to the one he had been wearing the other day. His eyes were focused on an I-pad on the table. He was alone. He raised his head as Lister came towards him. The drab light of the day reflected in the lenses of his round spectacles.

A waiter was quickly at the table. Moussa ordered the same thick, syrupy Turkish coffee. No biscuits this time. Lister looked at him and saw the white of his eyes behind the screen of the dark lens. He didn't want to say anything until Moussa addressed him. After a few moments, he glanced around the room, then he turned the I-pad to show Lister a photograph of an individual taken from what must have been a long lens camera.

"My colleagues located a man called Andrea Beletti. This is him," Moussa said.

The man in the photograph was walking along a Rome thoroughfare. It was difficult to judge his age precisely. He looked to be in early to mid-forties. He was wearing a dark, thigh-length raincoat and he was carrying a pouch-like document holder under his arm and a folded umbrella in the other. His hair was dark and thinning. He had a thin moustache across his top lip and a few days growth on his chin. His complexion was that of an Italian.

Moussa continued: "This was taken three days before on the Via Conducti in Rome. Not far from the office of El-Al. He admitted that he *was* working for Israel as an agent of Mossad."

Lister noticed the word 'was'. "What do you mean, was?" he asked.

Moussa took the spectacles from his eyes. His eyes were round and dark. The iris as brown as teak. "Our people in Rome interrogated him."

"Is he still alive?" Lister asked.

"That I don't know," Moussa replied.

"You must know," said Lister.

Moussa looked at him, steely-eyed. "This is a cold war we are fighting. There are no niceties in times of conflict," he rebuked.

He edged closer to Lister, so he could reduce the volume of his voice a notch.

"This man is working for Mossad agents in Rome, posing as a Palestinian sympathiser. He admitted that he recruited Hashem Abbas to carry out a mission in London." Lister said nothing. "This man is responsible for the atrocity that occurred in London on 1st March," Moussa added.

His eyes went to the waiter, who came to the table and placed a tray down, then he went back into the kitchen area.

Lister waited for a few moments to compose himself. "I wonder if he is the man who met Asim Malik in Amsterdam?" he asked.

"No."

"How do you know?" Lister asked.

"He has never travelled to Amsterdam," said Moussa.

"How do you know that?" Lister asked.

"Our people in Rome checked him out. He hasn't been to Amsterdam in over five years."

"Do you have a copy of the photograph?" Lister asked.

Moussa eyed him for a brief few moments, then he leaned over to one side, took a document holder, and extracted a printed copy of the same photograph on the face of the tablet.

"Is he married?" asked Lister. "Does he have any children of his own?"

"That I don't know," said Moussa. "He's an agent for Mossad, posing as someone who is helping the Palestinians regain their homeland. He deserves what is coming to him," he added.

Lister was philosophical. "When was the plot hatched?" he asked.

"Who knows. Maybe as long as a year ago. Maybe longer. Maybe shorter," replied Moussa.

"Where is he now?" Lister asked.

"I've no knowledge of that. He was interrogated by our people. He confessed to being an Israeli agent. He confessed he had orders to recruit an extremist in Rome and that he paid him."

Lister wondered if Beletti's body would be found floating in the Tiber. "How was Asim Malik recruited?" he asked.

"The same way as Abbas," Moussa replied. "He would have been recruited by an Israeli agent in London or even in Amsterdam. They were teamed up. Told to live in the same house and told to attack a Jewish target here in London."

"Who killed them both?" Lister asked.

"The Israelis, or even the British Intelligence service," said Moussa.

"M.I.5?" Lister was shocked at the thought.

"I don't know," replied Moussa.

He took the coffee pot, and poured a cup of strong black coffee. Once again, the aroma of full-strength Turkish coffee filled Lister's nostrils.

The door of the café opened and several people wearing office attire came in. The midday trade was just beginning to get underway. The opening bars of a lamenting Turkish ballad came over the air. Lister took a few moments to recap on what the doctor had told him. If there was a British connection in this then it opened up a new front in his investigation. He recalled what DI Taylor had told him about his meeting with Commander Stanley at Scotland Yard when Stanley had told him to dismiss the Israel connection.

"Why would the British Intelligence Service want to get involved in this?" he asked.

"It's a theory," said Moussa. "They may have been working together to assist the operation. The Italians recruited Abbas, the

270

British recruit Malik. They are – how do you British say – singing from the same song sheet," he said with a barbed tone in his voice.

Lister had no way of knowing if there was any truth in this. It may have been wild speculation at best, or fantasy at worst.

"Can I keep this?" he asked, referring to the photograph.

"Yes. But I shall deny I gave it to you if you say it came from me," said Moussa. He lifted a cup to his lips and took a sip of coffee.

"Of course," said Lister. He placed the photograph into the document holder he had with him. There wasn't a great deal more to discuss. If Moussa was telling the truth and he had little reason to doubt him, Beletti had confessed to his part in the operation to recruit Abbas.

"How do you think Abbas got into this country?" he asked.

Moussa took the cup from his lips and placed it into the saucer. "Use your imagination," he said. "A false EU passport, issued in Rome. These people have the knowledge and the skills to produce fake documents and to get people across open borders." He took another sip of coffee and savoured the taste on the back of his tongue as it raced over the taste buds. He didn't say another word.

Lister thanked him for his help and assistance. He stood up from the table, tucked his document holder under his arm and left. He never looked back at the doctor.

# Chapter 19

The possible involvement of the British intelligence Service was something that Lister hadn't anticipated. But it was only a theory. What had started out as an investigation into the actions of a 'Firestarter' had mushroomed into an international conspiracy to kill and maim young children in a bloody terrorist attack.

Lister considered his plan of action going forward. He had a contact within the British Intelligence Service. He had spoken to him before. Then it had been a request for information about the way the service undertook surveillance. This was different. This was about a terrorist incident that had shaken the nation and resulted in a well-respected Home Secretary losing her job and any chance of reaching the very top position of government. The truth was that ten school children had died on 1st March, but the repercussions were far reaching and affected more people than the victims and their families. Several political careers had been terminated. In a government reshuffle in the month following the event, the Home Secretary had expressed a wish to resign her post, though the smart money said she had been pushed.

Lister's contact in MI5 was a guy called Alan Henshaw. Lister wondered whether to ask him if he had any insight into the event. He may have heard something either on the grapevine, or directly from a reliable source. It was a risky strategy, but in order to

272

try and get to the bottom of this affair, he decided to contact
Henshaw.

Immediately after leaving the meeting with Dr Moussa, he
returned to his west London flat. He powered up his PC and sent an
email to Henshaw's private email. It was dubious to put it mildly,
but this was the only hope of contacting him and keeping it secret. In
the email he said that he needed his assistance, but he didn't say in
what regard. He didn't mention it had anything to do with '1-3'.

It was evening when he received a reply from Henshaw.
Henshaw said okay he would meet him for old times' sake and all
that. But anything he said was strictly off the record. Lister agreed.
Henshaw suggested that Lister meet him in a public house on
Shaftesbury Avenue, at two o'clock the following day.

## 23rd July

The 'Punch & Judy' public house was a small hostelry, right
in the heart of central London. The front was so narrow it was
possible to walk straight by it without noticing the bow-shaped
frontage and the *olde-worlde* black and white panel above. It was the
favourite hangout of several well-known – no longer with us –
actors, writers, and the like who were at the top of their profession in
the nineteen seventies and eighties. At two o'clock in the afternoon

the pub wasn't too busy with customers. The few patrons were a mix of people, several tourists, locals, office workers from nearby offices, and a couple of guys in dust-covered work overalls.

It was an old-style public house with two small rooms, a carpet on the floor and a juke box containing a score or more rock and roll classics from down the years. It had several round copper-topped tables, short stools, and loads of character. It was the kind of pub which hadn't changed significantly over thirty years. As Lister stepped through the entrance and into the lounge, he could hear 'Waterloo Sunset' by The Kinks playing on the juke box.

Alan Henshaw was sitting at a table by himself. He had a half pint pot in front of him, half full with a strawberry coloured liquid. Henshaw wasn't a large guy, nor was he distinguished. If you had to guess what he did for a living you would say finance officer in the Treasury or an administrator in a Whitehall office. Mundane was the best word to describe him. He didn't wear a badge that said he worked for MI5. He was fifty years of age. His dark hair was beginning to reveal grey specks in it. He was wearing a common style of sport jacket over a plain white shirt and tie. He had been a MI5 man for fifteen years. Lister had met him eight years ago at a social event in Oxford, where Henshaw was studying for an MA at the time. Lister didn't know a great deal about Henshaw's background. All he knew was that he was an information officer in one of MI5's central London locations.

Henshaw eyed Lister has he entered the pub. Lister sat next to him, and glanced around the interior. Meanwhile, Ray Davies sang:

Taxi light shines so bright
But I don't need no friends
As long as I gaze on Waterloo sunset
I am in paradise

"Let me finish my drink," said Henshaw. "Then we'll get out of here." Lister didn't reply. Henshaw quickly finished off the remaining liquid in the glass, then he got up from the table and led the way out, and into the weak, watery sunlight. They crossed over onto Haymarket, then onto Pall Mall and towards Trafalgar Square. The day was fine, cloudy but mild.

The number of people on the path had thinned out, and the traffic was moving at a decent pace for central London. At the end of Pall Mall, they crossed over the road and into the square. The entrance to Whitehall and the government quarter was across at the other side of the road that circled the square. There was a party of school kids taking photographs at the foot of Nelson's column. Other people were milling near to the lion statues. An open-topped tourist bus came around the square.

Lister and Henshaw took a clockwise route around the monument. Henshaw had pulled the collar of his jacket up and had sunk his shoulders into the jacket as if he was trying to hide his identity. This location was perhaps not the best, but at least they were two people in the crowd.

"Let's talk and walk," said Henshaw, then immediately took a moment to glance at his surroundings. "What can I do for you?" he asked.

"I'm doing some research into the 1st March bomb attack on the school in St. John's Wood," replied Lister.

Henshaw didn't reply. He kept his shoulders hunched and a gap of two feet between them. A flock of pigeons fluttered their wings then flew away and settled on one of the lion plinths.

"What about it?" asked Henshaw.

"According to some information I've picked up, it may have been an Israeli-led operation…" Henshaw remained mute. Lister continued, "…to discredit the former Home Secretary. What I would like to know is, is there any British intelligence service complicity?"

"Wow," said Henshaw. He was taken aback by his direct approach.

"I know. It's pretty serious."

"Why would there be?" Henshaw asked.

"I don't know. I'm just posing the question."

"Who told you this?"

"Let's just say a reasonably good source."

"Reasonably good?" questioned Henshaw.

"Is there any truth in it?" Lister asked.

"There's no smoke without fire," Henshaw said with a hint of theatre in his tone.

"Which means?"

"This is strictly off the record."

"Of course."

"It's possible that operatives of Mossad had a hand in the planning of the event."

"Why?"

"For the reason you've mentioned," said Henshaw.

"Was the bomber recruited by Mossad agents in Rome?"

"I have no direct knowledge of that," Henshaw said. He paused for a moment, reached into an inside jacket pocket and extracted a full packet of cigarettes. He put one between his lips and lit it with a cheap gas-fuel lighter. He took in a deep dose of nicotine.

"Their agents were purporting to be IS, or Islamic Jihad or some other alphabet soup," said Lister. "The arson attacks in north London were an attempt to create racial tension, and this would be used as the excuse for the 1st March attack."

Henshaw took the cigarette out of his lips. "The six points of the Star of David," he muttered.

"Who told you about that?" Lister asked.

"I heard the theory from a contact in New Scotland Yard."

Lister raised the document holder he was carrying. He extracted the photograph Farid Moussa had given him. "Do you recognise this man?" he asked. He handed the sheet to Henshaw. He paused, then glanced at the image.

"No. Who is he?" he asked. They started to saunter again across the square at a slow pace.

"Someone called Andrea Beletti. He's an agent for Mossad in Rome."

Henshaw passed the photograph back to him. "What's the angle?" he asked.

"He's believed to be the man who transferred forty thousand pounds into Asim Malik's bank account." Lister threaded the single sheet back into his holder and zipped it closed.

"Looks as if you've done your homework," said Henshaw.

By now they were nearly at the starting point of their walk around the square. The sights, smells and sounds of the traffic encircling the square filled the air. The sun had gone behind a cloud so the surroundings were bathed in grey shadow.

Lister didn't reply to Henshaw's remark. "Asim Malik was in Amsterdam a few months ago," Lister went on. "He was seen walking with a man of middle-eastern appearance."

"What's the significance?" Henshaw asked.

"He may have travelled there to meet someone posing as a Palestinian, or a member of some terrorist organisation. But he was actually a Mossad agent. This man may have given him his instructions."

"To do what?" Henshaw asked.

"To carry out the arson attacks." Henshaw didn't reply. "Did Malik know of the wider plot to bomb the school?" Lister asked.

"Probably. His credit card was used to buy the materials to make the bomb."

"You know more on this then you're letting on," said Lister

"Only the bare essentials," replied Henshaw. He took the cigarette out of his lips and tapped off a length of ash.

"It was all about stopping a British politician from expressing pro-Palestinian views and opinions," said Lister.

Henshaw dropped the cigarette to the floor and crushed it under his foot. He looked at Lister square in the eye. "Yeah. That's about the size of it," he said in a sarcastic way.

"What a fucking shame," said Lister.

"Believe me, the intelligence community are pissed off with the Israelis," said Henshaw.

"Is that supposed to make me feel better?" Lister asked.

"Not at all. Israel is an ally in the fight against extremist violence. We need them as much as they need us. Nine-eleven changed the picture. It's us against them. If I was you, I'd forget this investigation. You don't want to make enemies, do you?" Henshaw said.

"Is that some kind of a warning?" Lister asked.

Henshaw smiled. "No. Not a warning. It's free advice. If it was me, I'd ditch any investigation."

"Was MI5 involved in the plot?" Lister asked.

"Not at all," Henshaw said.

"What's going to happen?" Lister asked.

"About what?" Henshaw asked.

"British intelligence liaison with the Israelis"

"I don't have a crystal ball," Henshaw said. "If history is any guide, it will all blow over in a few months, and then go back to normal."

In the next few strides they had reached the southern end of the square adjacent to the crossing going over to Northumberland Avenue and Whitehall.

Henshaw pointed ahead. "I'm going on to Whitehall. You go down Northumberland. It was nice talking to you. Be careful how you go," he said with a crooked smile.

When the traffic lights changed from green to red and the little man flashed, they crossed over to the other side. Henshaw quickened his pace and walked away from Lister at a brisk gait. Lister watched him walk around the corner onto Whitehall and go out of view. Once Lister was on the other side of the road he turned back and returned onto the square. He raised his head and looked up at the silhouetted figure of Nelson against the backcloth of a dark rain filled cloud.

Within an hour of arriving home, Lister had collected all his working notes together. He sat at a desk and opened a new pad of writing paper. He had a set of sharpened pencils next to him. For the next few days, he hardly moved from the desk. In that time, he wrote the first seven thousand words of the report.

The following day he added another five thousand words. Then he did the key exercise - the editing phase. He reduced the word content by ten percent and put it into a friendlier format. He was happy with the finished piece. He wrote a summary of what he had learned during the past three weeks. He wasn't yet at the euphoria stage, as he still had plenty of work to do. Over the next hour, he wrote a two-thousand-word summary.

Then he went to his PC, turned it on and spent the next few days typing the words into a document. He didn't name names. He wrote his findings in such a way that names were not a necessary commodity. He gave the reader the information, the pointers and the direction of travel that would allow them to come to his or her own conclusion as to what the truth was. That a foreign intelligence service was complicit in the planning and the execution of the tragedy. He believed most things Alan Henshaw had told him, specifically that British Intelligence wasn't in any way involved in the planning or the execution.

Once he had written three drafts consisting of an executive summary, a short report, then the longer, far more wordy detailed report he printed off two copies of each. He gave the papers the rather cryptic title: '1-3. The Israeli connection?' with the question mark attached. It was his intention to post one set of papers to Helen Potter-Smith, and to give one to DI Steve Taylor for his appraisal.

Lister's next task was to contact Taylor and arrange to meet him. He sent a text message to his mobile phone. DI Taylor replied a few hours later. He agreed to meet Lister in one week, at the same place in Regent's Park. It was eleven weeks since they had first met in early June.

# Chapter 20

**Friday, 18ᵗʰ August**

The middle of August can bring some blisteringly hot days. This was one of them. It was one of those days when life couldn't get any better. All it needed was a glass of beer, some summer music, a comfortable chair, and a TV to watch a test cricket match, and the day would be complete.

DI Taylor and Reece Lister took the first path to the left and entered the parkland. Lister was carrying a document holder in his hand. Inside, was a plain manila envelope that contained a copy of each of the three reports he had written.

They sauntered on like a couple of friends taking a time out from the office. They turned onto a second pathway, and continued along the side of the wider stretch of the Serpentine Lake.

Just ahead was a vacant park bench. They sat down and surveyed their surroundings.

Taylor turned to Lister. "How do you feel? Now that your research is complete?" he asked.

Lister sighed out loud. "You know that feeling you get when you complete a long-standing project, that you've been working on, seemingly for ages? It's a feeling of euphoria, mixed in with a sense of achievement." Taylor didn't respond to his words.

"I'm getting out of London for a few days," Lister went on.

"Good for you," said Taylor. He adjusted the sunglasses over his eyes and dislodged a spread of perspiration from his brow.

"I need some down time and R&R," said Lister.

"You and me both," said Taylor.

They could just hear the shouts of the youths playing touch rugby on the field and just make out the people in the rowing boats on the lake, despite the shield of trees.

"What did you discover?" asked Taylor.

"A lot. A lot more than I thought to be honest. Like the involvement of Israeli intelligence in the plot that led to '1-3'" Taylor blew out a tuneless whistle. Perhaps sensing the enormity of what he had just said. "It's all in the report," said Lister.

He paused for a moment, lifted the document holder, opened the zip, and extracted the manila envelope. "I'd like you to read the three articles and give me your opinion." He handed the envelope to Taylor.

Taylor felt the weight of the papers inside. He said nothing. Several people were coming along the path towards them, like the young couple hand in hand, the young woman pushing a child's buggy, and the light complexioned man in a long, knee length dark raincoat. Taylor was struck by this last figure for a moment because he was wearing a raincoat, which seemed odd in this warm weather. The man had blonde, almost strawberry-coloured hair that was shaped in an odd way and didn't look natural. His cheekbones were sculptured like an Adonis like vision.

The young couple passed by, then the young woman pushing the child in the buggy. Lister and Taylor were silent. Taylor turned to look at Lister. He was going to say something to him when he was distracted by the man's sudden movement towards him. The man increased his pace, then he lurched to a side and seemed to be reaching inside his raincoat for something. Then it all went into slow motion. His hand came out from underneath the coat.

Taylor could hardly see what was in his hand against the dark of his shiny mac. It took him a second to see that he had pulled out a long black handgun with a silencer screwed into the barrel. The man moved his feet so he assumed an attack position with his feet apart and balanced. He raised the barrel of gun level with his right shoulder, aimed it at Reece Lister and squeezed the trigger. The resulting 'crack' was like the sound of a cricket ball gently hitting a cricket bat, rather like a resounding 'thwack'. Reece Lister was shot from a distance of no more than ten feet. Taylor was stunned. He could hardly move his feet, but he did and set to turn and run. The gunman swivelled his stance and turned the gun on Taylor. He took aim and squeezed the trigger.

The bullet hit DI Taylor in the upper back and entered his body in a spot two inches below his shoulder and two inches from his spine. It exited through his chest. The force of the bullet caused him to jolt forward and he lost his balance. Then he heard a scream, and the sound seemed to echo and resonate in his ears for a prolonged time. Despite being shot, his survival instincts took over and he tried to flee, but his legs felt heavy and he couldn't get any purchase on them. Within a second, he fell to the floor, face down. The next thing he was aware of was the shadow coming over him. In his mind's eye his life flashed in front of his eyes in a montage of images and visions. The next thing he was aware of was the manila envelope being wrenched from his grip. This was followed by the sound of someone running away, and more screams and shouts that converged into one sound.

He managed to roll onto his back and look up at the pale opal of the sky, then he saw a face appear over him and look down at him. He didn't know if this was a near-death experience or a past recollection appearing before his eyes. He saw the lips of the face move, but he didn't hear a sound. His senses were deserting him.

The last face Steve Taylor saw was that of a stranger or maybe it was an angel coming to claim him and take him to the afterlife. He closed his eyes, sighed for the final time, and felt his life slip away.

# Chapter 21

Reece Lister and DI Steve Taylor were shot dead in cold blood on a path in Regent's Park, approximately five months and three weeks after the 1st March bombing. They died within ten feet and three seconds of each other. A life near to the edge for both of them had ended in a bloody act of violence. Steve Taylor and Reece Lister died trying to preserve the truth. A personal commodity they both held close to their hearts.

In the immediate aftermath of their double slaying, the Met police and the security forces searched high and low for the assassin, the man with the strawberry-blonde hair, sculptured cheek bones, and the blue eyes.

DCI Lake was handed the task of leading a twenty-man strong team of detectives to find the killer of DI Steve Taylor and Reece Lister and bring him to justice. DI Hamilton was drafted in as her number two. Members of the Counter Terrorism Unit led by Commander Stanley joined the search.

In a painstaking operation that clocked up many man hours those witnesses who were near to the shooting, and could be identified, were traced and questioned. The Met put out a request for all those who were in the park on that day to let them have any photographs or video they may have taken. Several Met officers had to go abroad to interview some American tourists who said they had seen the killer walking away from the scene.

Within a minute of killing two people, the assassin was seen walking at a brisk pace through the park. As he neared a walkway over the edge of the lake, he was seen to throw something into the water. The Met underwater investigation team were brought in to search the lake. After several hours of looking in the water they found Lister's document holder and his mobile phone at the bottom of the lake. The document holder was empty. The manila envelope that had been in DI Taylor's hand was never found.

Just like the murder of the TV personality Jill Dando in Fulham, in 1999, the murder had been carried out by a professional assassin, who had melted into the surrounding area. Never to be seen again. It was thought his strawberry-blonde hair was a wig. It was perceived that the same man may have murdered both Asim Malik and Hashem Abbas, though there was no evidence to connect them.

The copies of the three reports Lister had written, and which he intended to put in the post to send to Helen Potter-Smith were never sent. The security service took away Lister's computer and erased everything on the hard drive. His attempt to reveal the truth about the 1st March, and who was responsible, didn't hang with the official version that it was the work of Islamic extremists. Islamic extremist terrorism was a malignant evil that had to be confronted come-what-may and defeated. If that meant bending the truth, then so be it.

The investigation wound down six months later, with no breakthrough in finding the killer. DI Peter Hamilton remarked to a friend that the investigation into the murders of Reece Lister and Stephen Taylor was like the devil's own advocates carrying out an investigation into devil worship. The chance of finding anything was remote, because they didn't want to find anything that would cast doubt on the official version of events. The findings presented by Reece Lister and Steve Taylor would only complicate things, and nobody wanted that.

The premise that all Muslims are not terrorists, but all terrorism in the 21st century is carried out by Islamic extremists, allowed the security forces to exercise elements of control over the decision makers, and nothing should be allowed to distort that mindset. Not even the truth.

Reece Lister and Steve Taylor simply had to go, and in the great scheme of things, they were expendable. Hence, they were murdered in cold blood. Just like Asim Malik and Hashem Abbas. At the end of the day, nobody knew if Hashem Abbas had ever made or planted a bomb by the gate at the entrance to the school. If the authorities said he did, and no one challenged that belief, then he must have been the culprit. Anyone challenging that notion had to be dealt with.

**The End**

# 'Six Amigos'

## Chapter 1

If ever such a thing as an eligible bachelor existed, then it had to be Rob Bennett. Let us consider the evidence. He was tall, dark, handsome, sophisticated and wealthy. He had it all. The looks, the charm, the swagger, the bed-side manner, and the physique of a guy who took his own personal fitness extremely seriously.

At thirty-two-years of age he had his pick of all the beautiful girls he knew. His profession was also what dreams are made of. He was a pilot for British Atlantic Airways. Flying from London to all points in North America.

He had been through most of the airline's prettiest stewards. After all, what more was there to do in the hotel during the layoffs between flights? When it came to settling down, he had chosen the girl he had met two years ago to become his life partner. She wasn't a stewardess for British Atlantic Airways, nor did she have any connection to the airline industry. Susan Charles was an interior designer who owned a shop in Kensington, west London. She had a growing reputation that had even spread to the TV. She had been a guest on several home make-over shows and had become well known on the TV circuit.

Bennett met Susan Charles when he was looking for someone to refurbish his Chelsea flat. She had been recommended to him. She came to his home to look at what he wanted. He liked what he saw. They had hit it off in a big way. Now, two years later, they were to be married in two weeks in a church in her home village, deep in the quaint and delightful Hampshire countryside. Like all fun-loving men, Bennett had decided on a once-in-a-lifetime stag party. He had invited six of his closest male friends to join him on a weekend jaunt to New York City, where they would drink, eat and party for two days before returning to the UK.

It was Clive Pennock, Bennett's best friend and best man who had taken up the task of planning the event. Pennock had made all the arrangements. He had persuaded Bennett that Manhattan would be a great venue for a stag party. Bennett agreed and asked Pennock to do all the ground work. Pennock said okay he would be honoured to arrange the itinerary for the two days. He had booked seven rooms in a midtown Manhattan, boutique hotel.

As an ex-British Army man Pennock had planned the party schedule with almost military precision. The seven friends would meet on a Thursday night in the hotel. After a quick bite to eat in the hotel restaurant, finishing at close to seven-thirty, they would trawl downtown to the pubs and bars in the Bleecker Street area. One of the guys knew a Lap-Dancing club in Soho where, until the early hours of the following day, they would watch the dancers shedding their clothes and dancing naked. From there it would be back to the hotel at three in the morning to sleep it off. On Friday afternoon, they would visit a few bars in midtown. On Friday night they had tickets in their own private box to watch the New York Yankees play baseball at Yankee stadium. With waitress service, of course. After the game, they would hot foot it back to midtown to visit a nightclub in Tribeca where the beers would flow and the boys would enjoy themselves dancing and flirting with the female patrons. Several of the guys had to be back in London on Sunday evening so the party would end at midday on Saturday. No doubt all of them would be several pounds heavier, the worse for wear, fatigued and several hundreds of pounds poorer, but they would have had a great time in one of the best party towns on earth.

Rob Bennett had known Clive Pennock for getting on for twenty years. They had been school mates in their home town – Bedford, before both of them had moved into the London area for work. Two of Bennett's other friends – Kurt Smith and Steve Cummins – were pilots for British Atlantic airways. One of his other friends – Tony Norman – worked in the City of London as a market analyst for Citibank. Danny Fordham was an ex-professional football player Bennett had played alongside when he had turned out for a semi-professional team based in north London on half a dozen occasions. Though he was a talented mid-fielder Bennett didn't have what it took to make it to the next level. He knew it so he called time on his football career at twenty-four years of age to concentrate on getting his wings and becoming a fully-fledged pilot for one of the big commercial airlines. After spending the best part of one hundred and fifty thousand pounds of his own money for three years training, he had succeeded. Today he was a flying transatlantic for British Atlantic. The sixth and final friend was Wayne Hall. Hall was a personal trainer and fitness guru who had gotten Bennett into shape when he needed to pass a physical examination for the airline. They had become good friends.

All his six friends were a similar age to Bennett and all had outgoing personalities. All six of them were successful in their chosen professions. They all shared not only a similar sense of humour and the will to win, but also liked to have a laugh and a good time.

Rob Bennett was really looking forward to spending the next couple of days in Manhattan with his chums and having the time of his life. When they began to reminisce about some of the things they had got up to, it was bound to create some great banter. The two days were sure to go off with a bang and create a sack full of memories to last a lifetime.

Chapter 2

On that Thursday afternoon, Bennett checked into the hotel at four in the afternoon. The hotel was a small, independent establishment, a couple of streets south of Madison Square Garden and Penn Station on a stretch of west 29th Street between 8th and 9th Avenue, in a spot where midtown begins to drift into Chelsea. It was an area he wasn't that familiar with. Airline crew tended to stay nearer to the main New York airports: JFK and Newark Liberty. He very seldom flew into or out of LaGuardia airport.

Bennett recalled Pennock telling him about the hotel after he was told about it by a colleague of his. It certainly was different. Each room was individually decorated on a theme, related to a classic movie. Bennett found himself in the 'Vertigo' suite, which had a full wall size image of a frantic, petrified-looking James Stewart in the foreground, hanging by his fingertips from a gutter of a tall building with the spread of downtown San Francisco in the background.

Bennett was assured the hotel had a great bar, good room service and a decent restaurant. Despite being a boutique hotel, it didn't come at a huge price for New York, just the seven hundred and fifty dollars a night for a room. Clive Pennock was in the 'Laurence of Arabia' suite, Danny Fordham the 'True Grit'. Tony Norman the 'Dog Day Afternoon' suite. Steve Cummins in the 'Gone with the Wind'. Kurt Smith the 'Wizard of Oz'. Wayne Hall was in the 'Mary Poppins', which would no doubt create howls of laughter.

Bennett knew from the text messages he had received that four of his friends had already checked in at noon. Danny Fordham had flown in from London with Tony Norman. Wayne Hall was here. Steve Cummins had come in from Boston. Kurt Smith was due in the next hour or so on a flight from Miami. Clive Pennock would be here shortly as he had just landed at JFK. All his mates were here and that pleased him immensely. They were going to have a great couple of days with loads of banter, laughs, stories; too much alcohol and far too much fun for a bunch of thirty-something-year-olds who should have known better.

Bennett hadn't seen any of his friends for some time. After all, he had been courting Susan Charles for the best part of two years. With the demands on his time and flying back and forth across the Atlantic, to all points on the North American continent, he hardly had the opportunity to see his friends. The only guy he had seen on a regular basis was his fitness trainer, Wayne Hall, when he visited him in the Earls Court Fitness Centre which Hall owned.

The plan was for them all to meet up in the hotel bar at seven o'clock, grab a quick bite to eat in the restaurant, then head downtown in a couple of taxis to Bleecker Street to begin the party, before descending on the strip club in Soho for eleven o'clock or thereabouts.

Bennett managed to get a couple of hours sleep, then at seven o'clock he went down to the restaurant. The dining room was decorated with full size posters from iconic baseball movies, such as 'Field of Dreams', 'Bull Durham', 'Moneyball', and 'The Natural'. Colourful, Tiffany style lamps hung from the ceiling. The small bar was well stocked with liquor bottles on glass shelves in front of a mirrored wall. The scent and sound of sizzling burgers and French fries filled the air. Several of the guys: Danny Fordham, Tony Norman, Wayne Hall were already seated at a table littered with empty bottles of beer. The party had started early, though Wayne was on fresh orange. He would probably get onto the harder stuff later. The three of them looked up as Rob Bennett entered the room.

'Here comes the condemned man,' shouted Danny Fordham. The other guys laughed out loud. The other half dozen people in the room looked up and observed the loud Englishmen. His friends raised their beer filled glasses to him and it was in this spirit that the friends met. All the guys were looking cool. All were in smart casual dress, but no jeans, or sneakers. After all they were going to the club later which had a sensible dress code. To avoid disappointment at the door they were dressed appropriately.

As Bennett sat at the table, Steve Cummins came in and immediately threw a pair of plastic handcuffs at Bennett. The others laughed out loud. "You'd better get those on and get used to it," said Cummins. Little did Bennett know the irony of what he had said and what was to come later.

"I don't want a tattoo and I don't want a weird haircut," Bennett protested. He had heard stories of how some stag party pranks had ended with the groom in handcuffs clamped to a lamppost or some other permanent fixture or how a stag had been put on a train and sent off on a journey to God knows where. Or guys who had gotten so incapacitated that they got a tattoo they regretted as soon as they were sober. He didn't want any of that 'thank you very much'. He had a feeling it was going to be a great two days. It would be a party he wouldn't forget in a hurry. Like one of those occasions that come back with happy memoires or adversely, send a cold chill down the spine.

Within minutes Danny Fordham was reeling off one of his favourite stories about an old ex-pro footballer he knew, who had gotten up to all sorts of things he shouldn't have. Fordham had a wicked sense of humour. At six feet two tall he had the height of a central defender. He had played football with Bennett at semi-professional level for a team in north London called Enfield Town. He had a footballer's physique and stamina, and a mischievous glint in his eye. He was like Bennett in many respects, though he had a fair complexion, while Bennett was much darker.

Tony Norman was a City of London investment banker who worked for an offshoot of Citibank. He was a polar opposite to Bennett and Fordham. He was five-feet five in his stockinged feet and at least three stones overweight. He had a podgy frame – no doubt the result of too much fast-food and too many late-night visits to the pub after work. Bennett had known him for nearly ten years, following a chance meeting in the sauna in a residential block they once lived in in Bloomsbury. Norman was originally from some place in the North of England. Despite living in London for the past fifteen years he still retained a soft northern accent. He said his father was a farmer who still had loads of valuable land in the Yorkshire Dales area. He wasn't short of a bob or two from his family ties or his occupation.

Wayne Hall was a tall guy who possessed the granite-like body of a serious body builder. No one was likely to tangle with him if push came to shove and shove came to a fight. He was a naturally fit guy with brooding good looks and porcelain skin. The kind of guy who worked hard to look good, but stayed on the straight and narrow and was a nice guy at the same time. Bennett had met him a couple of years ago and they had hit it off. Hall had helped Bennett when he needed to shed some pounds and get into shape. A fitness report, he had received from his employer, was less than flattering and pulled few punches. He had to get himself into shape if he wasn't in danger of losing his status. It was that serious. Hall had him first on the treadmills to build up his stamina and get his heart pumping, then provided him with a strict fitness programme of easy-going exercise and weights to get himself into shape. It worked. The next fitness assessment was in stark contrast to the previous one. He was no longer in danger of being downgraded to relief pilot. Bennett had continued the programme and saw Wayne Hall at least once a week in his fitness centre.

Kurt Smith and Steve Cummins were fellow pilots. Cummins real first name was Barnaby, but everyone knew him as Steve for some reason. Bennett had known them for eight and six years, respectively. In truth, there wasn't a great deal to say about them. They were both the same age as Bennett and flew virtually the same routes as him. Smith was an ex-RAF reconnaissance pilot, while Cummins had followed the same route into the industry as Bennett. He had financed his own training programme, and had achieved his wings after three years of intensive, on-the-job training. They were both steady guys and people he could rely on in a crisis.

That just left Kurt Smith and Clive Pennock to arrive and the magnificent seven would be complete. For the time being the five of them chatted and tucked into a light meal of burgers and fries with lashings of ketchup.


The final two party-goers, Kurt Smith and Clive Pennock checked into the hotel within five minutes of each other and soon joined their friends at the bar. Rob Bennett did the introductions for those who didn't know one another. The group were a well-balanced spread of guys looking for a good time and a good time is what they were determined to have. After all they were about to send one of their own on the next chapter of his life and down the road to a place called 'marriage'.

Within minutes of meeting Susan Charles, Bennett knew that she was the one for him. The moment he clapped his eyes on her slim figure, cute face and heard her bubbly personality he knew he had to have her in his life. He soon forgot about all the other girls he knew. He broke a few hearts when the news filtered out that he was engaged to be married. Or maybe, that is what Bennett liked to think.

It was a little after eight-thirty when the group left the hotel on West 29th street. The idea of kicking off the night with a couple of beers in a midtown bar was kicked into touch. The group were eager to get downtown to sample the happenings down there. Both Kurt Smith and Steve Cummins said they knew of a wine bar in Little Italy that had the best selection of chianti you could find in the city. They would start down there then move onto Bleecker Street and finally Soho.

For a Thursday night in June, the downtown area was busy both on and off the road and in the bars. They stayed in Little Italy for an hour and consumed a couple of bottles of chianti between them. From there they ventured the half mile or so to the Bleecker Street area, an area renowned for its music scene, trendy bars and comedy clubs where top-line comedians often appeared unannounced.

Over the next couple of hours, they must have entered a dozen bars, sampling the craft beers and the atmosphere. As the evening progressed the scene became even more lively as the students from the nearby New York University, Washington Square campus, came out to join the fun.

By eleven o'clock the guys were becoming progressively drunk and the vociferous chat was increasing. Several of the NYU female co-eds were hanging onto Wayne Hall and complementing him about his muscles and his British accent. At eleven forty-five Kurt Smith summoned the group together and suggested they get to the strip club which was only a block away.

The 'Private Eyes' club was a gentleman's establishment in which a dozen dancers or strippers were working the crowd on raised platforms that criss-crossed the floor. The patrons sat in leather upholstered chairs and sofas adjacent to the catwalks. All they had to do was raise their hand for a waitress to be at their beck and call.

The group of seven entered the club at just before midnight, each paying the thirty-dollar admittance fee at a window in the vestibule. Inside the large main room, the audience was primarily made up by guys watching the girls. Lights were flashing and the glitter balls attached to the high ceiling were turning. The sound of high-octane funky house music filled the air. On the raised catwalks, strippers in various stages of undress were cavorting to the sound of high tempo music.

There were several half-naked girls sitting in gilded bird cages on the end of metal bars suspended from the ceiling. It was like a scene from some 1970's hard-edged sexploitation movie. Other dancers twirled around poles placed at spots where the catwalks converged. This wasn't one of your down-at-heel strip joints in which some old birds danced for a few bucks. This was a venue for the discerning gentleman who had plenty of money and expensive tastes. According to the blurb in the entrance, the girls were some of the prettiest and sexiest performers in New York City. The quality of the dancers and venue was reflected in the cost of drinks and food. A five-minute private dance could set you back the thick end of three hundred and fifty dollars.

The guys sitting at a table summoned a waitress to take their drinks order. The atmosphere was vibrant, the music loud and the glitter balls were spinning to send shards of white light reflecting onto the crimson walls. It was a great venue. A long bar, on the sidewall, was manned by at least six female bar staff dressed in fancy black shorts, vests and bow ties. A couple of big, strapping guys in suits, patrolled the floor to keep an eye on the patrons to ensure nobody was getting too close to the girls.

The British guys were soon getting into the party spirit so much so that Danny Fordham and Tony Norman had disappeared with a couple of girls to each enjoy a private dance. One hour passed. It was one o'clock. One of the waitresses, a girl called Chelsea had taken Rob Bennett to one side. She had enticed him to sit at the bar for a chat. She was a tall, willowy blonde with plenty of sex appeal and a body to match, though she wasn't in Susan Charles league by any stretch of the imagination. What made Chelsea stand out was one of the nicest top-racks Bennett had seen on any girl in ages. She was wearing a thigh length pleated skirt and a white blouse that was flapping open to her navel.

He was sitting on a high stool at the bar with a half pint glass of beer in his hand. She was by his side, whispering sweet-nothings into his ear. He was drunk, but not that drunk that he couldn't understand what she was saying. She had her arms wrapped around his shoulders and kept offering to dance for him in one of the private side rooms. She would show him her Brazilian landing strip if he gave her two hundred dollars. He was tempted. She whispered into his ear and nibbled on his ear lobe. She would allow him to touch her if he agreed to pay an extra fifty dollars. He glanced back to the table where his mates had been sitting. The table was now empty. They had gone off in all different directions. The action on the floor was still in full swing. The drinks were flowing and the girls on the stage were dancing to the vibe. His glass was half-full and she was still nibbling on his ear. Her boobs under the white cotton blouse brushed his arm. She told him he could do anything to her.

Despite declining her offer to dance for him she stayed close to him and allowed him to buy her a drink. She was making sure that his glass stayed topped up. Maybe he shouldn't have told her he was a commercial airline pilot. Stupidly, he had told her what he did for a living. Maybe she saw the dollar signs appear in her eyes.

By one-thirty Bennett was beginning to feel worse for wear and a little out of it. Nonetheless, the music was still playing, and the night was still in full swing. He had no idea where his friends had gone. They must have been enjoying the show on offer.

Double vision was starting to affect him. He took his glass and lifted it to his lips and took a mouthful of beer. Then in the next moment something weird happened. He began to feel drowsy, as if a 'Mickey Finn' had kicked into his system. He felt a dizziness in his head. He looked at the bottles of liquor on the glass shelves behind the bar and caught his reflection in the mirror. Then in the next moment he felt as if he was going to faint. He tried to say something to the girl, but his words didn't make any sense. His eyes felt as if they were been weighed down. He was finding it difficult to keep his eyes open. He raised his head and looked at her, then in the next second her face seemed to splinter into three or four different obscure shapes. The sounds in the room increased in decibels. His eyelids closed and he felt himself sliding off the stool and slipping off to a place he had never been to before.

# Chapter 3

Rob Bennett opened his eyes. A wedge of bright white light blazing into his vision blinded him. There was a pain in his head and a whooshing sound in his ears. He tried to focus his vision, but there was a mist and double vision in front of his eyes. The surroundings were in two converging shapes. Beneath him he could feel the softness of a mattress and bedsheets wrapped around his chest, but the smell in the room was one that he couldn't comprehend. It was similar to the cold, fusty smell of damp mixed in with dust. Such was the confusion in his head he didn't know his name. It took him a second to realise who he was. It was as if a segment of his brain had failed to respond so he could hardly focus or grasp cognitive thought. He felt the softness beneath him and knew that his head was immersed in the cushion of a pillow. The light was blazing into the room through a window. It was an alien environment. He looked up to see a crack in the ceiling plaster. He wasn't in the hotel room. This was a strange room and the fusty smell was as powerful as an acrid scent. The room had plain, apple white walls. There was no picture of a petrified James Stewart hanging onto a gutter with the word 'Vertigo' stencilled across it. This was a foreign place. He had no idea of time or where he was. No idea of how he had got here or how long he had been there. It was an experience he had never had before and it worried him to the core of his soul. A moment passed then he could hear the creak of floorboards as if someone was outside the room. He didn't know where the sounds were coming

306

from. Suddenly, there was the sound of a heavy fist battering against a door.

"You in there," shouted the voice. The words were followed by two more thuds that shook the door. "Time's up," the person bellowed.

Bennett managed to raise his head from the pillow and lift the top half of his body erect. He was naked. As he came level, he felt a tremble in his head and a nauseating dizziness came over him. He breathed in the scent of damp and moisture. He felt the warm sensation of liquid in his mouth and a taste of vomit in his throat.

There was another thud on the door followed by a second shout of 'Time's up'. Despite the trembling in his head, he managed to swing his legs around and sit on the edge of the mattress.

"Okay," he replied as best as he could. He could taste the vomit in his mouth so he opened his mouth to allow a small amount of liquid to dribble out. Then as he looked back onto the bed top, he could make out the shape and feel the weight of someone on the other side of the mattress. He turned his head in a series of robot-like movements and clapped his eyes on the face of a woman lying next to him. She was a dark-skinned woman. The bed sheets were down around her waist. She was naked. Her breasts were flat to her chest. He managed to stand-up and step around the bed to an open space where his clothes were scattered over the floor. He looked back at the figure on the bed assuming that she was sleeping. From this angle it was difficult to see her face or gauge her age. She had red corkscrew hair that curled around her face. She wasn't making a sound. Not even a snore or the sound of a breath. Nothing. No rise of her chest as she took in oxygen or expelled carbon dioxide out of her nostrils. He had no idea who she was. He was going to call out, then he felt a thud in his chest. Whoever she was she wouldn't be answering his questions. She wasn't in a deep sleep. She was dead. There was a blueish tint on her lips and her skin had a grey pallor to it, as if the colour of life had been drained out of her flesh. The shock going through him had the effect of increasing his cognitive thought. He glanced to the window to see the dark shape of the side of a building looming high above. The walls of the room were bare and peppered with damp stains and patches of flaking plaster. There was a threadbare carpet on the floor. A tatty, three-drawer chest of drawers was placed next to a cupboard door.

Despite the dizzy feeling in his head and an unsteady feeling in his feet, he managed to pick up his clothing from the floor and put them on the mattress. He looked at the body on the bed. He was hardly able to comprehend what he saw. It was like some kind of weird dream. He asked himself if he knew her. Was she someone he had met previously? He didn't know her. He had never seen her in his life. He had no idea who she was. Or where he was. Or how he had gotten here. He had enough brain power to know he was Robert Bennett and that he was in New York City. Beyond that he had no recollection of meeting the woman or entering this room. He couldn't recall anything other than the moment he had lost consciousness in the strip club. After that he couldn't recall a thing and that was very disturbing.

Despite the wobbling sensation in his legs, he managed to dress himself then he stepped to the door, took hold of a bolt and slid it open. He took the door knob and gently pulled the door open and peered out onto a narrow, bare landing that was mostly in shade. There was a door to the right and one further along the corridor. There was a strong smell of trapped air and a fusty aroma. The wallpaper on the opposite wall was peeling off. A dust- covered light shade provided the illumination. Before he stepped out of the room, he glanced back to the body. He looked at her chest to check if he could see the rise of her breasts. There was no movement and no sound from her. Whoever she was, she had ceased to be.

There was no one around. He stepped out of the room, waited for a brief moment just in case one of the doors opened, then he closed the door behind him. Turning to his left he stepped along the corridor. He had no idea what floor he was on. There was noise from a TV coming from one of the rooms. As he came to the end of the landing, he clapped his eyes on the elevator door ahead. On the left side of the elevator was a flight of stairs going down to the next floor. On the other side were stairs going up to the next floor. Then he saw the sign on the elevator door which showed: Floor 4. Rather than wait for the elevator, he ventured down the staircase, went around a corner and down the next flight to the third floor. Light was pouring in through windows with the side of the building next door casting a shadow onto the stairwell. He didn't linger. He wanted to get out of this place before anyone emerged and clapped eyes on him. He was soon on the second floor then down onto the first floor which turned out to be the ground floor. As he stepped off the last stair, he moved out into a small lobby, a reception area that was covered with stained, grey and blue chequered carpet tiles. Just to the right was a reception desk come counter. A large dark-skinned man with large, bulbous eyes and frizzy, grey smoked hair was standing behind the counter. There were several notices on the wall. One asked the residents to vacate their rooms by ten o'clock. It was obviously a hotel of some description.

The man clapped his eyes on Bennett and looked at him with a kind of questioning expression on his face. Opposite the desk was a single panel glass door that led out onto the sidewalk. There was no one else nearby.

Bennett couldn't do anything, but look at the guy behind the counter. The chap didn't say a word. By the size of his physique, he could have been the guy who had rapped his fist on the door and shouted, 'time's up'. He didn't say a word on this occasion. He watched Bennett walk across the floor and step to the door. The exit was just a few feet away. Beyond the glass the sidewalk was bathed in sunlight. Bennett aimed for the exit. As he stepped outside, he took in a huge intake of air and ran his hands over his face. He still felt nauseous and unsteady on his feet. Nevertheless, he was out of there. He didn't have a clue to his whereabouts. By the preponderance of yellow cabs on the street and the school bus parked further along the sidewalk he knew he must be somewhere in the city. By the appearance of the stores and the general surroundings he knew he wasn't in one of the more affluent parts of the city. He set off to walk along the sidewalk. Ahead there was a drycleaner and an ethnic eatery. He passed a CVS store and a coffee bar. The area had an Afro-Caribbean feel. There was the fragrance of spicy food in the air. There was a DIY store on the corner of the street called 'Harlem Hardware'. Above that, the metal steps of a fire escape jutted out of the face of the building.

He still had no idea where he was. It was a complete mystery. By the sign above the store front he guessed he was in Harlem, therefore he was still in New York City. The bus coming along the thoroughfare said 'M15. Downtown Manhattan'. Now he knew for certain that he was still in the city.

The warmth of the sun hitting his head made him feel marginally better. The sounds of people and the rush of the traffic on the street echoed in his ears. He felt wobbly on his feet. The remains of alcohol or something else was still present in his blood stream. After a few yards, he paused, reached into his back trouser pocket, and felt the small wad of dollar bills. He pulled them out and counted the notes. He had fifty dollars on him and some loose change. An idea came to him. He stepped to the edge of the street, faced the oncoming traffic and raised his hand.

A cruising yellow cab quickly pulled up. Bennett opened the back door and climbed into the cab.

"Where to?" asked the driver.

"Where am I?" he asked.

"What?"

"Where am I?" he asked again.

The driver looked startled. "You're in Harlem," he said. "This is one hundred and thirty-second street. Where to?" he asked again.

"To West 29$^{th}$ and 7$^{th}$ Avenue. The Movie House hotel."

The driver set the meter running and pulled away from the kerbside.

"What time is it?" Bennett asked.

"Five before ten," replied the driver.

Chapter 4

The taxi driver drove out of Harlem and back into midtown Manhattan within forty minutes. He dropped Bennett right outside the hotel at ten-thirty. Bennett paid the fifteen-dollar fare and tipped the driver ten dollars. He was relieved to be back in the hotel, though it wasn't exactly home.

Once inside he went straight to his room on the fifth floor. The first thing he needed to do was to take a shower, get a change of clothing and try to take a short nap.

As he entered the room, he familiarised himself with the setting. The sight of the frantic-looking Jimmy Stewart seemed so apt. It was exactly how he felt. He fell onto the mattress and buried his face in the pillow. He still could hardly believe it. How the hell had he ended up in that place? Who was she? How had she died? Surely, he hadn't killed her? He felt anguish at the thought that he could have done something which resulted in her death.

Just then there was a knock at the door to his room. He climbed off the mattress, stepped to the door and opened it. Clive Pennock was standing on the corridor.

Pennock could see the state he was in. "What happened to you?" he asked.

Bennett opened the door wide and invited him into his room. Pennock ran his eyes over his stained clothing and his dishevelment appearance. "Jeez. You look like shit," he said, pulling no punches. "You look as if you've been dragged through a hedge backwards."

Bennett wiped his face, then ran his hands over the back of his head. "I feel like it."

"Where've you been?"

"That's just it. I don't know. All I know is that I'm in big trouble."

Pennock screwed his face. "*Trouble*? What kind of trouble?" he asked.

"Trouble you wouldn't believe."

"Are you going to tell me?"

"I woke up in a strange bed in a place I had no recollection of getting to."

"So?"

"That's not all."

"Like?"

"There was a dead body next to me."

Pennock's eyes widened and his mouth dropped open. "Good Lord. You're kidding me?"

Bennett shook his head. "I wish I was."

Pennock bit his lower lip. "When you say dead body, whose dead body?"

"This black chick."

"Who was she?"

"No idea."

Bennett stepped back a few paces and sat on the edge of the mattress. He put his hands over his eyes as if he wanted to banish the face of the woman from his memory. Pennock could see by his body language that his torment was genuine. This was no joke. This was serious.

"Look, maybe…" said Pennock. Bennett looked up at him. Pennock could see he was really shook-up. He stopped in mid-sentence. He changed tact. "Perhaps you'd better tell me everything."

Bennett took a deep breath. "I woke up in this room in God knows where. Turned out to be one hundred and thirty second street in Harlem."

"Harlem!?"

"Yeah."

"Someone was banging on the door and shouting something about, 'Time's up'. The room had stained, flaking walls, damp stains everywhere and a smell that I can only describe as gross. It was some kind of rat-arse hotel. My head felt as if someone had been using it as a football." Pennock wanted to chuckle, but forced himself to remain serious. "My clothes were all over the floor. I looked around. I didn't know where the fuck I was. Then I looked to the other side of the bed and saw her."

"Who?"

"The dead body."

"Describe her."

"Brown skin. Say thirty-five, I'd guess. Why?"

"Was she someone in the club? I noticed a couple of black girls."

"No. Not as far as I know."

315

"How do you know she was dead?"

"She was just lying there. Not moving. No sound. Eyes wide open."

"Jeez. How'd she die?"

"No idea."

"Okay," said Pennock. He blew out a breath. "We've got to manage this," he said. He took a few paces towards a window and looked down onto twenty-ninth street below. He turned back to look at Bennett. His face was glum.

"Did anyone see you leaving that place?"

"What, the hotel where I found myself?"

"Yeah."

"Yeah. A guy standing at a counter."

"Shit. Who was the person knocking at the door?"

"I'd guess it was the guy who was standing at the counter."

"This hotel sounds like the kind of place were the customers pay for the room by the hour. Was she a hooker?" Pennock asked.

"I don't know. She might have been."

"Depends if anyone saw you entering the place with her? How did you get to Harlem from the strip club in Soho? That must be some distance. Four miles I'd guess. You had to get there. Who took you?"

"No idea."

"What happened to you in the club? Last time I saw you, you were chatting to a blonde bird. A waitress."

"Yeah. I remember her. Called her Chelsea. She was trying to get me to pay for a private dance. I was drinking at the bar. Next thing I remember is feeling faint and slipping off the stool. Then nothing until I woke up in that room."

"When you heard the bang on the door. What did you do?"

"When the bloke shouted 'Time's up'. I got off the bed. Picked up my clothes and put them on. My head was throbbing like hell. I shouted 'Okay'."

"And?"

"By the time I got dressed, the bloke had gone. I got out of the room and took the stairs to the ground floor. That's where I saw the guy standing behind the counter."

"Was there anyone else around?"

"No. Just him. I stepped out of the front door, walked along the street for a hundred yards, then hailed a cab and came back here."

"Did the cab driver pick you up from outside the place?"

"No. Down the street."

"Yeah, you said that. Where did he drop you off?"

"Right outside here."

"Bad move."

"Why?"

"He'll know you're staying here."

"I didn't kill her," Bennett said in a defensive tone.

"I know that," Pennock replied. "Tell me did the guy behind the counter say anything?"

"Not a word."

"Good," said Pennock. He took a couple of paces back across the room. "Tell me. Be up front with me. How did she die? Did you…"

Bennett looked aghast. "I didn't kill her," he said in a raised voice. "I woke up in this room. Not knowing where the hell I was. Then I find this dead woman next to me. I had no idea who she was."

Pennock put his hands up in a disarming way. "I had to ask," he said. He blew out a long breath of air. "I had to ask," he repeated. "Jeez, this is crazy. A dead chick. Who would have thought it?"

Bennett looked at him with an anxious look across his face. "What am I going to do?" he asked.

Pennock didn't reply immediately. He looked down as if in deep thought then shook his head. "If you didn't kill her, you've got nothing to worry about. Go to the police. Tell them. Take them to the place. Explain it all. That way you'll be showing them you're innocent of any involvement in her death."

Bennett considered his words. His advice sounded pretty succinct. He thought that it was perhaps the best course of action. "You're right. Perhaps that's the best thing to do," he said.

"No doubt about it," replied Pennock. "Do you have any idea how you got to that place in Harlem?" he asked.

"None whatsoever. I woke up in this room that smelled like shit."

"Were you naked?" asked Pennock.

"Yeah. All my clothes were scattered over the floor. But at least I still had some cash in my pocket."

"Do you think you had sex with this woman?"

"I doubt it, but I don't know. Why?"

"If you did, they'll have your DNA. It will put you at the scene of the death."

Bennett ruminated on Pennock's words for a few moments. "Clive, I didn't kill anyone," he said in a soft, reflective tone of voice. "How would I have killed her?" he asked.

"Let me have a look at your hands," asked Pennock.

"Why?"

"See if there are any marks."

Bennett showed him his hands. Pennock examined them and even turned the palms over as if he knew what he was looking for. "I can't see any cuts or anything like that. Your knuckles aren't bruised. Maybe she was already dead."

"Yeah. That's possible."

"Maybe someone put her there. And you've no idea how you got there?"

"No. I remember sitting on the stool at the bar talking to that blonde, then the next minute I passed out and wound up on the deck. Then hours later, I'm woken by the sound of someone banging on a door."

Pennock didn't say a word. He looked totally stupefied as to what may have happened to his friend. It was like some weird tale he had read in a paperback novel or seen in a movie.

"What shall I do?" asked Bennett.

"Go to the police. Tell them what you've told me. Take them to the place."

"I'm not sure I know where it is."

"The guy at the desk saw you, didn't he?"

"Yeah."

"He'll recognise you."

"Yeah. I reckon he will. There were not many white people in that part of town."

"Shit."

"What?"

"If he saw you, he'll give the police your description and they'll make up a photo-fit."

"That's possible."

"More likely highly probable."

It seemed by his tone of voice that Pennock was going off the idea of going to the police. Bennett picked up on it.

"I don't much fancy the idea of going to the police," he said.

"Why?"

"I'll be detained for hours."

"That could be a small price to pay," said Pennock. "What's the alternative?"

"I get out of here. I'll get back home on a flight leaving tonight. I could be home by this time tomorrow morning."

"But you'll be running," said Pennock. "If that guy has reported it to the police, they could be looking for you already.

Trying to slip out of the country might be a bad move. You might not get out of the airport. You didn't say anything to the guy at the desk, did you?"

"No. Not a word."

"Good. That way he won't know you're a Brit."

"Just a minute I shouted out 'Okay'."

"That doesn't mean to say he'll know you're English. Does it?"

"That's true."

Bennett dropped his head, put his hands over his face and brushed the fingers through his hair. "Of all the dumbass things to happen." He looked at Pennock and could only give him a wistful look. "Where are the rest of the guys?" he asked.

"I don't know for sure. We all got separated in that club. I came back here at two-thirty with Kurt and Tony. I assume the rest of the guys are sleeping it off. Not sure what happened to Wayne or Steve or Danny. I reckon they all got back here together."

"Fucks sake!"

"What?"

"This mess."

"If you want my honest opinion, I think you'll be crazy to run away. Why don't you have a shower? Have some sleep. Sleep on it for an hour. See how you feel. Anything you decided to do I'll support you all the way. If you're up for going to the police, I'll come with you. They're bound to get to the bottom of it."

"You think?"

"Yeah. For sure."

"What if they don't? What if I'm arrested for murder? Fuck sake. Why me?" Bennett asked with an air of desperation.

"Eh. You're innocent. We'll get to the bottom of it sooner than you think."

Bennett looked at his best friend. "You're right," he admitted.

"I think it's the common-sense thing to do."

Bennett leaned forward and rested his hands on his knees. He considered his options, which frankly were few. Either he headed to the airport and tried to get onto a London bound flight or he went to the police to report finding a dead body.

"Have a shower and get some sleep," said Pennock. "I'll come back in an hour."

With that he turned away, stepped to the door, and left the 'Vertigo' room. He closed the door behind him and left Bennett alone to stew. The time was nearly eleven.

## Chapter 5

As soon as Pennock left the room, Bennett discarded his smelly clothes and took a swift ten-minute shower. On returning to his room, he slipped into a bathrobe, lay on the mattress and nestled his head into the softness of the pillow. He was feeling better, but still anxious and fearful about the entire episode. He couldn't comprehend what had occurred to him and why. It was like a dream. He was half expecting to snap out of it and discover it wasn't true. That it had been a terrible nightmare. Despite continuing to have a sore head and feeling ill he drifted off into a light sleep.

He must have slept for an hour or so before he was awoken by the sound of a ringing telephone. He opened his eyes and looked at the bedside clock. The time was a shade after twelve noon. Reaching out he took the telephone.

"Yeah."

"It's Clive. Quick, turn the TV on," he instructed. "Channel Seven Eyewitness News."

"Why?"

"Just do it," said Pennock in haste, before terminating the conversation.

Bennett pulled himself off the mattress, tightened the belt around the bathrobe and went to the television. He took the remote control and turned on the TV. The screen opened straight onto the local 'New York City Channel 7 Eyewitness News' channel.

A pretty female reporter was standing on a street in an urban setting, with a microphone in her hand, and talking into the camera. The caption at the bottom of the screen said: 'WABC- Eyewitness News Channel Seven.' The words inside a box said:

**'Body of female, aged thirty, found dead inside a Harlem hotel room.**

The news reporter said: "The police have not yet released the name of the victim or the cause of death. It's too early to speculate. The victim was found alone in a room on the fourth floor at just after ten o'clock this morning."

In the shot behind the reporter, a police officer dressed in the uniform of the New York Police department was standing on the sidewalk, outside the glass entrance that led into the building.

Bennett recognised the doorway. It was the exit of the hotel he had walked out of two or so hours ago. 'Oh my God!' he said to himself.

Just then there was a tap on the door to his room. He opened the door and Clive Pennock came in. He was looking sweaty, harassed, and concerned all at the same time. His eyes went straight to the TV screen attached to the wall. They didn't say anything to each other, just looked at the screen and listened to what the reporter was saying.

Off camera, the anchor in the studio asked the reporter if the police had a description of a suspect. She replied saying that the

NYPD would like to speak to a man aged between thirty to thirty-five years of age. Six feet, two. One hundred and fifty pounds. And who speaks with a British accent."

Pennock took the remote control out of Bennett's hand and turned off the TV.

"The less you hear of that the better," he said.

"What if I call nine-one-one and ask the police to come here?" Bennett asked, seeking his advice.

"No. Don't do that," said Pennock. "It might cause a commotion in here. Go in person to a police station. I think there's a police station on West 26th. I'm sure I noticed it. We'll walk to it and go there in person. It will look better. I'll come with you."

Bennett ran his hand across his mouth. He looked at Pennock. "Thanks," he said. He slipped the dressing gown off and proceeded to change into a fresh set of clothes.

"Take your passport for ID," Pennock advised.

"Okay. I'll do that."

As soon as Bennett was dressed and he had his passport in his possession the pair of them went out of the room, down the elevator and out of the hotel onto West 29th street. The sounds and sights of this part of the city reverberated like a never ending choreographed rumble of noise. The early afternoon was pleasant, though a whispering breeze was blowing along the sidewalk.

As they made their way to the end of the street and the junction with 8th Avenue, Bennett asked Pennock about the rest of the guys.

"What about them?" asked Pennock.

"Should we have told them?"

"No need to yet," said Pennock. "I wouldn't say anything until later. Let them find out later. Hopefully, it will all be sorted by then and we'll all get to the baseball game."

"Of course," said Bennett. He had forgotten they had tickets to watch the Yankees take on Baltimore Orioles in Yankee stadium this evening. He somehow doubted he would make it to the game. Something told him he was in deep trouble.

"Don't worry about it. I'll text Danny. Tell him we might be a little late leaving."

"Okay," replied Bennett. He was thankful that Pennock had it all under control and was taking the lead. It made him feel a whole lot better.

At the end of the street they turned right onto 8$^{th}$ Avenue and walked three blocks south to the beginning of West 26$^{th}$ street.

Pennock was correct. There was a small police precinct on a stretch of 26th street in the block between 8th Avenue and 9th Avenue. A couple of police cars were parked in the kerb opposite the entrance. There were no police officers in plain sight. The words: 'New York City Police Department, 26th Street Precinct' were attached to the façade above the entrance doorway in thin, one-foot high silver letters. A line of opaque windows ran along the wall for ten yards or so. Opposite, on the other side of the street was a children's playground behind a high, chain-link fence. A group of nursery-age children were playing on swings and roundabouts, with mothers and child-minders sitting on benches, watching in close attendance.

"You're doing the right thing," said Pennock as if there was some debate about it, which there wasn't. "Let me do the talking," he added.

Bennett didn't reply. Pennock pushed the door open and led him into the precinct. There was a counter directly opposite, at which a man of average height, dressed in a NYPD uniform, shirt and tie. He was standing, looking at something on a shelf beneath a foot-high glass partition. On a notice-board attached to the wall behind him there were the mug shots of several people wanted by the NYPD. It was a typical setting for a police precinct, though it was strangely quiet with a lack of activity and people. Opposite the counter were a row of white plastic bucket seats. A water cooler with paper cups was on one side of a solid looking door with a mesh wire glass window and a numbered security keypad.

As Pennock and Bennett entered the station, the guy behind the counter looked up and put his eyes on them. The two Englishmen stepped to the counter.

"What can I do for you gentlemen?" asked the cop. He was a good-looking guy with distinguished grey hair and nice soft mature features.

"My name is Clive Pennock. This is my friend," he turned to gesture to Bennett. "Rob Bennett. I understand the police found the body of a woman in a Harlem hotel this morning. My friend here might know something about it. Though he vehemently insists he knows nothing about her death."

Bennett looked at Pennock. '*For fuck sake*', he said to himself. He sounded as if he was already guilty.

The police officer looked at Bennett. "And who might you be?" he asked.

"Robert Bennett." Bennett slipped a hand into a jacket pocket, pulled out his passport and handed it to the cop. The officer maintained an unsmiling face. He flicked the passport open at the back page and looked at the details of the holder. "Robert Bennett?" he asked. He put the passport down on the counter.

"This is the man the police are looking for," said Pennock.

The cop gave Bennett a serious face. He reached out, took hold of a telephone and tapped a couple of digits into the number pad. He waited for a moment for a reply.

328

"Lieutenant Kaminsky," he said. "Please come to the front desk. I have someone here who has information regarding the discovery of a body in a Harlem hotel this morning." He put the telephone down the moment he stopped talking and thrust his chin towards the seats next to the entrance. "Take a seat," he advised.

Pennock and Bennett took a few steps back and sat in two of the seats opposite the counter. No sooner had they sat down, then the door to the right opened and a small man in a dark jacket, and matching trousers stepped into the reception area. He couldn't have been much more than five feet six inches tall. He had a slightly bulbous nose and an olive complexion. His round shape head was completely hairless. He couldn't have weighted more than one hundred and fifty pounds. He had an identification badge perched in the breast pocket of the jacket. Under the jacket, he wore a crisp looking pale blue shirt and a shiny red, white, and black striped tie that looked like real silk. He certainly cut the image of a polished detective. His brown brogue shoes were buffed to a shiny finish.

The uniformed cop behind the counter looked at him. "These are the gentlemen," he said. "Here with information about the body found in the Harlem hotel this morning."

Lieutenant Kaminsky looked interested. He put his dark, hazel eyes on the two men sitting in the seats. He took a step towards them. "Perhaps you'd like to come this way," he said. He looked to his colleague at the counter, but didn't say a word. The content of the message was passed between their eyes.

He turned to the door, opened it wide and held it open for the visitors. Pennock and Bennett rose out of the seats, stepped to the door, went through it and into a narrow corridor. Bennett was aware of the aroma of recently applied green paint to the plain walls. His nose puckered at the smell.

"Sorry about the fragrance," said the Lieutenant. "We've recently had the place refurbished. There's still work to do."

His accent contained a Hispanic edge, but he didn't look Hispanic. His name suggested he was of east European background. His English was more than adequate, though his accent indicated that he wasn't American-born.

He led them down a short corridor, through a door and into an interview room which had a square table and four straight-backed chairs placed under it. The aroma of fresh paint was stronger in here than it had been in the corridor.

"Take a seat," he encouraged. Kaminsky sat down at the table, rested his elbows on the surface and crossed his legs. The timepiece on his right-hand wrist looked oversize and expensive. Pennock and Bennett joined him at the table. Bennett was seated directly opposite the detective.

Kaminsky cleared his throat. In the overhead light the crease of his suit looked sharp. The shirt and the tie were of the finest quality.

"You have information about a death in a Harlem hotel. Is that right?" he asked. His words were precise. He didn't seem like the kind of person who used too many words. "Which one of you would like to tell me?"

Bennett leaned forward and set his forearms down on the table top. "Me," he replied. "Let me tell you." Kaminsky said nothing. He simply nodded his head in his direction. He retained an open front.

Bennett began. "This morning I woke up in a strange place. I don't know where I was. I was woken up by the sound of someone banging on a door. I honestly don't know how I got there. It's a total mystery to me. Next thing I look to my side and see a dead body lying next to me. Believe me. I've no idea who she was or how she died. Or how she got there in the first place."

"Let me say something," said Pennock. "Last night we were in a club in Soho."

"Which club?"

"The Private Eyes."

"A strip club?"

"Yes."

"Before we go on. Please tell me where you gentlemen are from?"

"London, England," replied Pennock.

"I thought so," said Kaminsky. "Why are you in the city? A convention?" he asked.

"We came here to party. For a stag party. It's Rob's stag party."

"You're Rob?" asked Kaminsky looking at Bennett.

"Yes."

"Okay. So, you're in a gentlemen's club in Soho. How did you get to Harlem from there?"

"That's just it," said Bennett. "I've no idea."

"No idea?"

"No."

"How many of you are on the trip?" Kaminsky asked.

"Seven," replied Pennock.

"Seven of you?"

"Yeah. But we all got separated in the club. No one knew where Rob had got to," said Pennock.

"I was sitting at the bar chatting to one of the waitresses. Then I suddenly felt ill and fainted. I guess I passed out."

"Did you get her name?" asked Kaminsky.

"Who?"

"The waitress."

"Chelsea."

"Chelsea?"

"Yes. That's what she said."

"So, let me get this right. You're in a club in Soho talking to a waitress called Chelsea. You suddenly feel ill and pass out."

"That's correct."

"Then you woke up in a hotel in Harlem next to a dead body?"

"Absolutely."

"And you've got no idea how you got to Harlem?"

"No. None at all."

"What time did you enter the club?"

"About midnight," said Pennock.

Bennett cleared his throat. "All I recall is chatting to this blonde at the bar. I suddenly felt ill and passed out. The next thing I'm in a strange bed in a strange room in a strange hotel and with someone I don't know."

Kaminsky shifted his position in the seat. He turned to a side and stretched his legs. The overhead light reflected on his bronzed cranium. The look in his eye was one of concentration combined with uncertainty at what he was being told was the truth. He clearly had his doubts that Bennett was telling him the truth.

"Can you describe Chelsea?" he asked.

"About five-nine tall. Slim. Long blonde hair that reaches halfway down her back."

"Pretty?"

"Yes. Pretty."

"How many of you were in the club?"

"All seven of us."

"Who are they?"

"Friends," said Bennett.

"We've all come over to party for a couple of days," said Pennock.

"What do you do for an occupation?" Kaminsky asked Bennett.

He hesitated for a moment. "I'm a commercial airline pilot," he admitted.

"Which airline?"

"British Atlantic," replied Bennett.

"Have you visited that club before?" Kaminsky asked.

"I haven't," said Bennett. "Last night was the first time I've ever stepped in the place."

"So, you're chatting to a girl. Drinking. What were you drinking?"

"Beer and wine."

"Is this the first time you'd ever seen the girl?"

"Who?"

"Chelsea."

"Yes."

"So, you're at the bar talking to her. You feel ill and pass out?"

"Yes."

"Will she recognise you?"

"Chelsea?"

"Yes."

"Yeah. I'd think so. We were chatting for a while."

"What about?"

"All sorts of things."

"Anything specific?"

"No."

"Nothing about taking her to a hotel?"

"No."

"How much had you had to drink?"

"Too much."

"Beer? Hard liquor?"

"As I said beer and wine mostly."

"Where were your friends when you were at the bar?"

"I honestly don't know. I looked at the table we'd been sitting at, but there was no one there."

Kaminsky sniffed. "Bear with me a moment, will you?" He got up from the table, went to the door and stepped out. He closed the door behind him.

Bennett looked at Pennock. "He doesn't believe a word of it," he said.

"Shhhh," said Pennock. He glanced around the room. "Whisper."

"Why?"

"There might be hidden microphones."

"He doesn't believe a word I said," said Bennett in a whisper.

"Why not? Listen. You're doing great. Anyone can see your telling the truth. It's your word against theirs. They can't prove anything."

"This wasn't such a good idea. It isn't going to end well," said Bennett.

"Of course, it will," encouraged Pennock. "You've got nothing to worry about."

The door opened and the detective came back into the room. He didn't re-take his seat, choosing instead to stand by the side of the table. "I've just been talking to my colleagues in Harlem. I suggest I take you back up there. Are you okay with that?"

"Certainly," said Bennett.

"We've nothing to hide," added Pennock.

Kaminsky smiled at him like a crocodile smiling at meat dangling on the end of a hook. "My colleagues in Harlem are awaiting. Let's go."

Neither Bennett or Pennock said anything as they rose from the table. Kaminsky led them out of the interview room, down the corridor, back into the reception area and out onto 26th street. He took them to a bronze coloured Honda Camry parked by the sidewalk. Both the Englishmen climbed onto the back-passenger seat. They were soon in the hustle and bustle of the early Friday afternoon midtown traffic.

Bennett reflected on the interview with Kaminsky. It seemed like pretty low-key stuff. The detective's questions didn't appear to have any great base in investigation. There were no really probing questions. He had just reacted to what Bennett had said. Maybe this was his style. Maybe the in-depth interrogation would begin when he arrived at the hotel to meet the cops waiting there. Then he considered the possibility that the police had established that the woman in the bed had died of natural causes and therefore it wasn't a suspicious death. Kaminsky had never uttered the word, 'homicide'. If the truth be told he hadn't said a great deal. And he wasn't saying much now as he drove uptown.

Was he deliberately down-playing it because he knew he had the killer in the back of his car? Bennett looked at the dashboard, noticing that there wasn't a radio unit and no other obvious indication that this was a police detective's vehicle. Maybe this wasn't genuine, but the police precinct and the uniformed officer had looked real enough.

Chapter 7

As the vehicle reached Columbus Circle and Central Park West, a cell phone rang. Kaminsky took the call, hands-free. "We're on our way. Five minutes," he said. He ended the conversation and concentrated on getting the car around the turn and driving onto Central Park West.

After two hundred yards, he turned right onto the 65th street transverse and cut across Central Park, then along East 65th street before turning left onto Park Avenue. No words were exchanged.

It was another ten minutes before they reached Harlem with its mixture of tenements, ethnic eateries and small business premises. Kaminsky seemed to know where he was heading. He drove along Adam Clayton Boulevard, then turned onto 132nd Street.

Bennett immediately recognised the area. There was the DIY store on the corner of the street called: 'Harlem Hardware', and the CVS store just along from that.

One hundred yards along the street Kaminsky arrived in front of the six-floor building that had the sign; 'Hotel' above the glass enclosed entrance. A blue and white NYPD police car was parked outside. A cop dressed in a dark jacket over his blue shirt was standing adjacent to the door with his hands resting on the thick lip of the utility belt around his waist. The black leather holster containing his firearm was tucked tightly against his right-side hip. Kaminsky pulled into the sidewalk and stopped behind the marked police car. He killed the engine, then looked out across the pavement to the front of the hotel.

"Is this the place?" he asked Bennett.

"Yeah," he replied.

"Let's go in. Which floor were you on?"

"The fourth," Bennett replied. His mouth was dry and there was a soreness in his throat. The thumping in his head had all but gone, along with the scent of vomit in his nostrils, but he still felt a little giddy.

"Show me the way," said Kaminsky.

"I'm not under any caution, am I?" Bennett asked.

Kaminsky's eyes went to Pennock first then back to Bennett. His nose appeared to twitch as if he smelt something rancid in the air. "Not at this stage," he replied. It was as ambiguous as it was non-committal. It didn't put Bennett at ease. He glanced at Pennock who looked slightly stunned by the notion that his friend had almost admitted to some kind of wrongdoing. Bennett thought he was being up-front. He had nothing to hide. He was co-operating with Kaminsky and the NYPD.

The door to the hotel came open and a large, thick-set African-American man in a brown and olive chequered jacket and thorn coloured trousers emerged onto the sidewalk. He had a quick word with the officer standing by the door, then he put his eyes on the Camry. He had an identification badge attached to his jacket. He was a big fellow with thick black to grey bushy hair. A thin moustache ran along his lip. He looked haggard, and stressed with too much police work.

Kaminsky opened the driver's door and climbed out of the vehicle, Pennock and Bennett followed his lead. Kaminsky led them across the sidewalk to the glass door. In the background the sound of activity on the street filled the void of silence around them. A truck was delivering merchandise to the CVS store. Kaminsky turned to Bennett, took him by the elbow and shepherded him through the door and into the hotel lobby. It was the same place. There was the counter to the left. It wasn't manned at this time. The stairway going up to the next floor was to the right of the elevator shaft. The same blue and grey tiles on the floor. The entrance door came open and the big plain-clothed officer in the brown and olive check jacket came in. He looked at Kaminsky. Kaminsky introduced him has Detective Clarence Brewer.

"Is this the guy who handed himself in to you?" Brewer asked Kaminsky.

"Yeah. It's him."

"Let's take him up. Who's he?" he asked looking at Pennock.

"His friend," replied Kaminsky.

"Okay. I'll lead the way," said the bigger of the two detectives.

He moved towards the stairwell and led them up three flights to the fourth floor. Bennett was aware of the same fusty smell, the threadbare carpet under his feet and the stained wall plaster.

As they arrived on the fourth-floor landing, they turned down the corridor to see another uniformed cop standing in front of the door to the room. On seeing his plain-clothed colleagues, he stepped aside. Clarence Brewer led the way along the landing to the door, took the handle, opened it and went inside. Bennett and Kaminsky were right behind him with Pennock bringing up the rear. Bennett didn't want to see the body on the bed. He cringed at the prospect of seeing her again.

The bed was still unmade, but the body had been removed. The light in the room was less vibrant and sharp than it had been at nine forty-five. Inside, there was a young, plain clothes detective who was holding a notebook and pen in his hand. He was by far the youngest of the three detectives. No more than thirty years of age. He was dressed in a more contemporary style when compared to his two colleagues. He looked at Kaminsky who acknowledged him with a nod of the head.

Kaminsky seemed to relax a touch. "Is this the room?" he asked Bennett.

"Yes."

"And you don't know how you arrived here with the victim?" Kaminsky asked.

"No."

The young detective took a step forward. "So, you've no recollection of getting here or who she was?" he asked.

Bennett looked at him. The man was in his early thirties. He had a freckled face, fair eyebrows, and blue-green eyes. He looked a bit new school. Like a modern detective from some TV series. The badge clipped to his jacket said he was Detective Louis Mulvane.

"No," replied Bennett. He was conscious that he was giving one-word answers. The young cop wrote his response into his notebook.

"You don't know?" asked Kaminsky in a blunt, brusque tone of voice. "Perhaps you had better give Detective Brewer your version of events."

Bennett thought his world was caving in. They clearly suspected that he had killed the women. He felt his heart beating like a drum. "How did she die?" Bennett asked.

"Who?" asked Detective Brewer.

"The woman in the bed."

"We haven't established the cause of death yet," said Mulvane. "Too early to say."

Bennett felt his heart beat slow a touch.

"You must have known her to end up in bed with her," said Brewer, again in a brusque manner.

"Do you usually pay for sex?" Kaminsky asked.

Pennock was going to interject and say something, but held back. Bennett noticed his reluctance and was instantly deflated.

Mulvane glanced around the room. "This isn't the kind of place a pilot would stay, is it?"

"Unless he's come to have sex with a prostitute," said Brewer.

Bennett shook his head. "I've never paid to have sex with anyone," he said. He wasn't prepared to crumble under the pressure. He was keeping his end up and staying as level-headed as possible.

"So, why on this occasion?" Mulvane asked.

"I never did."

"We found three, one hundred-dollar bills in her purse," Brewer said.

"All new and crisp," added Mulvane.

"I never gave her the money."

"Did you use protection?" Mulvane asked.

"For what?"

"Intercourse."

"I never had sex with her."

"But you don't know you didn't. If you can't remember anything how can you be sure?" Mulvane asked. The cops were working in a triangular pattern of interrogation, though it appeared to be haphazard.

"Would you have any objection if we took your DNA?" Kaminsky asked.

Bennett shook his head. If he was going to get out of this, he had to maintain his innocence. "Not at all," he replied.

"Where had you been last night?" Brewer asked.

Pennock cleared his throat. "We'd been to a strip club in Soho."

Brewer looked at him. "I wasn't asking you," he snapped.

"The Private Eyes strip club," said Bennett.

"And what time did you leave?"

"I don't know for sure. I passed out at the bar. Next thing I woke up in here."

"What were you doing in the club?"

"It's my stag party."

"Stag?" Brewer asked as if he didn't understand the meaning of the word.

"A party before I get married in two weeks."

"How many are in your party?" Brewer asked.

"Seven."

"Where were the rest of your party?"

"When?"

"When you supposedly passed out."

"I don't know. We all sort of got scattered. I'd guess you'd say."

Before either of the cops could ask another question, there was a sound of a cell phone ringing. The young cop, Mulvane, stepped to the door, opened it, and went out of the room.

"There's seven of you in a strip club and not one of your friends saw you pass out or saw you leaving the place?" Brewer asked.

"No."

"Perhaps we had better interview these guys," Kaminsky said. "Maybe you left with the victim. Maybe you picked her up on the street outside. It's a place where hookers hang out waiting for

344

tricks. Maybe she agreed a price with you. So, you came all the way out here to this place to screw her. Maybe you paid her for sex."

"That's preposterous," said Pennock. Brewer gave him a withering look.

"It's not true," said Bennett.

"Why would he come all the way here to have sex with a prostitute?" Pennock asked.

"Why does the sun rise in the morning?" asked Brewer in a rhetorical tone. His expression seemed to have hardened and his barrel chest was far more prominent.

"That's the way it may have happened," Kaminsky said.

Bennett was dumfounded by the turn of events. The implied accusations. He was up to his neck in deep shit. The detectives clearly thought he had met the victim in the club or outside on the street and they had come here for sex. In other words, the victim was a sex worker who was turning tricks. But why would he travel four miles to have sex with her? It didn't add up, but this is what the detectives had concluded.

Detective Brewer cleared his throat. "You were in the club and you were talking to a girl called Chelsea. Is that correct?"

"Yes. I was talking to her for some time."

"What about?"

"All sorts of things."

"Like what?"

"Favourite movies. Places. That sort of thing."

"Movies. Places?" Brewer asked, as if he didn't believe a word of it.

"Yeah. I was sitting on a bar stool. She was standing by my side."

"And she's one of the waitresses?"

"Yeah. One of the waitresses. She served us some drinks when we first got in there. She asked me if I wanted her to dance for me."

"And did you?"

"No. I'll admit that I was tempted. But I turned it down. I was just happy to chat to her."

Brewer grinned. "So maybe you could link up with her later. Is that correct?"

"Maybe," admitted Bennett.

"So, you were looking for sex with someone?" Kaminsky asked.

"If she suggested we go. Then maybe. Yes," he admitted.

Pennock sucked on his teeth. He was listening to his friend backing himself into a corner. He was admitting too much.

There was a tap on the door. The door opened and the young cop came back in. A negro male accompanied him. It was the guy who had been standing at the counter when Bennett walked out.

Kaminsky looked to the man. "Do you recognise this man?" he asked, nodding his head towards Bennett.

"Yeah. Sure," he replied. "He's the guy who came in at three o'clock this morning with the dead woman."

"You sure?" Kaminsky asked.

"Yeah. I'm sure."

Bennett was stunned. "W…What," he said. "There must be some mistake," he protested.

"Don't say anything," said Pennock.

"Wait a minute. I've never met the woman in my life and I never came here at three this morning."

"This guy says different," said Brewer.

"Don't say a word," said Pennock, substituting 'anything' with 'word'.

Bennett shook his head vehemently.

"And is this the same guy who left the hotel this morning?" Kaminsky asked.

"Sure," the fellow repeated in the same unequivocal tone.

Kaminsky looked to the younger detective. "Make a record that the clerk positively recognises Mister Bennett as the man who arrived here with the victim at three o'clock this morning."

The young cop did what he was told and made a note in his notebook.

Bennett was stunned by the way things were panning out. Not for the first time he wondered if it was true. Had he actually picked up a prostitute from outside the strip club to come here for mutually-agreed sex? Could it be that he had had some sort of memory relapse?

He heard Pennock's advice ringing in his head and thought for the first time about asking for a lawyer to be summoned. The young cop led the desk clerk out of the room.

Kaminsky ran a hand over the back of his neck. "No one sees you fall off the stool and pass out?"

Bennett sucked in a breath. His head was spinning. The shit he was in had got a whole lot deeper. He didn't reply.

"Listen," said Kaminsky. "Did anyone see you pass out?"

"The girl must have done."

"Who?"

"Chelsea."

"Perhaps we need to speak to her. Get her account of things."

The door opened and Detective Mulvane came back into the room. Kaminsky looked at him. "Contact the manager at the Private Eyes club in Soho. Ask him if there is a girl called Chelsea who works there as a waitress. If yes tell him to get hold of her. We'll need to interview her."

The young cop nodded his head. He looked at Bennett with a look that said he was as guilty as hell. He stepped out of the room once again.

Chapter 8

They hadn't been in the room for more than fifteen minutes. Through the threadbare net curtain at the window the light of the day was raining in, along with the street sounds behind the hotel.

If Chelsea confirmed he had fallen off the stool and passed out, then at least they would know he was telling the truth. He felt relieved that he might be finally getting somewhere. She might tell them who had picked him up and what had happened to him. He considered for the first time that someone had spiked his drink and maybe tried to put him in the frame for the murder of a prostitute. Crazy as it might sound, that could be the only solution to this mystery.

Two minutes passed before the door to the room opened and the young cop returned. He looked at Kaminsky. "I spoke to the manager of the club. He confirmed that a waitress called Chelsea was in the club last night."

Bennett felt a weight lifting off his shoulders. He wanted to say *thank-God for that,* but kept his mouth closed.

Kaminsky looked at him through a pair of narrow eyes. "Sounds as if that part of the story might be true," he said in an almost grudging tone, but he didn't say which part. Bennett looked at Pennock who had a sombre, concerned look on his face. Was he considering the possibility that his best friend could have killed the girl? Maybe.

Bennett knew that if he was arrested it wouldn't look good at all. He would need to do some explaining to his employer. They wouldn't take kindly to one of their pilots being arrested even if he was later released with no charges. His career as an airline pilot was on the line here. There was no doubt about it and he knew it.

Detective Brewer looked to his younger colleague. "Call the manager back and tell him to tell the girl to be at the club in thirty minutes from now. We want to hear her side of the story. She'll either verify his account or she won't."

Bennett said nothing. He wanted to say *good* but once again thought better of it.

The young cop nodded to Kaminsky. He withdrew a cell phone from his jacket pocket, then went out of the room.

Kaminsky looked at Bennett. "Who organised the trip to New York?" he asked.

"I did," said Clive Pennock.

"Why Manhattan?" asked Kaminsky.

"We all thought it would be a good choice. It's only a seven-hour flight from London and there's loads of things to do. That reminds me we're due at Yankee stadium tonight for the Yankees versus Baltimore." He looked at his watch. The time was coming up to twenty past two.

"Okay," said Kaminsky, then in a rather dour tone. "We'll see about that," followed by a gap before he asked him for the names of the other people on the trip.

"Why?" Bennett asked.

"We may need to interview them in time," said Kaminsky.

"Kurt Smith and Steve Cummins are both airline pilots," said Bennett.

"Who else?"

"A guy called Danny Fordham."

"What's he to you?"

"An ex-team mate. I played soccer with him at a semi-professional level."

"Any team I know?"

"No."

"Who are the others?" Brewer asked.

"Tony Norman works in the City of London for a bank."

"That's four. What about the other two?"

"Wayne Hall."

"What's your connection to him?"

"He's my personal trainer."

"How long have you known him?"

"A couple of years."

"Who else?"

"Clive of course."

"Who's Clive?" Detective Brewer asked.

"Me," said Pennock. "We've been friends for the best part of twenty years."

"Okay that's fine. They're all good friends then?"

"Yeah. I'd say so."

Bennett was downbeat. He was still reeling from the fact that the desk clerk had identified him as the person who had entered the hotel at three o'clock this morning with the woman who was found dead in the bed. It didn't seem plausible.

The door opened and Mulvane came back into the room. "I spoke to the manager again. She'll be there in the club waiting for us," he announced.

"Anything else?"

"She told the manager that she recalled talking to an English guy at the bar."

Bennett wanted to say 'told you so', but didn't.

"Doesn't mean to say it was you, does it?" Kaminsky said to Bennett.

"What'd you mean?" Pennock asked.

"I bet that there were more than you seven Brits in the club. The Private Eyes club attracts a lot of visitors from overseas. If she did speak to an English guy, it doesn't mean to say it was you. She'll have to recognise you face-to-face."

Neither Bennett nor Pennock responded.

"Before we go downtown is there anything, you'd like to tell us?" asked Brewer looking directly into Bennett's eyes.

"Like what?"

"Like anything you've missed. Anything you'd like to admit to. It's your chance to clear the record."

Bennett pursed his lips. "I've nothing to admit to. I've told you the truth."

"All right. We'll go downtown and speak to the manager and the waitress. She'll either corroborate your story or she'll give us some other information."

"We'll take my car," Kaminsky said.

With that the five of them, the three NYPD detectives, Rob Bennett and Clive Pennock stepped out of the room, walked along the corridor to the elevator and rode down to the ground floor. Detectives Brewer and Mulvane placed themselves one on each side of Bennett to ensure he didn't try to flee.

## Chapter 9

They were soon stepping out of the hotel and passing the policeman in uniform who was still standing by the door. The blue and white NYPD police car was still in place. At three o'clock in the afternoon the avenue was busy. Overhead the sky was full of white cloud that masked the sun. The sidewalk was damp and there was a fragrance of rain in the air. A shower had dropped over the dusty street in the past few minutes. The temperature hovered somewhere between warm to chilly in a short time frame.

Kaminsky climbed into the driver's seat of the Camry. He asked Pennock to sit in the front passenger seat. Bennett was told to sit in between the two police officers on the back seat. They were in effect preventing him from attempting to get out en route to Soho.

Kaminsky pulled away from the kerbside and set out for the drive south through Harlem and down to the lower part of the island. The traffic was heavy and moved in fits and starts. Buses, cabs, private vehicles, and delivery trucks vied for space on the avenues and streets that criss-cross Midtown like a giant snakes and ladders board. No words were spoken by any of the five occupants. Bennett could feel the presence of the two cops on either side of him. He wanted to scratch his backside, but he couldn't get his hand free. He still couldn't grasp the magnitude of the situation he found himself in. It was something that happened to other people, not to him.

He felt like he was in some kind of weird out of body experience. Like a plot that even the most creative of authors couldn't imagine.

It took Kaminsky the best part of twenty-five minutes to drive from Harlem to lower Manhattan. It was three-thirty when they arrived outside the entrance to the Private Eyes club in Soho.

Bennett recalled going through the front door, paying the thirty-dollar fee at a window inside the entrance, then stepping into the main room were the girls were dancing on the raised stage. The music was loud, but not ear bursting. The glitter balls were turning and the lights were aimed on the catwalks were the girls were either semi-nude, totally nude or in the process of becoming nude.

As soon as the car came to a halt, all five men got out, stepped across the sidewalk, and went to the closed door. Detective Brewer and Mulvane kept their eyes on Bennett. He wouldn't run. Not now. He had nothing to run for and nowhere to run to. He wasn't guilty of anything except for his own stupidity. He should have raised the alarm the second he discovered the body next to him. Going back to his hotel was a stupid thing to do. It made him look as if he had something to hide. If he had his time again, he would have asked the man on the desk to call the police. He had panicked. Who wouldn't? He hoped his actions wouldn't place him in a more perilous position than he was already in.

The notice in the glass panel by the side of the doorway said the club was open Monday to Friday: 10pm and 3am. Saturday: 9pm to 4am, Sunday: 10pm to 2am. Private parties could be arranged by prior arrangement. There were no photographs of the artists. There was only a plain looking board over the doorway that said, 'Private Eyes. A Gentleman's club, Bar and Restaurant'.

The young cop knocked at the front door. The door opened and a man in a chest hugging plain shirt appeared. He was a middle-aged guy with a solid torso, slick black wavy hair curled to the back of his neck. He looked Latino. A gold band at his right wrist and the thick medallion chain around his neck all added to the image. He eyed the men, knowing who they were, then stepped to a side and allowed them in.

The men entered then went through into the large open room with the raised catwalk and the crimson colour backdrop. The club was empty. There were no spotlights penetrating the gloom, no sound, and no audience lapping up the entertainment.

Over to the left two people were sitting on stools adjacent to the long bar. One was a barman who had served Bennett. The other was a female with long, straight blonde hair that reached to the small of her back. The girl Bennett knew as Chelsea.

The group of six men took a short series of steps to get up to the higher level, then they approached the area in front of the bar. Bennett was pensive. He couldn't guess what she would tell the police. If she did the right thing and confirmed that he had passed out then any suspicion on him might be watered down, though there was still plenty of hurdles to jump before he was scot free.

Chelsea was wearing a two-piece sports outfit. A grey sweatshirt which had pink piping and a matching pair of jogging pants. Bennett looked at her. He felt his heart give a lift. She could explain what had happened to him and that he couldn't have killed anyone because he was incapacitated. As they came close, Chelsea and the man by her side stepped off the high stools, and turned to face the group. It was a strange scene. All capped by the openness of the floor around them. The silence. The lack of smells and the lack of activity on the catwalks.

"Are you Miss Chelsea Manson?" Kaminsky asked.

"Yes," she replied. She was taller than Kaminsky and only a couple of inches shorter than Brewer and Mulvane who were both close to six feet tall.

"Do you know this man?" Kaminsky asked and pointed to Bennett.

"Yes," she replied.

Bennett wanted to smile, but remained expressionless. She was still very cute. She was wearing the merest hint of pink lipstick and eyeshadow.

"This gentleman says he was talking to you at the bar and that you offered to dance for him. Is that correct?"

"Yes," she replied.

"He says that he felt ill, slid off the stool and fainted. Is that correct?"

She instantly screwed up her face and pinched her eyes closed. "Hell. No. That's not correct."

Bennett was stunned.

"Excuse me," said Kaminsky in a raised voice. "He told us he fainted."

She shook her head. "No. That's not true."

"What?" asked Bennett.

"Quiet," Brewer snapped.

Chelsea put her eyes on Bennett. "He was perfectly fine. We did chat for a while. Once he had turned down my offer of a private dance, he went to the other side of the bar to talk to a brown-skinned woman."

"That's right," said the barman. "I saw him."

"That's not true. Believe me," protested Bennett. He was almost on the verge of crying.

"I told you to be quiet," Brewer snapped.

"Which dark-skinned woman?" Kaminsky asked Chelsea.

"She was perhaps thirty. I'd guess. Red hair. Probably a hairpiece. Done in loose curls and ringlets."

"I saw him chatting to her," said the barman.

Bennett's jaw fell open. He could only stare at him in disbelieve. He was mindful not to say a word. He was being shafted. He couldn't ever recall talking to the woman described. Maybe he had. Maybe he was going mad. Maybe he had killed her. Maybe he was being set-up.

"What do you say to that?" Kaminsky asked.

He wondered whether to stay silent, but his sense of innocence was too strong. "I don't know what she's talking about. I never spoke to that person. Might it be someone else."

"No. It was you," said the barman.

"That's right," said Chelsea. "I saw you leaving her with."

"Is that right?" Brewer asked.

"Yeah. I offered to dance for him but he turned me down. Next minute he's leaving with that other woman."

"And you never saw them again?" Mulvane asked.

"No. They left the club together," she said.

"What? This is crazy. I don't know what the hell she's talking about," Bennett said in a stunned tone.

A cell-phone sounded. The younger cop took a call. He stepped away and it was possible to hear him say: "Yeah…No…Is that right?" then something inaudible.

Kaminsky and Brewer looked at each other and raised their eyebrows.

"How well do you know your friends?" Detective Brewer asked Bennett.

"What the guys with me?"

"Yeah."

"Very well."

"Could one of them be setting you up?"

"Why would anyone do that?" Bennett asked.

"I don't know. Can you think of a reason why anyone would want to drop you in trouble?"

"What? One of my friends?"

"Yeah."

"No."

"Who are they?" Kaminsky asked.

"Well there's Steve, Kurt, Wayne, Tony, Danny and Clive of course."

"What's he do?"

"Who?"

"Let's start with Steve."

"He's an airline pilot. Like me."

"How long have you known him?"

"A few years. Six I'd guess."

"Kurt. How long have you known him?"

"Eight years. I think."

"Tony?"

"A few years."

"Danny?"

"Ten years."

"Wayne?"

"A couple of years. Look what are you getting at?" Bennett asked.

"How long have you known Wayne?"

"Two years."

"So, you don't know him at all?" Kaminsky remarked.

"How about other friends?" Brewer asked. "Think. If you didn't kill her as you say does anyone have something against you and would want to put you in trouble?"

"I don't think so."

"A jilted girlfriend, maybe?"

"I can't think of anyone."

"Do you know anyone in New York? Any friends?"

"Not really."

"Therefore, no one wants to set you up?"

"No. Not that I can think of. Okay I've left a few women in my time, but I don't think anyone would want to do this to me."

"So, you've been a bit of a rake. Have you?" Kaminsky asked.

Bennett looked sheepish. "If you want to put it that way then yes. Probably," he admitted.

Brewer said nothing. The young cop ended his cell phone conversation and stepped back to join the group. He moved close to Kaminsky, leaned into him, and whispered something into his ear. Kaminsky listened to what he had to say.

A moment passed before Kaminsky put his eyes back on Bennett. "We've just got word from our investigation team. The woman was a thirty-two-year-old prostitute called April Showers. She was the victim of a homicide. She died by strangulation."

Kaminsky stepped a pace nearer to Bennett and looked him in the eye. "Robert Bennett. I'm arresting you on suspicion of ..." he stopped in mid-sentence as if for dramatic effect.

Bennett was petrified. He felt the floor sliding away from under his feet. He wanted a huge hole to appear into which he could disappear. In the next instant Detective Mulvane moved around him, took his arms, pulled them back and snapped a pair of iron handcuffs over his wrists.

"...For having a truly great party," Kaminsky said in a raised voice.

In the next moment, something quite extraordinary happened. The overhead lights came on and the sound system sprang into life. A wide door opened and a group of people emerged. It took Bennett a few moments to see they were his six friends. They were hand-in hand with six girls. There were whoops of laugher intermingled with cheering. Meanwhile the barman pulled a massive bottle of champagne from under the counter and popped the cork. A spray of champagne spewed from out of the bottle.

"Happy stag party," shouted Pennock as the opening riff to 'Start me Up' by the Rolling Stones belted out of the sound system. Pennock grasped hold of Bennett and gave him a hug. "Congratulations. You've just been pranked," he announced.

His six friends encircled him. They were all laughing. The cops were smiling. The barman and the chap with the slick back hair were pouring champagne into a line of crystal flutes. The brut was flowing like Niagara Falls.

Rob Bennett was stunned beyond words. It took him a full ten seconds to realise what was going on. He had been tricked, hoaxed, duped, scammed, stung. Use whatever verb you wish. He wasn't under arrest for murder. He wasn't going to be sent to jail for the next thirty years. He wasn't going to lose his job. The relief he felt in his heart was enormous. It was all a trick; a charade, a set-up. He had fallen for it, hook, line and sinker.

His friends and the girls were all beaming from ear to ear. They must have known what he had just been through. Clive Pennock was laughing his head off.

Chelsea, if that was her real name, came behind Bennett and took hold of the handcuffs. "It's time for your private dance," she announced. Bennett was led like a lamb to the slaughter, onto a catwalk to a cascade of lude cheering from his six amigos. Chelsea forced him to sit down in a round backed chair. Then in full view of the others and standing a foot away from him, she began to gyrate her hips to the tempo of the music.

Bennett's heart was thumping like a football that was being simultaneously kicked by a dozen boots. The relief was like something he had never experienced before. Chelsea took the bottom of the grey sweatshirt and lifted it up to reveal her shapely boobs. She pulled the sweatshirt off, took her breasts and squeezed them together. Then she dropped her hands. Took the cord holding the pants up, untied them and gently, sensuously let them slide down her thighs.

She danced close to him for five minutes. She was like a Playboy playmate. All blonde and naked. Rob Bennett was a sucker for a beautiful woman. He was a sucker for a prank. Because that is what had happened to him.

Kurt and Steve were now dancing with two of the girls on the catwalk, whilst over by the bar everyone was drinking champagne and laughing out loud. There was a Jeroboam sized bottle of champagne on the counter. The music was now classic 1970's Motown. The disco lights were flashing.

# Chapter 10

The party continued for the next hour and a half. There were at least twenty people at the bar. The three pretend detectives were still here, quaffing champagne. Smiling, laughing, and enjoying themselves. The girls had put some clothes on. The music was at a low volume and the guys were sitting at a big table, chatting, reflecting on what had just happen to their mate. The time was close to three-thirty. Clive Pennock had just reminded everyone that they were due at Yankee Stadium at seven o'clock. A stretch limo would pick them up from outside the club and take them back to the hotel so they could freshen up. The party would continue in the Yankee Stadium hospitality box.

All the guys looked tired and whacked. In a moment of quiet, Bennett went to sit next to Clive Pennock who had a fresh glass of champagne in his hand.

"How did you do it?" he asked. "Set me up like that. It was amazing."

"Easy," he replied.

"How?"

"A couple of years ago a friend told me about a company called E.E.M. Extra Event Management, based here in New York. They arrange events and create scenarios for people to be pranked. I spoke to the rest of the guys and we all thought it would be a great idea to do one for you. It's your stag-do. You might only get one. So, we wanted to make it memorable."

"You certainly did that. Scared me shitless. You had me well and truly screwed."

Pennock grinned. "Yeah. It was good. Worked like a dream. I told them all about you. What you liked. They came up with the plan."

"Wow. How did they do it?"

"Planning, I guess."

Bennett glanced towards the bogus police officers. "Who are these people?" he asked.

"They're all actors."

"You're kidding!"

"No. Straight up. I was told about them by my friend. That's why I choose New York for your party. They're said they'd be able to set you up with a scenario you'd never forget."

"It worked."

Pennock chuckled out loud. Bennett looked at his friends, reached out to the table and took hold of a glass of champagne and lifted it to his lips. His wrists were still chaffed where the handcuffs had rubbed against the flesh.

"What about these girls?" Bennett asked.

"They're the real deal," said Pennock.

Bennett smiled. He didn't want to ask Pennock how much all this had cost him. It must have run into the thousands of dollars. It had been worth every penny. It was something he would never ever forget for as long as he lived. "How did they get everything to fit?" Bennett asked.

"They thought of every what-if possibility. Every scenario."

"Like what?"

"Just say you panicked and tried to call nine-one-one from that hotel room. They had anticipated this scenario. In that case, the call was routed to them. Just say you had tried to revive the girl, they would have managed that and created a new story line. These people are just brilliant at what they do."

"Amazing," said Bennett. "But what about the police station? How did they manage that?"

"It wasn't a real police station. They mocked it up to look like a police station. They had set it up in the hour before we went in."

"Incredible."

"You could smell the new paint on the walls," said Pennock. "That was a bit of a give-away."

"Of course," replied Bennett as if he should have known. "What about the girl in the bed?"

"That's her speciality. Playing dead. She was never dead."

"What about the news reporter on the TV?"

"It wasn't a real news reporter. It was an actor. They had it wired into your room on a continuous loop."

"Jeez," said Bennett.

"The lengths they had gone to to make it all look real and the way they managed it was breath-taking."

"You're not wrong. It had me convinced."

"But you did well," said Pennock. "You didn't crack under the pressure. All the guys are proud of you."

Bennett had to smile to himself. Indeed, he hadn't cracked under the pressure. Maybe it was down to his pilot training.


The party in the club wound down after another hour. Bennett's friends all thanked him for bringing them to New York. They were having a whale of a time. It was the best stag-party they had ever been on.

Bennett had to admit it was pretty awesome. There was still more to come. They were due to go to Yankee Stadium later. Maybe he would discover that he was pitching for the Yankees. He couldn't wait to discover what else the guys had lined up for him. He laughed, then cringed at the prospect.


THE END

About the author....

Neal Hardin lives in Hull, England. He is the author of several novels, novellas and short stories. His first published novel, 'The Go-To Guy' was published in March 2018, by Stairwell Books, based in York, England; and Norwalk, Connecticut, USA.

Before retiring in 2016, Neal worked in the Education sector for over 21 years. He enjoys travelling whenever possible. He has visited the United States and Canada on many occasions, along with Japan, China, Australia and other countries. He follows his local football team and enjoys most sports and working out in the gym. He continues to write and enjoys the discipline of writing and constructing great stories.

Neal Hardin is also the author of...

*Dallas After Dark*
*A Gangland Tale*
*The Four Fables*
*Moscow Calling*
*On the Edge*
*The Wish-List*
*A Titanic Story*
*The Taking of Flight 98*
*Perilous Traffic*

All these novels are available to purchase on Amazon

See me on Twitter   @HardinNealp

Printed in Great Britain
by Amazon